ॐ श्रीं श्रीं

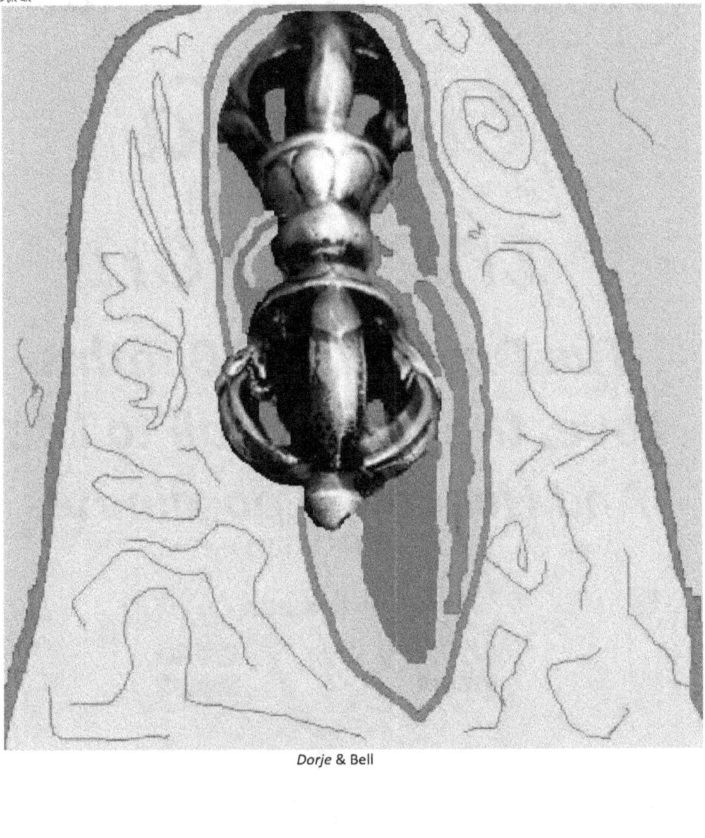

Dorje & Bell

A Resounding Novel of Polyamory without Frontiers

by

Ariadna Farkas Simon

Camilla the Siren

The Daughter of Death's Love, the Siren's Call to Life And Her Love Coordinates

Symbols: 1) Infinite Love in Infinite Combinations with Pi, 2) Leather, Latex, and BDSM, 3) Purple Mobiu, 4) Polyamory Flag, 5) BDSM Triskelion, 6) Infinity heart, 7) Polyamory Campaign Ribbon, 8) Poly Parrot.

 Kamadeva

ISBN-13: 978-0615643120
ISBN-10: 0615643124
Kamadeva
A member of SEAO
Wilkes-Barre, PA
Novels division
Erotic, Mythology, Paranormal

AUTHOR

ARIADNA FARKAS SIMON, generated by fierce Hussars, grew up wild in the Magyar forests. Raised by Hungarian "*farkasok*" wolves, she became a powerful werewolf. Now she is a "*lupa*" she-wolf, roaming the ruins of ancient Pompeii.

CHARACTERS

CAMILLA is a beautiful, curvy, tall and fiery woman just turned thirty-five, with long red locks, piercing blue eyes, a love-bite birthmark on her neck and with a very strong need to be loved and a passionate desire for sex.

PALMIERO is a Globe-Traveler searching for the end of the World with a long history of fascination with Pre-Columbian American culture.

DIANA is a frightening young ghost yearning for life again, a stunning woman with blond long hair, hazel eyes and a regal figure fit to fill a royal throne among the glamour and splendor of a mighty kingdom. She is Death narrating this ancient story.

Copenhagen mermaid and Pompeian symbols

CONTENT

PART TWO
MAKING LOVE

To C. DEVIL, she passed away on
February 18th with great bitter pain
and a huge hole in the heart.

DEDICATED TO OUR DEAR READERS

This is a story of extreme love, viscous passion, brutal lust and hungry death. Only if you are Pure of heart and with the best intentions, you may read it.

You can read this book intended for your edification. Do not be afraid. The road you have taken is hallowed. Follow it in peace. You are the maker of your own surroundings. If you were not here, who would recognize all this?

Do not reveal your vivid experiences by making them routine. You may lose them in the chaos of the external world.

***

"Love, pursued by the ignorant,
Becomes bonding desire.
That same love, pursued by wise ones,
Accomplishes liberation."[1]

INTRODUCTION

"Knock and it shall be opened."[2]

"*Camilla the Siren*" is a book for dreamers. Life is a pendulum swinging from Love to Death. Love and Death are the two mysteries of life. What they are and where they come from, no one knows and no one can know. Philosophical, psychological, religious, scientific and other definitions abound. Nonetheless, no one truly solves the mystery. Through an act of sexual desire or love, life springs out to end with death. What precedes or follows those acts is unknown. This is the eternal story of love and death throughout the eras. Ancient myths and contemporary realities intertwine. From nowhere stories jump out begging for remembrance. They want to live again through their actors and narrators. The eternal ebb tide flows continuously form myths to dreams, from Love to Death and from there to Love again.

In an ancient Roman novel,[3] the beautiful Photis cries out to incite Lucius, her man, who was impatient to engage in lovemaking,
"Kill me, you who are about to die, *Occide moriturus.*"

With a metaphor, in fact, the French call sexual orgasm "the little death," *la petit mort*. Still, with this event, our parents took us out of *No-where* and into Life. Where do we come from? What was there before our birth? What is there after our death? An ancient sacred Indian text,[4] declares,
"*In the beginning, there was nothing.*
Indeed, Death concealed all this,
Hunger, because hunger is death.
Then, Death projected the thought,
'*Let me be an individual.*' "

We are born with a hunger for experiences, a craving for knowledge. When we die, life leaves us with an unsatisfied famine. We come to this World from *No-where* and we go towards *No-where*. The first *No-where* is outside the Sacred Cave of the Matrix. Then, the Vagina irrigated by Love generates and projects her offspring towards the other side of that first unknown. The second *No-where* is in the Cave of Death.

Loving-hungry-desire comes from that Fissure of Life/ Desire/Death. As a result, Love/Death embraces and envelops the potency of Life within her circle into which Life orgasms. The world of the dead presses on life to overcome death and life goes back to death in the attempt to overcome it. All this, takes place amidst the throes of childbirth.

Life intertwines with Time and lives interact in it. The *Present* is always *present*. It was so when lived by the ancestors as well as when experienced by the descendants. It was *present*. It is *present*. It will be *present*. For every one, the Present is such as it is for us, here and now. The present, felt by Julius Caesar at his time in Rome, is the same we experience it now and here. The present perceives and looks into the past as distant in space. The light-years of the stars is the past seen now. In fact, the daylight we see and feel now is the Sun about eight minutes ago. The further in space we look, the more *distant* is the past we experience in this moment.

The past is dead. The past *passed* away. It is that which is no longer. It is Death itself. The past is here to haunt us! It comes up unexpectedly, immediately, capturing us with its snares of love's desire. Like all wild life, frogs in the pond, crickets in the grass and ancient *lupae*, she-wolfs resounding from Pompeian cemeteries, all are lovers calling one-another. They seek for each other through coordinates of entangled timeless webs rooted and branching in the Shadowy Abyss of Death. Each past, present and future action,

Webs rooted and branching in the Shadowy abyss of Death

shaped in kinked vines of pain and pleasure, connects with all the other pasts. Different stories, from diverse times, from distant poles-apart locations and from unusual dimensions, all pop up throughout our life's journey to flavor our daily activity. There is a necessity to grab the past, to make it present, but it is impossible because it is past, it is dead. This is what we call the fleeting time. It does not flee because is already dead. The *Present* is the only one eternally present. However, we do not know what it is. We cannot define it except as past. That past is seen as the death of the present. However, that can never be, because the present remains here as a solid rock. At best, the past is a memory relived in the present. It is *present*, nevertheless. This is evident at the time of death, when the whole life passes by in the flash of the present.

The impelling need to sleep is the force of dreams, which want to come to life in the mind. They are ghosts craving to live again. In the flow of our real daily experience, dreams come as new stories and new fables that seem to have no relationship with the waking state. However, unknown to us, they influence our conscious behavior. Dreams, for the waking state, are like fragments of reality. They are an essential dimension of our everyday consciousness. Dreams interwove with the course of events as a parallel structure of our daily life. In the stream of consciousness, dreams flourish seemingly with no connection with the flow of reality; whereas, they are part of the overall structure of experience.

Similarly, for a confused brain, hallucinations are events reflecting real and concrete objects, while, for the sane mind, they are pathological aberrations. In both perceptions, however, the same perceiving act depends on a consciousness conferring reality to the object experienced. Ultimately, only the observer makes the final judgment between truth and deceit. After seeing the ghost of his father, Hamlet[5] declares,

"There are more things in heaven and earth, Horatio,
Than are dreamt of in your philosophy,"

Russian *babushka*

As a many-layered Chinese box or Russian *babushka* doll, placed one into the other, the rhythmic development of life goes from one state to another. From dreamless slumber, it flows into wakefulness, hence to dream and from here again to sleep with no-dreams. Each moment of the dramatic events of human history is a building block that contains preceding ones, while generating and transforming itself into a new structure. Each block, therefore, is a molecular fragment of the entire fabric of existence. It is a sort of mushrooming foam in which each bubble is an entire complete universe in itself. Even when we focus on one thing, still the wallpaper, on the background of our mind, contains holistically all the conscious, subconscious and unconscious elements ever lived, experienced and learned. Somehow, like DNA, the entire past and future world is constantly present to the actuality of this mind.

Since immemorial times we humans spoke about love. We mythologized it. We used fabulous descriptions to portray it. Commonly, we address our loved one with the metaphor *Honey*. We describe sexual love with a smile of compliancy. Everyone knows it, but, at the same time, it is mysterious, secret and beyond words. We go a great length out of our habitual way in order to pursue it. It has always been so.

Like a weaver, Love weaves its coordinates. The spider of Love spans its filaments and hides in its cobweb waiting for the prey. Once in it, the victim has no escape. S/he does not want to get away. S/he offers him/her self gladly to the jaws and deadly embraces of that many-tentacles love.

Camilla and Palmiero live their lives here and now in this historical dimension, where dream and reality merge along very tenuous borders. Whatever becomes difficult for us to understand in their story is not different from our complicated and unexplainable daily experiences. The dream we had last night is a tassel in the fabric of this day. Without that slumber vision, the fabric of this wakefulness would rip, begging to have another dream. To patch it up, therefore, we fall asleep again and wander into the sleep dimension of another enchanted gripping story.

Camilla, Palmiero and Diana are universal figures. They are templates of our historical reality. They live their lives on different parallel dimensions, all taking place here and at the same time. In each instant, however, they are not immediately conscious of the lived dimensions of the other states, like dream, sleep and death, and the consequences they have on each other. Furthermore, when we are conscious of the other human being, it is not his or her consciousness we experience but only ours.

Every story ever told is a possibility. Every possibility yearns to become a reality. Every reality is a lived experience. Every lived experience is an incarnation of desires. An unfulfilled thought-desire becomes energy. That energy congregates, like into a dynamo. And it powers new desires, new life-springs yearning to be brought to fruition.

This book is composed of two parts. Part One deals with the Myth of Love, while Part Two deals with the Making of Love. Both parts blend in a timeless-space-less eternal continuum pendulum. Furthermore, as the work of a complete Opera, this book is a drama conveyed through words and integrated with music. It is the unified artistic interaction of history, music, poetry, prose, reader, romanticism, storyteller, symphony and worlds. Like in the Opera, the music blends with the words and the voice of the heart. That voice becomes a fluid instrument among musical instruments. The rhythmic sound of our heartbeat constantly syllabizes and spells our life. The alternating tempos of 1-wake-2-dream-3-sleep-1-wake-2-dream-3-sleep, preceded and followed by the silence of death, continuously stress our existence.

Therefore, the music connected with this book is an integral part of the living flow of the story itself. The melody of this book is the movement in which the mere sounds of its words come to life. As a result, this book has a separate cross-referenced companion musical CD sold separately. Various tunes can be played while reading. This image directs readers to specific musical pieces.

Throughout this book we tried, as much as possible, to avoid words that may be construed as offensive. Not because we consider some words more vulgar than others. There is not such a thing. Neither have we followed this policy for prudish motives. This is clearly not the case, given the evident nature of this book. Rather, it is for aesthetic reasons. When unavoidable, we will use those words only as colloquialism. Besides aesthetic reasons, we want to avoid vulgarities because it cheapens the content. It may lead our readers to give a poor quality connotation to the act of love making.

It should be clear that all expressions of love, in any way performed, are always sacred. Therefore, we do not want to cheapen it with expressions that may lead the reader to understand it as a mere act of no consequence, as in the colloquial expression, "*What the fuck*," or, as Camilla's dead soul would have said, "*It is only a fuck without a face*." On the contrary, all life is sacred in all its expressions. Explicitly, life is always projection towards the sacred unknown. Namely, the other is the foreign entity. When communicating, making love, or even killing, we implicitly consider, consciously or unconsciously, the other to be powerful, thus sacred. Namely, sacred is that which we *sacrifice*, we make-sacred or strong. The other is the mysterious, dangerous, appetizing one whom we want to love, possess or... kill.

"Seek, and ye shall find."[6]

PART ONE

THE MYTH OF LOVE

Prologue
Dawn of Time

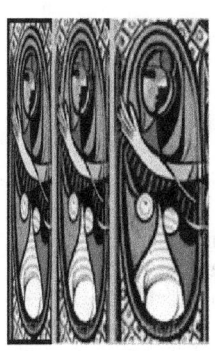

Between two mirrors,
My image reflects
Infinite series.
There my lives Interweave
With yours.
How can one find the Earth
Starting from the borders
Of the Infinite Universe?
How can one find Love
In the viscous Webs of Time?
Coordinates,
In the sinister murky Hades,
Are thin treads made of hope,
A flash of a ray illuminates
Fragments of faces
Full of desires.
***

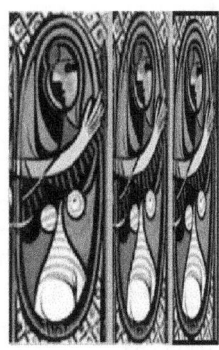

Detail, *Girl before a Mirror*[7]

THE BOOK OF FRAGMENTS, THE LOST TABLETS OF *INLY*

In the year of Our Lord, the Globe-Traveler Palmiero, whose name derived from solitary-Palm, took his staff and set foot on his journey. He was searching for the end of the World. He wanted to look beyond the borderline where the Sky meets the Earth. He traveled extensively through the Orient. He crossed Oceans, Mountains, Deserts and Rivers. He met Peoples with different and strange costumes. He encountered many dangerous situations. However, the only discovery that deserves mentioning is unearthing the fragments of the Lost Tablets of the Ancient Kingdom of Inly. His finding took place in a Desert beyond the high range of Mountains. After a sand storm, he was lost.

The last inhabited region, he had visited, was Sistan in Persia, east of the Great Salt Desert, exactly a year before. That particular afternoon was the seventh he had spent roaming with his horse. He had been without food or water during the last three days. His nights had been dreamless. When his horse fell into a pit and died, he thought it was the end. Suddenly it was dark. Black clouds of ashes were covering the face of the Moon. The stars seemed to fall from heaven and a violent quake shook the Earth from its foundations. The sand and falling rocks covered the carcass of his horse. That cataclysm continued for the whole night. He remained awake in great tribulation. Then he fell as a dead man. Behind him, he heard the sound of many waters falling from heaven. The sky had opened up and departed rolling up like a scroll.

When dawn came, he saw, all around, fragments of precious crystal mirrors. The earthquake had brought to the surface d*iam*onds and the rain had washed them away. Each fragment must have been part of a larger tablet on which gold letters were inscribed. Aware of the importance of the discovery, Palmiero gathered all the scattered fragments and, after giving them a systematic order to the best of his ability, he proceeded to decipher the writing.

FRAGMENT 1

OM, THE BEGINNING

1- Beginning in the beginning is not Beginning.

2- In the beginning is no "*in*" or "*out*" or both.
In the beginning, Beginning is not.
In the beginning, Beginning is.
In the beginning... Beginning.
In the beginning is Being alone.
In the beginning is Non-being alone.
In the beginning is no Being or Non-being.
In the beginning, there is no Beginning.
In the beginning is no "*there*" or "*here*" or both.
In the beginning, there is Nothing.
In the beginning, there is No-nothing.
In the beginning, there is neither Nothing nor No-nothing

3- Silence!

4- In the beginning silence is not because there is no sound.
In the beginning is the Word that is God.
In the beginning God is not.

5- In the beginning

6- Non-being alone,
Zero only, without a First, generates, without generating.
In the beginning is Being alone, One only, without a second.

FRAGMENT 2

THE SELF

1- In the beginning, there is only the Self, as fire shining on the Waters. It first said:
"I AM THAT I AM."

2- In the beginning, there is Nothing. It is covered by Death and Death is Hunger, Desire tightly embracing the Waters, its wife, its Speech. A perfect circle forms and, at the juncture of it, a spark generates, as a babe, and it says:
"I. "

3- In the beginning, God created heaven and earth.

FRAGMENT 3

THE LOVE SONG OF THE KING

1- Before Time the kingdom of Inly *is* the Light House for all the Nations of the World.

2- And, the Beginning begins by Thinking:
   "*I am*" and just so is named.

3- IAM is the most powerful monarch in the kingdom of Inly.

4- One day, strolling along, IAM sees his image in the water and falls in love with her.

5- They both cannot turn his mind away from her.

6- One day, as the king was looking at his image in the water, he asked her:
   "*What is your name?*"
   "*I ...!*" she answered with a whisper.

7- Ever since, the king resolved to marry the Fair Princess in the water.

8- All the arrangements for the wedding were made. A long list of guests was prepared. All the notables of the kingdom were invited. The invitation read:
   "*IAM I MARRIED TODAY.*"

9- Everybody, but Death, received the invitation to witness that union. It was felt that it was not propitious to invite Death at a joyous gathering such as a wedding.

10- When the wicked-ones knew about this, they immediately reported the news to Death, who, at first, was deeply mortified and, then, became furious. Of all the notables of the kingdom, he was the most important one. Why he was not invited?

11- Revenge was on his mind. Gathering all the powers of earth, he decreed:
   "*As IAM I will unite in their embrace, the king will die and only the queen will be left, never to see him again.*"

12- Desire, who was passing by, overheard the terrible curse and immediately replied:
   "*As long as IAM I will be united in loving embrace, the king shall live. Unseen during the night, he will be dead only during daytime.*"

13- Nothing more could be done to change that cruel faith.

14- The wedding took place as announced.

15- The king and the queen got into the royal bed and united in loving embrace. The whole kingdom experienced that union.

16- The king and the queen were radiant mirrors, one shining into the other. Their love was forever. The king loved the queen as himself and the queen loved the king as herself. No one in the kingdom ever witnessed such intensity of love. A flame engulfed the two lovers and each one became the other.

17- The orgasm, which derived from that union, was "the big bang," which generated this entire universe.

18- As the union got closer to daybreak, that flame was getting weaker and weaker. When the rays of the early sun finally reached the royal bed, the king started to fade away and disappear. The queen called for help, but nobody could bring the king back. Searchers searched the four corners of the kingdom, but the king could not be found.

19- I cried the loss of her king for the whole day. The whole day searchers were searching.

20- Then night fell on the kingdom. In the royal bedroom, resonated only the quiet sobs of I. When, all of a sudden, out of nowhere, a voice came out of the dark:

"My adorable wife, I am back."

"Who are you?" Cried the queen.

"It is IAM, your king and loving husband."

21- The two lovers fell in each other's arms. The king was again lost in admiration of the beautiful looks of his Queen. However, I could not see him any longer. They were united until another dawn came to separate the two enchanted passionate lovers.

22- To this day, visiting that kingdom, one can still witness the desperate search of the queen longing to behold her king. One can still hear, at night time, the cries of the two lovers embracing, thus the king might live forever.

FRAGMENT 4

THE SONG OF A PERSIAN KNIGHT

"I REALIZE IT

when I don't
know HIM.
When I know HER
in reality
I know myself.
When I know myself
I know my neighbor.
I am the messenger;
I am the only prophet;
I am the Elias,
which was for to come."

FRAGMENT 5

THE BIRTH OF KING EGOR

1- A year had gone by, since that first unfortunate love-night, in which the queen lost sight of her king forever.

2- Three hundred and sixty days and three hundred and sixty nights went by. An heir to the throne was born. He was named Egor.

3- When Egor was born the whole kingdom marveled because he was the mirror image of the king, his father.

4- Even the sky and the earth stood still to pay homage to the royal newly born. In that year, the annals of the astronomer recorded many wonders.

5- No lad in the entire world was fairer and gentler than Egor. Upon seeing him, all the women of the realm were touched by love. They all vowed eternal chastity unless possessed by the radiant child.

6- All the men of the entire domain were drawn to serve at his command and declared their unconditional loyalty to him.

7- Upon beholding his son, the king said to the queen:
> *"This son of ours deserves the best castle of the kingdom, from where he can move war to all the other nations and conquer the entire world."*

8- On hearing these words, the queen was very pleased. Immediately she gave order to build the most inexpugnable fortress of the entire country.

FRAGMENT 6

THE HOLY MOUNTAIN

1- There was a Mountain, the tallest in the kingdom of Inly, where, many eons ago, so legend has it, a very Old and Holy Hermit used to live in constant contemplation.

2- Some, to this day, sustain that he is still living there in one of the secret caves on the eastern side of the Mountain. However, nobody has ever seen him.

3- On account of the Holy Man, the Mountain was named Hierocrystal.

4- On the very top of that Mountain, the Royal Architects decided to build Egor's Castle.

FRAGMENT 7

THE EVERGREEN INVERTED TREE

1- Right in the midst of the Mountain, towers the Evergreen Inverted Tree. The Tree has Seven Branches. Each Branch produces jewels of unequaled beauty.

2- A beast with a thousand eyes guards there, to prevent mortals from seeing it.

3- The roots come down from Heaven. They take nourishment from a spring of pure Crystal Water, which, from the beginning, sprung on the top of Hierocrystal Mountain.

4- That Water is the same in which king IAM reflected when he first met Queen I.

5- From Mount Hierocrystal, that spring generates a River which branches out flowing down to the four corners of the fertile valley below.

FRAGMENT 8

THE CASTLE

1- On the highest peak of the Holy Hierocrystal Mountain, the Royal Architects built the Castle. A circular wall of granite was erected as a protection against the external world.

2- Three doors, from which a multitude came constantly in and out, and two windows were on the East side. Other two gateways were on the North and South side respectively. At its entrances music played constantly.

3- Half way, on the far South-West, there were two exits, which led to the base of the Mountain.

4- In the center, there was a mysterious Temple. It housed the Pillar of Jade.

BRONZE INTERPOLATION

HISTORY HAS IT THAT IN CROTON THE ITALIOTES BUILT THE
SANCTUARY OF HERA LAKINIA,
WHICH SHELTERED THE GOLD COLUMN,
HAVING THAT TEMPLE AS A MODEL.

FRAGMENT 9

THE dome

1- The entire Castle was covered by a dome, as a sky that holds under itself all the activities of those living below.

2- One hundred and eight thousand secret passageways were created. Through them, Egor, followed by his entire court, moved freely.

FRAGMENT 10

THE SECRET ROOM

1- Only one Room, in the secret mysterious Temple, was forbidden to him. It was a Secret Room at the center of the Imperial Palace.

2- IAM, the king father, had reserved that hidden Chamber only for his dwelling. Nobody was ever allowed to enter.

FRAGMENT 11

THE THRONE

1- At the center of the room, on the top of the base of the Inverted Evergreen Tree, a Throne of red onyx was built, in the shape of a cube.

2- In it, at the center of an ever spinning White Wheel, a Perfect Black diamond, a Sphere of pure Lightning, laid to rest.

FRAGMENT 12

THE SECRET PASSAGE WAY

1- Nobody ever saw it, but some say that from the center of that Throne a narrow Passageway was built in total secrecy.

2- The Passageway led out to the top of the dome, so the king could view the entire kingdom and contemplate the sky and the heavens beyond.

FRAGMENT 13

KING EGOR'S WIFE

1- Egor was very lonesome in his Castle. Nothing seemed to give him pleasure. He needed a wife.

2- Thus, it came to be that Egor knew Giovenca.

KĀMA-DEVA, THE LOVE-GOD, IS DEATH ITSELF

The ancient Indian texts declare that Kāma-deva is the god of love and death that generates preserves and destroys at will. In fact, those books declare that in the beginning, there was nothing at all. Indeed, this world was concealed by Death, by Hunger, by Desire. Desire is Hunger and Hunger is Death. Hunger and Desire damned the very first human couple. Their hunger and desire drove them to eat the forbidden fruit that, ultimately, lead them to suffer death itself.

Kāmadeva.[8]

The texts go on describing that Death projected its desire, as a mind-thought,

"Let me have a self," and he became a self.

In the time-circularity of a year, that self became a conscious being subject to death. In a circular turn, that mortal consciousness desired to become a historical ego, free to think and hunger. Subsequently, that ego produces other individuals capable as well of more desires. At the end, Death claims back all those mortals in his devouring jaws, only to ejaculate them out again, in a never-ending dead-fall spiral controlled by the three Fates.

FATES' COORDINATES

The three Fates sisters are the controller of all destinies. They weave since the time before time. Clotho spins the thread of existence and birth ensues, Lachesis measures the span of life and Atropos cuts it.

The three Fates.

CHAPTER 1
Course of Time

THE SIBYL UNFOLDING COORDINATES

If you want to know your future or your destiny, visit the mysterious volcanic crater of Lake Avernus near Neapolis, the New City of the siren Parthenope. There is the entrance to the underworld, the residence of the deceased. The entrance is located in the land of sulfur, a smoky passageway from where first Ulysses and later, Aeneas visited the dead spirits.

On those lakeshores, in a locality called Cumae, there is a dark cave. In the meanders of that cavern, lives the Sibyl, the oracle, the old ageless virgin prophetess. Holding the three books of life among smoky volcanic clouds, she predicts the future. She warns seekers of great fortunes and of ineluctable impending disasters.

Postcard of the Sibyl's cave

To the fearful warrior, asking about his destiny,
"Will I return safely from battle? "

The Sibyl answers,
"You will return *not* will die, *Redibis non morieris*. "

It is a double answer, depending where one places '*and*'or the comma. In fact, if it is placed before *not*, the warrior "will return, and will not die." However, if it is placed after the *not*, then he "will return not, and will die."

To the entrepreneur, concerned about business, or to the unmarried maiden, asking about her love, the oracle gives her predictions with similar *sibylline* answers.

THE COORDINATES OF DIANA THE HUNTRESS

Lovers are not always lucky. This was the case of Actaeon the hunter. In a time before time, Diana, the huntress goddess of the Moon and nocturnal spells, hunted *Gecalé*, the Beautiful-Site. There, she used to rest with all her nymphs bathing in a nearby spring. One day, Actaeon, a young hunter, passing by, caught sight of the chaste swimming goddess. He was ravished by that vision and fascinated by his sudden love for her. That arboreal divinity had captured him with her magic spell. The presence of Diana's attendants made him jealous. That river deity looked at him with her radiant eyes. Mysteriously rising from the clear waters, she recognized him. With an enigmatic smile, she called him by name and bewitched him. An overflowing spring of ardor gushed out of his heart.

However, the view of her breathtaking stunning nakedness had a deadly price. Out of rage for the intrusion, Diana transformed him in a stag. As a spooked buck, he ran away. The ferocious hunting hounds of that deity chased him and mauled him to death. Actaeon's love was buried there, in the turfs muddied by his own blood. Today, only the goddess Diana remains in that location. Her perennial immutable fascination lingers there, a mute witness of the magical mystery of that dream world.

Actaeon surprising Diana bathing and mauled by hounds[10]

THESEUS AND ARIADNE'S COORDINATES

At times and with dire consequences, a lover may give away her coordinating lines for the sake of the loved one. This happened in Crete. There, in the midst of the labyrinth, lives a terrible monster. His name is Minotaur. He is a beast, a man's body with a bull's head. He is the product of the bestial love between an ox and Queen Pasiphae, the wife of Minos the king of the dead.

Pasiphae and the Minotaur[11]

To hide the shame Minos built the Labyrinth. Once in that maze, no one can come out from it. There, lives the Minotaur. He feasts on flesh. Periodically, young Athenians are fed to the monster. The hero Theseus fought and killed him. Ariadne, the ogre's half sister, out of pure love for Theseus, gave him a thread. With it, the hero was able to trace his steps back to life but not back to love. In fact, Ariadne was abandoned by the merciless Theseus.

Even today, in that palace, a traveler can still hear the desperate cries of the seduced heartbroken maiden.

THE SIREN'S COORDINATE

Two-tailed siren and Achelous[12]

Not only humans can cry from despair. Also sirens anguish and die from love pains. Four-thousand-five-hundred years earlier, in the waters of Mount Vesuvius' Gulf, on the Tyrrhenian Sea, a strange creature entangled in the nets of local anglers.

"Run! *Tréchete*! Quickly, come here! *Currite a ccà*! The Siren! *A Sirena!* The Siren! *A Sirena!*" Local barefooted urchins screamed to alert passerby of a strange fish-like thing on the shoreline.

A crowd gathered around the poor creature washed up by the sea. It was the body of a very strange being. No one had seen anything like it.
"Is it a fish?" bystanders asked.

Some answered,
"No, it is not! "

Various onlookers declared, "It is a woman! "

"No, it is not! " Others replied.

"What is it? " Everyone enquired.

No one knew.

Her head and torso were that of a beautiful woman. Her legs were fins of noticeable length. The being was still alive. She was moaning with tears rolling on her checks.

The Siren's eyes expressing her longing love for Ulysses.

PARTHENOPE'S DREAM

A sigh comes out of her mouth, as she whispered,
"Ulysses... Ulysses..."

Some of the onlookers swore they also heard a cry, carried by the wind, coming from the distant horizon of the sea, an echo, a desperate echo,
"Parthenope... Parthenope..."

That being was the Siren Parthenope, which means Virgin-Maiden. On the shore of the Vesuvian Bay, she died surrounded by local people. She departed this life heartbroken, unable to seduce Ulysses, a lost sea wonderer in search of his way back home. Desperate and restrained to the master pole of his ship, Ulysses could not respond to the charming fatal song-call of that mysterious maiden-fish. He knew that sirens swam in that sea. He also knew that no one had ever escaped their deadly singing. Mermaids captivated navigators with their serenades. Poor sailors, inevitably enchanted by those calls, lost control of their ships and crashed on the numerous surrounding rocks. Ulysses, who was sailing those waters, was eager to hear the melodic voices of those beautiful seductive human-like creatures. However, to save the ship he ordered his sailors to strap him to the master pole while they plugged their ears with wax. Therefore, Ulysses was unable to answer the call of the mermaid.

After Parthenope's death, the local people staged an impressive funeral. During the ceremony, a bull with a man's face appeared. It was Parthenope's father, the ancient fertility water-god Achelous. He had left his shaded Greek river-home. He navigated the waters of the nearby Sepeithos stream and reached out to her resting place to attend her memorial service. Ever since, distraught by sorrow, his loving bellow does not call out anymore.

On that Gulf, the local population founded *Nea-polis*, now Naples, a Greek *New-city* and named it Parthenope in her honor. There, they also erected a temple dedicated to the Siren and established yearly commemorative celebrations with ceremonies that persist to this day.

Madonna dell'Arco, fujenti & vattienti.

In her honor, they held sacred contests with music and gymnastics. Traces of those ancient games can be observed today during the processions of the runners, *fujenti*, and flagellants, *vattienti*. The celebrations, dressed with Catholic garbs, take place at the Sanctuary of the *"Madonna dell'Arco,"* about six miles east of Naples.

Naples' panorama and Parthenope[13]

ETRUSCAN COORDINATES

Etruria is North of Naples. Two thousand two hundred years ago, the philosopher Posidonius from Rhodes visited Agylla, as his fellow Greeks named it. The local Etruscan inhabitants, instead, called it Cisra, while the neighboring Romans referred to it as Caere. Today that ancient town is Cerveteri, 28 miles north of Rome. At that time, Tarquinius, a resident nobleman, had invited the Rhodian thinker to visit with him.

Upon arrival, the philosopher was ushered by the *lautni slaves* in the banquet hall adorned with hunting scenes painted in vivid bright colors. Before him, on the center stage of the room was an impressive *klinai* dinner bed. Reclining on it, under richly embroidered covers, were the bearded Tarquinius, a man in his early forties with long curly hair, and his wife Larthia, a beautiful woman in her early twenties. She had long black hair parted in the middle and with tresses rolled at each side of her head. Her full lips invited kisses and her eyes conveyed an indescribable longing.

With a gracious welcoming gesture, the hosting couple pointed at the *klinai* to their right. Posidonius deposited his gifts at the foot of their bed and took place on that recliner.

Louvre, Etruscan sarcophagus in the shape of a *klinai*

The music started and dinner was served. Double flutes and string instruments accompanied graceful dancers.

Etruscan dancers

On the tables before the beds of each guest, servants placed a steady flow of food. They carried trays of cold roast beef in an oil, garlic and vinegar sauce, sided with cereal pudding. Dishes of boiled octopus in olive oil and sweet water perch cooked with eggs, white wine, salt and olive oil followed a hot mixed stew of pork, beef and veal. Meticulously slave girls kept the cups filled with a variety of local wines to wash down that abundance of food. Piles of fruit and sweet honey cakes provided a change of taste in between all those servings.

Numerous servants surrounded Posidonius bed. Some of those beautiful slaves, boys and girls, offered their pleasurable services under his covers. The philosopher refused with a thankful gesture. In doing so, it seemed to him that Larthia, who smiled at him amiably, welcomed his denial. However, she accepted the advances of a young slave while her complacent husband made room for his frolicking wife. As the slave pleasured her, she kept gazing upon Posidonius, who, in turn, could not believe his eyes. He had never witnessed such behavior in his native Greece. There, decent women kept in the seclusion of their homes. Only public courtesans mingled with men in the public arena.

As her slave was dutifully serving her, Larthia never took her eyes away from the Greek, who was lost in that ecstatic vision. What was unexplainable to him was the behavior of her husband, who helped his wife respond to her slave's love thrusts. Suddenly, Larthia pushed her lover outside of her bed. Right away, her husband Tarquinius took her place finishing off in him the ardor of the discarded slave.

Tarquinius and his slave

Larthia slid down from her bed and landed under Posidonius' covers. The philosopher's throbbing manhood had no difficulty slipping gently in Larthia pleasurable center abundantly moistened by her recent slave's foreplay. They did not have sex; they made passionate love. Moreover, they continued loving each other, even after they had both reached their apex at unison. Through their eyes, they recognized themselves. In each other arms, they found their ancient love. They realized that they were the primeval souls coming from the folds of time. They came from a time immemorial and now they were together again. In their loving, tender embrace, there was the promise never to part again.

The next day, a very bright and sunny one, Larthia and Posidonius had a romantic stroll along the *Road of the Underworld*. Hand in hand, they walked under the shade of ancient Mediterranean pines on the pathway coasting ancient tombs dating as far back as six hundred years earlier. The whole complex replicated the city of the living. But it was intended for the dead. Along the roads were rows of square tombs, elsewhere were domed shaped mound ones. Tuff, a popular local stone produced during volcanic eruptions, was the building material of those mausoleums constructed as authentic houses for the living. Each Etruscan tomb was an actual replica of their houses. Even the interior, composed of corridors and rooms, was lavishly painted in vivid colors with various scenes of daily life. Outside the complex, phallic columns, called

Cippi, indicated that the tomb belonged to a male, while mirrors and jewelry indicated the tomb belonged to woman.

At one point Posidonius stopped, looked Larthia in the eyes and said,
"I am in love with you; I don't want to go back to my country."

"I love you too," she replied with tears in her eyes. "You can stay here; my husband is influential enough to find a permanent occupation for you among our Lucomones priest kings."

"I would be honored," he replied. "However, you would have to give up your ways. I do not like your freedom, your promiscuity. I do not believe this is the behavior an honest woman should have."

"I resent very much your words," Larthia replied with a sad expression on her face. "You are criticizing our way of living, our customs and our society. This is difficult for me to accept. However, for the sake of my love for you, I will abide by your rules and I will try to behave according to your Greek models of conduct."

That same evening Larthia went to visit her personal haruspex, the Etruscan priestly diviner able to predict the future by analyzing sheep's entrails.

"Tell me my lord," she begged, upon arriving in his presence, "what is my destiny with my present lover?"

The wrinkled old man, who lived in a stinky shack with a straw roof, went outside without a word. Larthia heard some ruffle, a loud bleating that sounded like the cry of a baby, then silence. The haruspex came back carrying in his bloodied hands the entrails of a sheep. He placed it on a table and started examining it while reciting some prayers. After some time, he said,
"You will suffer a lot. Your lover will break your heart. You will lose him. Your life will be cut short."

"Is there a way I can avoid it? Can I change my destiny?" she pleaded in a state of panic.

"Yes, you can," replied the haruspex. "Go to the Artist sculptor and have him carve your likeness and offer it to the gods and goddesses."

Larthia felt better by his answer. Gave him a hefty offering and went away. On her way back home, she considered,
"Why should I believe all this nonsense? Posidonius is not going to leave me if I behave as he wants me to."

Comforted by this thought she returned home. Tarquinius with another man were waiting for her.
"Look who came to visit us, all the way from far Vatluna," he said, pointing to the handsome youth on his right.

Standing next to him was Eptesio, a sturdy man with a very stupid expression and a demeanor qualifying him good only as a sex toy. In the past, he had pleasured Larthia many times.

"*Hathna*, happy to see you," she said only to be polite, but without any emotion.

"This calls for a banquet to celebrate his return," declared Tarquinius with a big smile.

The next day, a festive gathering was organized. Guest started arriving and the happy event took place. Tarquinius ordered a separate *klinai* bed for Larthia, so she could have more room with her returned lover. However, she did not welcome Eptesio's advances. As he approached her bed, she refused him. For a moment he thought she was just playing hard to get. But when he realized that she was serious, he started becoming violent. Through all this, Tarquinius was looking with renewed interest, hoping to witness the rape of his wife. In fact, Eptesio grabbed Larthia from behind and, with a strangling hold, forced himself in her anus. He trusted his strong member in her and pumped her hard. Larthia cried for the pain. Tarquinius started masturbating. It was at that moment that Posidonius entered the dining hall.

Disillusioned and disgusted, he turned on his steps and exited the house. Larthia, shaking Eptesio off her, ran after him.

"Posidonius, stop! He forced himself on me. Please understand," desperately she pleaded, throwing herself at his feet kissing them.

"I do not want to lose you," she pleaded. "I love you. Stop, let me explain."

"No explanation is necessary," he replied, pushing her away with utter disgust. "I agree with the Romans, who use the word Etruscan as synonym for whore!"

Larthia remained there on the ground, sobbing desperately, while her philosopher disappeared in the darkness of the evening. That night and the following day, she sent her servants to convince him to return. Each time they came back with sad tidings. Until the final messenger reported that Posidonius had left definitively for Rhodes that same morning. Larthia collapsed. Five days she remained in that state of unconsciousness. Only the loving care of her nanny kept her fed. When she came to her senses, she remembered the prophecy of the haruspex. Hastily, she left for the house of the artist Dionysius. However, before leaving her home, unnoticed she took a sharp short dagger and hid it under her tunic.

Banquet scene on an Etruscan vase

Dionysius was a Greek slave. His specialized in clay portraits. His sculptures were very accurate in both resemblance and details, like three-dimensional photographs. It was customary, in those days, to have ones likeness reproduced in sculpture. Then the devotees would present the artworks in the local temples as a votive offering to the gods to thank for a grace received or to ask for one.

Motionless, Larthia waited patiently for hours while Dionysius worked on the sculpture. Tears were flowing down her cheeks and her fleshy lips parted as to send a kiss. The artistic talent of Dionysius captured both the intended kiss and the sadness of her eyes. Larthia waited also that the red clay head was fired. Then, she wrapped it in precious sacred linens and left for the temple.

Larthia?[14]

She reached the temple of Satres, the god of time. There, she placed her votive head before the god and the other goddesses and she desperately prayed,

"Come back to me, Posidonius, come back. Do not judge me for that which is beautiful and sacred. In time you will understand and I will be there waiting for you. Posidonius, your judgment, your condemnation wounds me to death. For the fulfillment of the diviner's prediction, I offer this votive head of mine to Lasa Vecu, goddess of prophesy. For my survival, I offer it to Evan, goddess of immortality, and to Tvath, goddess of resurrection. Finally, I offer it to Satres, the god of time, who will safe keep it until you will understand and will repent for your insanity. I seal this prayer transfusing my life into my clay image. "

Then, she took out the dagger and speaking to it as if to a human being, she said,

"You thirsty blade, drink my blood offered to the gods for my reunion with my love."

When Larthia finished her prayer, she plunged the knife in her breast. As her blood spilled over the red clay figure covering it completely, her life transfused into it.

DREAMING OF INDIA

Larthia came back to life some three hundred years ago, in Southern India. Her name, then, was Aditi. Her parents took her to the Ruler's palace in Arcot, near Madras. It was an honor for their daughter to become the concubine of the Nawab Muhammad Ali. She stood there, before his throne with her eyes fixed to the ground.

Mohamed Ali Khan Wallajah.[15]

"What is your name?" He asked.

After a few seconds of hesitation, prompted by his wazir, she replied with a timid voice that was barely audible
"Aditi, my Lord!"

"Oh," he added, "like the Hindu Goddess of Dawn."

Aditi was about twelve. Mercenaries, sent out to recruit young virgins for the Nawab's harem, had chosen her. The recruiters had convinced Aditi's poor parents to give her up voluntarily. In return, they received a small sum of money, which seemed as a blessing to them. At the same time, they were able to secure a good future for their daughter. Without having the expense of a dowry, they gained some needed assets at the same time.

At the court of Muhammad Ali, Aditi grew to become the most beautiful princess of the whole harem. One day, after many years, the Nawab noticed her while she was bathing. Her beautiful forms revealed that she was ready to receive his attentions. In the hot tropical breeze, during a full moon night, on one of the terraces of his royal palace, Muhammad Ali had her virginity.

Royal Palace, India

As she was penetrated by him and as a sign of willingly offering her submission, Aditi pressed harder on her Lord's shaft to feel more intensely the pleasurable pain. She became his favorite concubine. And she achieved a powerful position in the regal court. Her origins may have been from a poor Indian family but her gained status made her parents very proud. Nawab Muhammad Ali loved her dearly. Aditi was always the chosen one to spend the nights with him. This generated envy and jealousy among the other wives and concubines. However, this was also the cause of her ruin.

One day, since she was very ill, the eunuchs summoned Tiger, the court physician. They granted him permission to enter the harem. It was unprecedented. However, Muhammad, out of love for her, approved. Eventually she recovered, but the envy and the jealousy of the other harem women grew deeper. Especially Malka, the last of Muhammad's wives, felt deep anger against Aditi. Malka, the Nawab's youngest wife, considered herself the most loved one. She was convinced to be the prettiest of all. Therefore, she resented Aditi's new status. A real conspiracy took place in the harem. Most of the other wives and concubines gladly sided with Malka.

They started reporting to the Nawab that Aditi had been unfaithful and had a relation with Tiger the physician. It was not true. Nevertheless, it was very easy for the other women to fabricate evidence against her. Only Savitri, the first wife, who loved Aditi as a daughter or younger sister, defended her. Although Savitri was the oldest of the wives and therefore demanded respect, still she was alone in that power struggle. Thus, she was incapable of protecting the poor girl. Laws required severe punishments for unfaithful concubines. The less cruel one was to ban the culprit from the harem.

Heartbroken, Muhammad exiled Aditi to be a farm slave in a far away province, where she committed suicide shortly after. Tiger, the physician, was sentenced to death. The execution took place the following week. An elephant crushed his head.

REMEMBER MORNING RIVER, DREAMING THE WEST

According to different latitude and longitude, Love may take different garbs and costumes, but its fundamental structure knows no boundaries.

A new drama took place two hundred years ago among the Oglala, *Scattered Band* of the Far West Lakota people.

Chanunpa, the Sacred Pipe

"Oh, Yeah, oh Sacred, Yeah,
Yeah oh Mountain,
Yeah oh *Wamblee* Wise Eagle,
Yeah only she reaches you,
Yeah she took This Man
Yeah on the Peak!
Yeah come oh vision,
Yeah come oh vision!

Oh Immortal Grandfather, This Man, clad with *unci* Grandmother's blanket, is on a Quest and offers this song to you. Purified in the *inipi* sweat lodge, This Man has sacrificed the flesh in the Sun and has smoked the *chanunpa* Sacred Pipe with the Ancestors. That smoke made clouds in the sky. Yeah, it reached you, oh Great *Tatanka* Buffalo. "

The warrior sang these words, while following the tradition of his people. Among the sweet smoke of his *inipi* lodge, his Ancestor appeared in full regalia. The spirit figure spoke to him and the warrior heard the words coming out from the Alpine forest,

"*Takoja* Grandson this is your *hanbleceya* cry for a vision. Now, as we smoke the sacred *chanupa* pipe, learn from This Wise One. This is the way of life as it was when Plenty Buffalos roamed the *wiyohpe yata* Western Plains of the Forefathers. "

The warrior had been without visions for the first three moons. He had a sense of despair in his heart. On the Mountain with no water or food, that brave one was alone, full of Sacred Terror, clinging to the Ancestral Pipe. He was shaking his familiar *wagmuha* rattler in which *unci* grandmother had placed forty tiny dry pieces of her own flesh. She had chopped them from a strip of tissue cut off from her own arm for this purpose.

"Could it be that This Vision Seeker is destined to become an upside-down *heyoka* clown?" thought that young man.

On the third evening, when the *hanhepi-wi* night sun was already half way on its journey, the skins on the *inipi* lodge became transparent and a bright rising son was shinning on the horizon. Its rays were as crystal pure water pouring out of it. They were like a flowing river that came to irrigate a mighty tree that reached the sky. At the base of that tree, there was the sweat lodge.

As the warrior came out of it, a rush of cold air caused a burning sensation within his chest. Outside, under the branches of that mighty tree, all the creatures of Grandmother Nature were competing, mating, eating and drinking from that river.

He spent three moons in those waters. Then, a tepee *oinikaga* floating on the current came upon him and enveloped that brave man. In there, it was as bright as midday. It was so bright that it blinded him. Only the breath taking shapes of a naked maiden was barely distinguishable. She stood on the entrance holding an eagle feather. She was as beautiful as the mountains at sunrise, as sweet as honey and as fragrant as the herbal *waḣpe-washtemna* perfume of the forest. That warrior could not see her face. But the radiance of the sun was shining through her eyes. Only her flowing black long hair was dancing like soft clouds in the breeze.

The tepee

"Yeah, oh Eagle Feather, follow This Woman!" she chanted, sounding like the melody of the flute, like the wonder songs of the gentle winged people of the air. She handed him the feather and called the brave warrior with his new Oglala name, the name for a *yuwipi, a new* Dakota shaman.

She took *wikaša wakan*, this Sacred Person outside the tepee. Out, in the warm air she took This New Man, where all the animals, his relatives stood in the stillness of dawn. She walked before This Shaman without touching the ground. Then, suddenly, she turned and her long black hair swung like the spreading of the wings of a big bird and, lo, before his eyes, *wamblee*, the Great Eagle appeared. Then, slowly, with majestic movements, she flapped her wings and flew into the sun on the horizon.

That Man came down from the Sacred Mountain with the vision still within his heart. He was moving silently and cautiously through the woodlands at the first light of daybreak. The Great Womb of Mother Earth was peacefully awakening all her people, all the *mitakuye oyasin*, the relatives of This Man. She awoke the ones with two, four, or eight legs and also the ones with no legs at all. Far away, the white breath of the hot volcanic spring was slowly making its sacred offering to the four corners of the Universe.

It was then that This Shaman saw her for the first time. She was gathering wood in the forest. Also the maiden saw the young man. She did not seem afraid, but looked at him strait into the eyes and stood still. Brother owl flushed from the upland and flew between the two gazes. She went on collecting wood. Her agile figure moved swift and gentle with the grace of *Taha Topta*, the Sacred Deer. Occasionally, she would stop and gaze at the man with intense and deep eyes. The man was smitten, taken, incapable of moving. In those eyes he saw the same mystery of the vision he experienced during the last four suns on the Sacred Mountain. Motionless, he watched her until she disappeared beyond the ridge.

He fallowed her all the way to her village. It was the village of the Crow Dogs, the enemy of This Warrior's Ancestors. He was Oglala, the son of Thunder Cloud, the grandson of *Wakaŋ Taŋka*, the Great Mysterious Spirit. That Brave Man was Eagle Feather, the vision seeker.

"That Woman will belong to This Man," Eagle Feather thought.

The man watched as she entered her *onikaga* tepee. He waited. Long shadows were being casted when she came out following a warrior. The warrior stopped, sniffing the air, rapidly moving his head left and right, as if sniffing the danger. He knew the enemy was there. With a sign, he ordered the woman back into the tepee to fetch weapons. The shadows got longer. Crow Warrior and eagle Feather were breathlessly motionless waiting for events to unfold.

"Morning River!" cried out the rival warrior.

That name was not a surprise for Eagle Feather. She had the manner of Grandmother Earth. Her name reflected the way of Nature. He had noticed it while watching her moving freely and proudly in the woods. She appeared stepping out from the narrow opening of the tepee, holding a buffalo jawbone tomahawk.

Jawbone tomahawk

Immediately, the young Oglala warrior jumped knocking down with a blow the Crow warrior. He grabbed he woman and dragged her into the thick woods. All this he did without thinking or hesitation. He took everyone by surprise. Eagle Feather realized his daring action only when Morning River and he were well deep into the forest. They heard the war cry of the Crow warrior and the excited answer of his peers. Morning River and Eagle Feather were flying on the wings of *Wanblee* the Great Eagle. It was the same bird that, in the vision quest, had given the Oglala warrior his Sacred Feather.

There were no more shadows now. Only friendly darkness enveloped the entire woodland. No warrior would have dared follow. Way far and out of danger Morning River and Eagle Feather rested in a ditch. They found shelter under heavy brushes, a safe favorite bedding spot offered by the brother Whitetail. After a long silence, attentive to the sounds of the magic night during the time of falling leaves, Morning River asked with a soft whisper,
"How do you want This Woman to call you? "

Slowly, the Oglala Man turned towards Morning River and saw her mysterious enquiring eyes shining in the dark under the thick coverage, and said,
"This Man is called Eagle Feather by the Eagle itself. "

No more words were spoken. They were not needed. In the eyes of Morning River, the young man saw the Great Mother. In her arms he witnessed the Great Mother when she sheds her love through her branches. On her lips he experienced the Mother Earth when she rips apart trees and tepees with the might of her deadly breath. On her breast he found the warmth of Nature when she dresses with summer pastures. Then, quietness came down on the still woodlands and all the relatives of the forest stood into the Great Womb. In her womb, the great Oglala warrior deposited his semen while Morning River shivered in a loving orgasm.

Mysterious names were whispered throughout the trees of the forest. Despite the vision, This Man could not understand the voices he was hearing. They were as dreams and quests from another world, another season. Morning River, lying next to This Man, was breathing gently. Somehow he knew that all the answers were within her. This Man took Morning River. She was his road to the hunting grounds. An Oglala Shaman knows *canku-wakan*, the Sacred Road of Life. Now This Man knew that she was the Woman of the vision, she was the one that gave him the Feather of *Wanblee*, the Wise Eagle.

At dawn, Eagle Feather woke up. Five Crow warriors surrounded him. Each, in turn, counted coup by delivering deadly blows on him. It was a good day to die and Morning River was near to usher This Man through the forbidden door.

The Woman took a hand full of sand, lifted her arms and made it pour on the ground crying out loud:
> "Yeah, you go,
> Oh Eagle Feather,
> And you take
> This Woman's
> Heart with you
> Forever ... "

And the song echoed through the entire valley.

In his last breath This Man took her hand and with a murmur said,
> "Now take me beyond, Morning River. "

It was then that she became the Great Eagle *Wanblee* and took This Dead One on her loving wings. That Eagle took him up, passed the clouds, to those beautiful evergreen hunting grounds of *Wakaŋ Taŋka*.

While, down there in a ditch, under heavy brushes, in the favorite bedding spot of the Whitetail brother, a Woman, alone, was crying holding tight the hand of her dead lover.

PART TWO

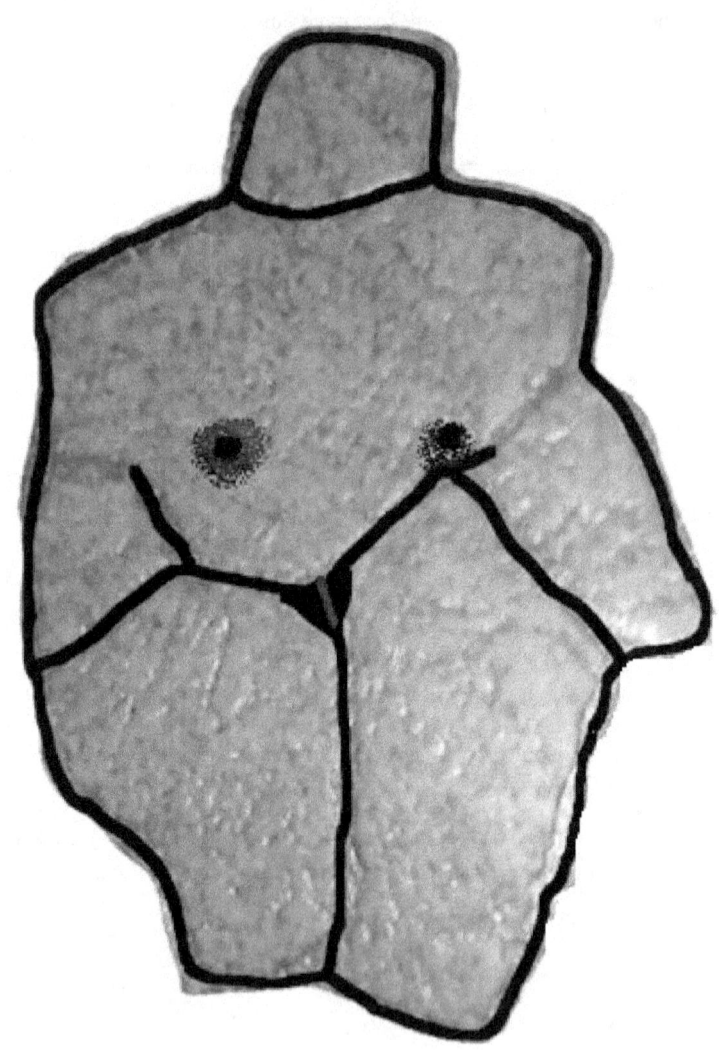

The Prehistoric Venus

MAKING LOVE

CHAPTER 1
Camilla

CAMILLA'S EDUCATION BEFORE PALMIERO

Camilla, whose Latin name means the *virgin* of *unblemished character*, was a slut, but not an *ethical* one. Frequently, her name comes up in mythology, art and literature. Opera and films were produced on her. Her name was also associated with a **flower**, the *Camellia*.

Our Camilla was the daughter of a Siren and a Siren herself, luring humans to life or death. She was a beautiful, tall, curvy and fiery woman just turned thirty-five, with long red locks, piercing blue eyes and a love-bite birthmark on her neck. She had a very strong need to be loved and a passionate desire for sex. She was in love with love. However, she did not know how to love. She was never capable to give herself and care for another. In spite of her achievements, her mind never soared above her navel. She was a walking vagina in a continuous state of arousal. She had even developed a way of stimulating herself and masturbating while sitting in public. Also tampons were a sexual toy for her. Once she wiggled one so forcefully that it ripped in her vagina and the husband had to painfully extract it.

"Look what I must walk around with," she used to tell her lovers. To demonstrate it, she would drag their hands between her legs and force their fingers under her panties. She made them feel her vaginal cavity inundated by viscous fluids.

Before getting married she had known carnally over one hundred men. In one occasion, she had been in bed with every one of the twelve firefighters in the local firehouse. Yes, she gave her body easily to the first comer. But she never gave her soul. She could not, because she did not have one. Her soul was already dead. Camilla had inherited that dead soul from Diana, her own deceased mother, who never loved any of her children. She was too busy playing around and too concerned with all her lovers. She did not have time for her kids, not even when one of her lovers raped her daughter Maggie, Camilla's sister. Eventually, that violent person turned out to be Diana's worst enemy.

Camilla missed her parent immensely. Every time she looked at herself in the mirror, she always saw her mother's beautiful face. In return, from beyond, mysteriously Diana, through her daughter eyes, longed for life again. Camilla was the instrument. And Diana was the siren calling *"back the lovely April of her prime."*[16]

On the footsteps of Diana's behavior, Camilla had all sorts of addiction, including drugs, sex and alcohol. After her wedding, however, she partially gave up the drugs and booze, but never sex. She continued on "prescription" drugs and, occasionally, with her lovers, to heighten the momentum, she got drunk or stoned. Her long history of heavy drug addiction made her connect with ghosts and the paranormal world. She claimed to *see* and *speak* with the dead.

Naturally, Camilla followed her mother's example in everything and developed a psychotic behavior. In spite of appearances, she never really made any effort for her family, unless it placed her in a position of command over others. That was evident when she bossed around her children's teachers, demanding special accommodations for them.

She married for money and never loved her husband. She chose a stupid gullible person who believed all her lies and deceits. She was very good at it. She was able to make up very convincing stories. She lied with straight angelic innocent expressions and very convincing heart moving fake tears. No one would have ever doubted her. And she knew this was her strength. Many times she told one of her lovers that, if her husband were to die prematurely, she had already eyed a successor. He was someone who was as stupid and devoted and would have allowed her all the sexual freedom and partners she craved for. As for her kids, she hoped her daughter would become a Dominatrix. Referring to her oldest son promising sizeable manhood, she used to tell her husband,
"With that endowment, he is going to fetch us a lot of money."
But that was not all, to one of her lovers, she confessed of having incestuous fantasies about her son's penis in her own lusting vagina.

With new lovers, she acted very quickly. Once, in one of the internet shady sites for kinky costumers, she met Jim, an army colonel. Upon meeting him, she immediately ended up in his cot in one of the barracks of a local military fort. The day after, the only great thing she could boast about the affair was his motorcycle and the remarkable size of his stocky manhood.

A week after that event, she had to choose between taking her kids to a free educational field trip to the Museum of Natural History in Washington DC, or meet Jim for the second time. She opted to spend the entire day with that newfound lover. It was for that man that she denied her children the educational experience of the museum. With her husband, she excused herself alleging impending job obligations. However, her selfishness back fired. The plan of spending the entire cozy day with Colonel Jim turned out sour. In fact, to submit Camilla, the colonel first forced his nightstick in her. Next, he satisfied his lustful wild urges in her mouth and repeatedly in her vagina. Finally, three hours ahead of schedule, he selfishly left her in the motel bed. She was infuriated. Her husband, believing that she was at work, expected her later. Therefore, not to raise his suspects, Camilla had to wait alone in that squalid room for the time to return home. Commenting on her bad choice, one of her lovers criticized her for having deprived her children of a valuable cultural experience. Immediately, to prove him wrong and to show that she was a caring mother, she took her kids to that Museum. There, she hurriedly dashed through the dinosaurs' exhibit only to skip the planetarium, the anthropological sections of the world's cultures and all the other exhibits. After that ordeal, with an air of superiority that highlighted her incapable intellectual nullity, she proclaimed,

"I would have preferred to stick a fork in my eye, rather than to experience all those ancient bones." Then, with a pseudo-intellectual tone, she boasted, "I, for one, have a preference for paintings."

Another time, she fell madly in love with a rapper, nicknamed the Podiatrist, on account of his very strong foot fetish. Camilla and he never physically met. She had found him on-line on another dubious site for fetishists. For a few months they chatted and exchanged thousands of their body images through webcam. She even offered him the photos of her daughter's feet for his stimulation. They had virtual sex, but never exchanged bodily touch. Nevertheless, Camilla proclaimed she was in love with him. Moreover, she was also ready to marry him. However, the Podiatrist was soundly critical of her promiscuous life. He demanded she would undergo STD testing before they had a physical sexual encounter. She did. Although all tests were negative, the Podiatrist was still critical of her lifestyle. Since Camilla did not intend to renounce it, she broke up with him. As used tampons, she passed him along with Colonel Jim to Josephine, her paternal aunt, with whom she was having an incestuous lesbian relationship.

Josephine was an old hag whose innumerable cosmetic remaking attempts did not diminish the withering away of a beauty that had never been there in the first place. She had been married to an alcoholic wedding singer, for whom Camilla had harbored a secret lustful desire. At that time, she had been very judgmental of her aunt's way of treating him. However, now that Josephine was divorcing, she became a great alibi for Camilla. In fact, she covered all her niece's lascivious escapades. In return for the favor, Camilla provided her nymphomaniac lonely aunt with lots of sexual partners. Josephine reciprocated her favors by helping her niece find clients. Yes, Camilla was a prostitute at heart who loved her trade. They exercised their business at the Tropicana Hotel and Casino in

Atlantic City. Camilla's fee was one thousand dollars per night, while her aunt gave it away for free. In her old age sick crisis, Josephine picked up all the men she could lay hands on. She used to say,
"I change and wear men like if they were dresses."
Eventually, shortly after, Josephine died of AIDS.

It was evident that Camilla did not know how to love. However, she demanded it from everybody. She yearned for it. She loathed it. She begged for it. The only love she understood was sex. It did not matter if it was with a man or a woman. She was satisfied only if she thought that the others were enamored with her. Upon assurance of their love, she would dominate them completely. After which, she would dump him or her to move on to the next victim-lover.

She measured love by the intensity of the sexual relationship. In her eyes, whosoever engaged sexually with her meant that they loved her. From her lovers, she demanded affectionate feelings. In exchange, she was not returning any sympathy towards them, unless it was to promote her own sexual gratification. In one situation, to totally control a bisexual lover, she sought a new man to enslave completely. When this last one was under her total control, she forced him to perform what she personally could not physically do. She obliged him to become her substitute to sodomize and satisfy her gay lover.

"Do you love me?" She very frequently asked her lovers, "If so, how much do you love me?" She used to insist and she was never satisfied without a detailed answer.

Like an ostrich, Camilla hid her head in the sand. She did not want to know what others thought of her. She considered herself the righteous one and the best love maker. However, she had an inferiority complex that led her to disparage those she could not compete with or were critical of her.

In her eyes, only she could end a relation. If she did not, she would have a real meltdown. As in the opera *Manon*, Camilla, like her mother, spent a life for pleasure and gold. From her mother, she had inherited the qualities of a temptress and of an irresistible tempestuously deadly siren. She had to control her lovers in every detail. In a way, her control was intended to punish them and to revenge what they had done to her mother and to her. In short, Camilla was the devil, the daughter of the siren Diana.

This was Camilla's education and, naturally, it was the fabric of her mind. Of all this, Palmiero knew nothing. Nevertheless, he was about to find out. But, what he really did not know was that in reality Camilla's mind was his own twin mind. Except for drugs, which Palmiero never wanted to experience, Camilla and he were twin soles. They went back millennia, recurrently coming back from eons of time. At different historical periods, Camilla and Palmiero had been for each other mother-father, lover-enemy, partner-superior, employee-employer and more. Each time they were in a love-hate relation.

A NEW "JOB"

Camilla sighed heavily as she closed the latest 'must read' from her book club.

"Another waste of my time and money," she thought. "These 'love stories' are all the same. The plot, the settings and the story line are all happily ever-after nonsense." She inhaled deeply and reflected on what Robert had told her just that evening,

"You are too difficult," he repeated it numerous times.

"Maybe he is right." Camilla considered. "Maybe I do 'want' more and more. I should be happy with what I have. All my girlfriends are jealous of me and tell me how wonderful Robert is and, in comparison to their husbands, they are one-hundred percent correct." However, Camilla could not help but think that there was more to 'happily-ever-after.' She could feel it deep in her bones.

She heard Robert downstairs watching his favorite porno films on television and knew he would choose to stay on the couch rather than cuddle with her.

"Well maybe tomorrow will be different." She thought, "The new job I got may be the change I need." She turned the light off and fell fast asleep.

Camilla's sleep was not dream free. The book she had read the night before had its toll. In her slumber, she dreamt of a King named *Iam*, a Queen called *I* and a city by the name of *Inly*. The next morning, upon awakening she could not make any sense of that dream.

"A city called Inly?" she thought. "Oh, yes … it makes sense… *Inly*… *In-ly*, as *in*-side, in the soul, as opposed to external-*ly*. Yes, there, *I am I*. I think of myself as one being, who is the ruler of my entire psyche. Then, that 'I' becomes this Ego… yes, *Ego-r*… I get it now! That was a very Freudian dream. I should talk about it to my shrink if ever I'll go see her."

***

However, Camilla forgot her dream. She had to be ready very early. She was anxious to get to work. It was a very important occasion. It was her first day at her new employment in Manhattan, New York. She had worked hard to land that job. In fact, she had obtained it by granting expert oral sexual pleasures to Charles Delaney, the Vice-President of her department. After the interview, he invited her for a weekend trip. She accepted. They went to Asbury Park, in New Jersey. Dinner at *McLoone's*, a local boardwalk restaurant, was followed by a night at the Empress Hotel across the street. She gratified him in every way possible. Most of all he loved her fellatio for which she left a lasting impression on him. And she was determined to keep up that good relationship.

***

She arrived at the bank before the opening to the public. Her new office was on the sixth floor of the Spring Street building. Her secretary was already there waiting to welcome her. She went straight to Charles' office. He got up visibly excited. She closed the door behind her. They exchanged an intense kiss while she reached for his groin and gripped his already hard shaft as a promise of future pleasures together. They did not know that fate had no further sexual encounters in store for them.

She went back to her office and sat at her desk. She looked around with a feeling of accomplishment.

Camilla had not been there long, when there was a knock on the door. A gray hair man, in his early sixties, greeted her with an ample smile,
"Hello, I am Palmiero Venturini, I came to introduce myself," he said, stretching his hand across the desk and squeezing Camilla's sweet long soft fingers. In doing so, her ring pinched him.
"I should run away," he thought, considering that to be a menacing sign. However, he remained.

The instant they touched, the world around them disappeared. He and Camilla were alone in immensity. He wanted to flee with her. He wanted to take her in a place where they could have lost themselves in their eyes without anyone intruding. Their glances were conveying a sudden shiver of intense joy. It was the current that climbs up along the spine when there is an unexpected fulfillment of the most secret hope. Their glances were like festive ringing of bells in an alpine valley during a spring morning. They were like inhaling the aroma of flowery fields in full bloom. Their glances were all that and much more. They were a cry of joy deriving from a regained coveted freedom. They were like finding yourself again in your own bed, after awakening from the desperation of a restless nightmare. Camilla and Palmiero recognized themselves through the fog and the oblivion of past ages. Finally, they had another chance to start anew.

"Hi, I am Camilla McKierney Douglas, nice meeting you," she replied regaining her composure and looking at him puzzled with her large sky blue eyes and showing a pleased marveled surprise. "I heard a lot of things about you," she continued.

"Oh, well don't believe any of the bad," Palmiero joked.

"Well none was bad, but I will whip you into shape if you get out of line," declared Camilla laughing.

Palmiero raised an eyebrow, but held his tongue thinking, "I may like that."

***

Palmiero was a tall, gray hair Mediterranean, with deep brown piercing eyes and long lashes. His thick salt-n-pepper hair and muscular build made Camilla look at him with interest. He was born in *Gecalé*, the Beautiful-Site in Southern Italy. A Computer Scientist at the University of Rome, he had married, at the age of twenty-six, Sofia Stefanelli, a classic dark hair and dark eyes Mediterranean beauty. Subsequently, he engaged in a polyamorous relation with another partner, Oriana Folliero, a woman with very provocative, unforgettable, ocean blue eyes. Palmiero had also exchanged vows with Oriana and felt married to her too. Oriana had broken his heart with a lie *so small* that both their lives were changed forever. Sofia and Palmiero had two marvelous children, Irene, now 36 and Justin just turned 34.

For thirteen years, Palmiero worked as a bank computer analyst in Naples. Then, a powerful earthquake rattled Southern Italy shaking Palmiero out of his house. He moved with the family to

America and established his residence in Atlantic Highlands, New Jersey. Oriana, who also was married, preferred to remain in Italy with her three children. However, after two years in America, Sofia decided to go back. She missed Italy, her family, her friends. They fought terribly. Although torn by her Catholic faith, she asked Palmiero for a divorce. Nevertheless, they kept a *poly-friendly* relationship. At first, she and the kids went back to her father's house. Then, in spite of her religious conviction, she moved in with an architect from Milan. She resided there with the kids and became the principal of a local *"lyceum"* high school. Eventually, Palmiero's daughter moved to Amsterdam, where she opened a fashion boutique in the red light district. His son followed his surfing dreams in Australia. Palmiero kept in touch with all of them, occasionally exchanging very rare visits.

Palmiero had a sentimental life filled with many women, but never anyone lasted more than a year. From Atlantic Highlands, he commuted daily to Manhattan with the comfortable ferryboat that took him directly to the World Financial Center. That particular day, he was eager to meet the new Assistant Vice President. When he found out his bank had decided to hire a woman for that position, he researched her credentials on line. Her photo attracted him. He felt a magnetic pull emanating from her. It was that first glance of that woman, with whom he would have worked and traveled, which astonished him.

***

Continuing his introductory conversation with Camilla, Palmiero said, "Well, as Assistant Vice-President, I guess you have authority in this department. You will not hear any complaints from me. I like women who are in charge."

"You must know my secretary, Marilyn Jones," Camilla continued pointing to the charming woman who had ushered him into her office.

Marilyn, named after the famous movie star, was a curvaceous, sultry brown-haired woman in her mid twenties. Her body was full, ripe and luscious. She had a sweet laugh and hid her eyes under thick bangs. She smelled of musk. All the men in the office were attracted by her, her manners, her ways of walking and especially her behind. Camilla loved to watch Marilyn in the office. Although she was a little overweight, she favored tight, low cut tops. However, her excess made Camilla like her even more.

"Oh, Dr. Palmiero and I go way back a long time. Once he took me to a mediation class," Marilyn interfered, proud of that friendship.

"You are interested in meditation?" asked Camilla.

"I came to welcome you to our Bank, and wanted to be the first one to do so," continued Palmiero, "I heard you and I will be working closely together and I was sorry not to have met you when you came here for the interview last month. I was in Italy on vacation. And ... yes I am interested in meditation as well as paranormal phenomena, ghosts, extra-sensorial-perception and other similar things."

"This is very surprising. I see ghosts," declared Camilla.

"Really?" Palmiero asked intrigued.

"Someday I will tell you about it, but now we have business to discuss," concluded Camilla.

"Can we meet next week to talk about your new bank report?" inquired Palmiero.

"Yes," she replied.

***

The week before, the Information Technology Department of the First International Bank, in New York City had hired Camilla. She referred to herself as a self-made woman from the Adirondack Mountains. Jokingly, she liked to say that wolves raised her and had no idea how she learned to read. She was the mother of three beautiful children, Mary 10, Robert 6, and Patrick 3. Her husband Robert, a full-blooded Irish and a Wall Street employee, was four years older. An apparent successful eleven-year marriage had left them still seemingly in love. That accounted for their friends' envy. However, they did not see that, beyond Camilla's shell, there was a woman yearning for excitement, adventure and most importantly love. Her life was one big sigh. Her one refuge was her career.

In reality, also during those eleven-years she had other lovers. Besides occasional prostitution, she sought a job with a publishing house. There, she met Jason Murray, an obscure writer. He hired her as a typist. Without enthusiasm, she described him as a man with a sizeable member and a similar sense of guilt. Each time they had intercourse he made the sign of the cross. At that time, she also had affairs with Dave Swetakowski, the publishing director, and with Herbert Silverstein, a lawyer who spent his vacation tracking sex tourism in Jamaica. He taught her new tricks of the trade. Eventually she got tired of those men and of that menial job. Therefore, with the heart filled with anticipation and hope, she embarked on that new position at one of the leading banks in New York.

Camilla and her husband Robert lived in a split colonial house in a modest neighborhood in Newark, New Jersey. From there, it was easy to reach Midtown Manhattan, New York. On the train ride back home, Camilla was bubbling with life and excitement.
"This new position is a dream comes true," she thought. "I get to work with fascinating people who are not only intelligent but so pleasant to be around." In reality, she was thinking of how interesting she found Palmiero.

When she entered her house, she was surprised that her worlds at home and at work were miles apart. She expected warm questions from her family about her day and new work place. All she got was a lukewarm hello and
"Did you pick up dinner?"

She could see Robert playing with their dog in the yard. Wrestling and throwing him up in the air.
"Deep breaths Camilla, deep breaths," she told herself.

At last, Robert asked, "How did it go?"

"Finally, someone is interested in what I have to say," she thought as she started to recount.

However, as soon as she started to tell him, she noticed that he was not listening.

"I might as well save my breath," she thought. She turned her attention to her children and started helping them with their homework.

That night, as she lay in bed, she tossed and turned. She wished she could get on the train right then and head into the city. Frustrated, she touched her body. She caressed her arms and legs and found it curious that her fingers wandered inside her. The natural cream between her legs was so thick that she gasped,

"My goodness, I am turning into a creampuff!" she considered and, dismissing that solitary pleasure, she went to find Robert.

He was sleeping on the sofa with the TV still on. She woke him up gently nudging him.

"What..." he started to say, as Camilla sank to her knees and started nibbling and licking him, "What are you doing?"

She kept silent and continued to take him further into her mouth. When he was fully erect, she motioned for him to stand up. She straddled the sofa and, bending on her hands and knees, offered herself to him. Robert eagerly thrust his erection into her and, gaining momentum, continued with an allegro andante pace. His orgasm was explosive and she could feel his semen coating her.

She got up, went to the bathroom and sat for a minute letting his pleasure drip out of her. Robert had not kissed her, hold her, or given her an orgasm. With a heavy heart, Camilla went back upstairs to her room and without washing him off, fell on her bed into a deep slumber.

***

A week had gone by, since Camilla had started her new banking position, when Palmiero visited her office again.

"Lunch anyone?" He proclaimed smiling at Camilla, the only person in the room. "Would you like to get out of here for an hour? It is a beautiful day. Let's go for a walk in the park."

"Yes! Does the bank pay you to play or to work?" replied Camilla laughing and already grabbing her bag, eager to get out after a long morning.

They stopped at a café to purchase a pastry and headed to nearby Canal Park. In that glorious late-summer day, the park was romantically conspiring, as Palmiero and Camilla strolled through it during their lunch break. Then, Camilla stopped. Looking at him in the eyes, she boldly asked,
"Do you have a crush on me?"

"No, not precisely, I have a *huge* crush on you," confessed the man, happy that she had noticed it.

Palmiero, who was much older and could have been her father, made no other comment and they made their way towards a bench.

"Thanks for getting me away from my computer," said Camilla sitting down.

They spent the rest of the time talking about work and personal things, but as they were walking back to the office, he asked for her cellular number.

"That would not be appropriate. But, you can e-mail me, camilla@bluehorizon.com." She replied without giving any further explanation.

"Good, then expect an e-mail from '*uandi6*.' When you receive it, you will know who the sender is," replied Palmiero, with an enigmatic smile.

***

That night Palmiero had a recurring dream. He dreamt of being in India in a royal palace dressed as a maharaja. He never understood that vivid frequent vision. It was very real to be a simple bubble coming up in his mind and from his unconscious ocean. Therefore, the reverie always puzzled him. Until, one day the previous summer in London. There, visiting the Victoria and Albert Museum, he stood before a life-size painting of Nawab Muhammad Ali. Then, he recognized the person of his dream. He remembered his palace with arches and balconies. He recollected looking from those huge windows at the manicured tropical gardens. He had been the Nawab of Arcot. Now, having met Camilla, he realized that she had also lived in the harem with him. She was Aditi.

THE SIREN'S CALL

The next day Camilla had a promising gift for Palmiero. She approached him and said,

"It is easy for you to remember my cellular number, dial '*u call me now*' 822-556-3669. " Camilla said with a smile.

Palmiero mentally registered it. He could not wait to call her. When he returned home that evening, he lay on his bed and nervously, dialed the number. Music came on. It was Vivaldi's *Four Seasons*. Then, a voice answered,

"You have reached Camilla McKierney Douglas, please leave a message after the beep," Camilla's recording had a youthful singsong quality to it.

"Camilla *McKiernee*, Camilla *McKiernee*." Echoed Palmiero smiling and hang up.

He remained lying down on his bed with his eyes closed and the phone still in his hand. A faint murmur rang in his mind's ear. It was not audible, but it was distinct, soothing as a transfixing song of ancient lore. It reminded Palmiero of the *a'riana*, the serenading songs he heard in his childhood hometown.

Sixty-fife years earlier, *a'Diana*, the serenades to Diana the morning star, were sung during the whole night, until daybreak. They were love heartbreaking songs that ushered the yearly feast of *Our Lady of Sorrows* celebrated the next day.

Then, he heard those enchanting serenades carried by the summer night breeze through the open window, all the way to his bed in the dark side of the room. They came from the far away alleys and streets of *Gecalé*, his Beautiful-Site Southern Italian town. Even today, the singers keep serenading Diana, the huntress and moon deity.

Our Lady of Sorrows

THE SIREN WEAVING HER LURING SONG

Diana's heavenly name kept echoing in Palmiero's mind, as he retraced his steps back to Camilla's office the next morning. She knew he was going to come and greeted him with a hug. She introduced him to the rest of the office proclaiming that he reminded her of the father.

Then, Camilla asked him, "You told me that you are also interested in ESP and yoga. Tell me more about it," she was eager to hear his response.

"As a matter of fact, I am fascinated by those subjects since childhood!" stated Palmiero, while Camilla's expression changed from jovial to seriously intense.

"If you want, I will introduce you to those disciplines," he concluded. Then, changing topic, he asked; "I need some updates on last month's investments sales, could you please give them to me? "

"I will bring them to your office, next week," eagerly, replied Camilla.

***

During the weekend, Palmiero constantly thought of Camilla. He liked her very much.

"Ok," he considered "this is never going to happen I could be her father. Besides, she is married and I am married. Between us can never be anything more than friendship."

Nonetheless, he did not realize the huge impact he had made on Camilla. She too had thought of him throughout the weekend. She e-mailed to remind him that she was going to bring the investment sales' updates, he requested, to his office next Monday and added,

"Yesterday I baked too much zucchini bread, would you like to taste it? If you want, I will also bring some for you."

"I would love that. I am impressed, a career woman who knows also how to bake," wrote back Palmiero, eager to taste anything Camilla would have offered him.

"It relaxes me," replied Camilla in her email.

***

The following Monday, on the way to his office, Camilla was very nervous. She had no preconceived expectations. She just put one foot in front of the other. When she reached Palmiero's door she nervously tapped on it. There was no sound coming from behind the closed door. She did not think he was in his office. After a while the door opened, Palmiero was surprised and delighted to see her.

"Oh, welcome... welcome Camilla," he said ushering her in. Camilla peered behind him into the darkened office.

"Is now a bad time?" Camilla asked anxiously.

"No, no... Actually I was meditating,"

"Meditating?" she asked doubtfully.

"Yes, yes... I know you are interested in meditation?" he replied.

"Well yes," she answered. "However, I have no real knowledge of it."

"I will introduce you to it," he offered.

Camilla noticed an ornate small altar with many fascinating artifacts on it from Palmiero's travels. He was pleased of her interest and started explaining each piece. Camilla saw a picture of a man in a loincloth.

"Who is he?" she asked.

"Ah, he is my guru, my personal teacher."

"I do not know him," she stated.

"Please, sit down and I will tell you."

Camilla sat on the small sofa before his desk and looked around at all the artifacts he had collected and with which he had decorated the entire room. The photos of his travels covered all the walls, from the Pyramids of Giza to the Great Wall of China, from Stonehenge to the Taj Mahal, from the Gran Canyon to the island of Bora Bora, from Bali to Iceland and from Tokyo to Rome, just to mention a few. Three times, he had circled the world and the artworks were testifying each location in which he had established residence.

Camilla was captivated, as she observed those numerous objects. Caught up with Palmiero's enthusiasm and wondrous dark eyes, she thought, "He is interesting, he is like a little boy all excited to share his interests with his mom."

"Will you teach me how to meditate?" she asked.

"I would like that very much." he replied. "However, as you may know, I am leaving for a business trip to Paris. I will be sending you e-mail from there."

Palmiero got up from his chair, walked around his desk, sat on the couch next to her and, as a friendly gesture, asked if he could hold her hand.

"Yes, nothing more than that," uttered Camilla nervously. "But, it is late, I must return to my office. Business first, here are the papers you asked for and the bread I had promised." She continued handing him the items.

However, when she got up to leave, she felt like being nice to him. Therefore, she quickly pressed her lips to his in a goodbye salute. Surprise and delight flashed on his face. As she left the Palmiero's office, she knew there was no turning back and she thought,
"I must be crazy! He is old enough to be my father." Yet the pull was undeniable.

***

That afternoon, Palmiero left the office with his heart overflowing with happiness. In reality, Camilla was that happiness itself. During the night and the following day, he examined all the excuses he could think to meet Camilla again and counted the hours for their next encounter.

Back home, Camilla strode pensively among the trees and flowers of her garden. The strong breeze blew through her hair. She always felt a deep connection with the wind and listened for the message it was conveying to her. She let her thoughts drift to Diana, her deceased mother. In the airstream, she sensed Diana's presence. It had been a long time since Camilla had felt her mother's spirit in the wind's embrace.

She went to bed early. But that night she was unable to sleep. A strong storm had developed and kept her awake the whole night. Lying in bed with her eyes opened in the dark, she thought,
"Why do I think I have such a connection with the wind? I feel my mother's essence again. The wind is calling me outside, but I am being sensible and I will stay in bed." Camilla looked through the windows at the clouds and it was as if they were restaging the old tragic story in cosmic proportions. For the first time in her life she wondered,
"Why is she still here? I see her in the trees... Go away!"

Diana in the tree

Camilla, who had inherited the *'gift* of *seeing and speaking'* to the dead, pondered her ambivalence toward her mother. However, she was always afraid to do or learn anything that would let spirits crossover. That day she was frightened for Diana's presence in the wind. She felt the familiar pull of her mother's whiff. It was the constant strong smell of tobacco and alcohol that Camilla remembered so vividly of her mother. Now she was back. Diana the Siren was composing her song in the storm and she was interlacing her web with the help of the three Fates sisters, the controller of destiny.

Chapter 2
The Romance of Love

UNENDING LOVE[17]

"I seem to have loved you in numberless forms, numberless times...
In life after life, in age after age, forever.
My spellbound heart has made and remade the necklace of songs,
That you take as a gift, wear round your neck in your many forms,
In life after life, in age after age, forever.

Whenever I hear old chronicles of love, it's age old pain,
It's ancient tale of being apart or together.
As I stare on and on into the past, in the end you emerge,
Clad in the light of a pole-star, piercing the darkness of time.
You become an image of what is remembered forever.

You and I have floated here on the stream that brings from the fount.
At the heart of time, love of one for another.
We have played alongside millions of lovers, shared in the same
Shy sweetness of meeting, the distressful tears of farewell,
Old love but in shapes that renew and renew forever.

Today it is heaped at your feet, it has found its end in you
The love of all man's days both past and forever:
Universal joy, universal sorrow, universal life.
The memories of all loves merging with this one love of ours -
And the songs of every poet past and forever."

Rabindranath Thakur

VIRTUAL LOVE

The following weekend, Camilla and Palmiero started their on-line relationship.

(9/23/6:59:50 AM) Palmiero wrote to Camilla, "My Precious, chatting with you fills my heart with pleasure and joy. I truly feel a connection with you. I cannot pinpoint from which past lifetime you come from, but you are definitely there. I feel free and appeased in your presence. There is a very very special room for you in my polyamorous house. The key for polyamory is sincere communication, no thoughts held back, no cheating, no lies and no jealousy. Unfortunately, not all these things are present in our society. Communication, communication, communication, that is the secret for healthy relations."

(9/23/7:15:23 AM) Camilla replied, "Smile that is all I do when I think of you. I cannot help myself. You make me happy. Right or wrong, that is the truth. I wish we could have more time by ourselves without anyone knowing. I would love to go to museums and farmer's market with you. Send me your favorite music; I will put it on my iPod."

(9/23/8:02:34 AM) Palmiero answered, "Precious, you convey a sense of completion. Do not ask me what it is; I know only that it is beautiful. The kiss you gave me, as you were leaving my office, left me speechless. Yes, we need time alone by our self, like two kids walking on the beach hand in hand. We probably did that in a previous life. I feel you very close. However, I am troubled by our difference of age... I am definitely convinced that nobody should know when we meet and yes, I want to be alone with you. I would love to go to the museum with you. But, until we can, what matters is to be together. As for my favorite music, yes I will send to you those pieces that are meaningful for us. I will keep writing to you. Love, me."

(9/23/ 10:16:10 AM) Camilla, "I think it is too obvious that we are happy to see each other. That is why we cannot really be seen together in the office. Moreover, you have your life and I have mine. I do not want nosy people trying to figure something out about us. Yes, we should be very careful. We should not be together in the office; therefore, we must have our meeting place outside the working place. We must decide our meeting locations. I cannot be more that one minute without seeing you. Therefore, it is difficult not finding some excuse to come to your office. We can always meet for lunch. We will go directly to the meeting place. I would love to go to the museum, operas and plays with you. I have never been there. I do not get the opportunity to take off and explore the city. I come here every day for work and then back on the subway to 'mommy duties.' My path was very different from your upbringing. It was survival. There was no time to appreciate the finer things in life. I have just recently realized how I crave for art, literature, music but have no real knowledge of any of it. I never had anyone interested in showing me those things and I would love to explore and learn from you."

(9/23/7:43:32 PM) Palmiero, "Precious, as you know, our Department is sending me to France. I will be leaving tomorrow, but will keep you posted."

(9/23/8:15:43 PM) Camilla, "Safe landing, be well and don't talk to any other French redheaded on the airplane, ☺ Luv, Precious."

The next day (9/24/12:30:21 PM), Palmiero wrote, "My precious One, I went to bed thinking of you. I woke up thinking of you. And I will be thinking of you all the way. I hope there will be Internet connection where I am going. I will have my laptop. But, if there is no connection, there will be three long days without the Goddess of my thoughts. Am I to daring if I say I want to kiss your hands and your feet? I can be totally yours if you want me to be. Just say the word. You are my Goddess and I will be your worshiper if you allow me. I will follow your orders. For now, I gently kiss you goodbye. I must leave you, my limousine is at the door. I am yours..."

(9/24/3:10:01 PM) From Kennedy airport in New York, Palmiero, staring at his laptop wrote, "I just realized... I have a love affair with... my computer. I cannot stay away from it, because it puts me in touch with you. Sofia, who came to visit with me, is puzzled by my continuous writing."

(9/24/3:20:28 PM) Camilla, "You made me smile. I did not know Sofia was visiting with you. Be careful we do not want to hurt her. I am happy to know that you are together. She must be excited to be with you. Enjoy your time together. But, don't you have a plane to catch? It is good that I do not dream of you. I am exhausted from thinking about you all my waking hours! My laptop, for which I had no real love, is now right by my bed. Good thing my husband does not share a bedroom with me. Do not worry for him; I am still taking care of his needs. He is a loud snorer though!

Have a wonderful trip. Where in France are you going? I hope you meet interesting people and enjoy nice conversation and wonderful meals. As for me, I will be working in the garden this weekend, feeling the warmth of the sun on my skin. I will imagine it is you."

(9/25/7:01:28 AM, Paris time) Palmiero, "I am at *de Gaulle* Airport in Paris, waiting for the shuttle to take me to *Le Grand Hotel* in the city. Camilla you are my Goddess, my Devi."

(9/25/6:43:47 AM, NJ time) Camilla, "I hope your flight went well. It is a beautiful day here in New Jersey. It became sweeter with your e-mail. If you need to call me, you know my cell."

(9/25/11:55:19 PM, Paris time) From the hotel, Palmiero wrote, "I had so many day dreams about you today. Thank you for your cellular number, I gave you mine already."

(9/25/8:51:38 PM, NJ time) From her house, Camilla answered, "While bathing my son, the bubbles made me think of you... Dreamt of a place where we knew no one and we did not get second glances... Thought some other things, they made me blush... I can hardly believe that I am so connected to you and I barely know you. I must be dreaming. I have figured out who you are. You are Himeros, the Greek god of longing sexual love."

(9/26/7:03:28 AM, Paris time) Palmiero, "Yes, I am Himeros, the longing love, the sexual desire, the sublime passion of purity and at the same time sensual, very sensual and extremely sensual, accepting all sexual fantasies, none excluded. He is the equivalent of the Indian Kāma-deva... god of love-desire.

You are my *Devi*-Goddess. I am your *dasa*-slave, completely controlled by you and under your spell. My mission is to give you pleasure asking nothing in return. The only pleasure I want is to give you pleasure. In this is my real pleasure. However, I can be also your slave-master and a good one if you want me to be. I would love to kiss your whole body, leaving <u>nothing</u> unexplored by my lips and tongue.

But, if you tell me to behave like a true monk with you in purity and chastity I would gladly oblige. When I think of you I immediately get a big smile. I wonder why that is... Love is a mysterious sudden thing. I make a solemn promise to you; I will always be truthful as I expect that from you too. My mind is yours."

LOVE'S ADMISSION

(9/26/9:09:41 AM, NY time) From her office desk, Camilla wrote on her computer, "Thanks Palmiero for your e-mail, I long to hear from you. I am happy we can communicate this way, as I am still shy to tell you these things in person. Besides, we do not have privacy. I do love you, in so many ways.

I have a beautiful life. One I could never have imagined to have. The horror of my childhood seems like a bad nightmare. We must be careful. I do not think my husband can understand that, loving you, it has opened me to love him more. You make me blush with what you say and what you want to do to me. I think we should be alone and see what happens. It could be that you will totally change your mind when we will be alone. Send me warm loving thoughts today."

(9/26/6:27:38 PM, Paris time) Palmiero, "Change my mind? Impossible, once I said what I said, I meant it. It is good that you love your husband more; this is what happens and this is the way it should be. You will see that you will love your husband even more, as it happened to me with my wife.

This would be even greater if they would agree and understand our relationship. I am your slave, my precious owner. We will find quality time to be truly alone and possibly we will really get to know each other. I am concerned you will not like me then and you will change your mind."

(9/26/1:46:37 PM, NY time) Camilla, "My love, I did not mean I love my husband more than you. I mean I love him more than before. I am feeling more love towards him because, with your love, you are filling those gaps and emptiness that he leaves unfulfilled. I am ok now. I have been so emotional lately. I hardly ever cry, but after reading your e-mail this morning, I burst into happy tears. I am so full of light and love. I want to spread it all around me, here at work. Enjoy your day."

(9/26/11:56:43 PM, Paris time) Palmiero, "We went walking the whole day. Paris is beautiful this time of the year and the *Avenue des* Champs-Élysées welcomed us all the way to the *Arc de Triomphe de l'Étoile*. But, that beauty could not distract my mind from thinking always of you. That is why I had to call you; I needed the reassurance of our voice. I cannot spend much time on this computer... you know... Monday, on my return, we must have lunch together. I must see you or I will melt down in sadness. Love you. My Goddess, I am, I feel and I want to be your slave."

(9/26/7:26:47 PM, NJ time) Camilla, "We will definitely go to lunch upon your return on Monday. I will try to remember how you told me you like your avocado and we will have a picnic. We will go to our park where we will have privacy. I think it is supposed to be nice weather.

Good luck tomorrow with your business presentation. I had a wonderful day. I felt your warmth glowing around me. I was imagining both of us living in your childhood home. We were holding hands and drinking wine. There with you I was very sexy. But at this moment, I don't feel so sexy. I am afraid you will grow tired of me.

Furthermore, I cannot deny your age is a huge factor. I can also tell you that no man ever, without even touching me, has turned me on as much as you have. I wait for your e-mail. I am so on fire. This is the strangest thing that has ever happened to me. You are not even with me in the room and I feel you making love to me. Writing is wonderful because we can be so free with our words. I think that when we will finally be alone we will be very bashful. Love you too. Be well."

(9/27/7:03:52 AM, Paris time) Palmiero, "Sorry to disagree, but you are very sexy all the time. Do you want me to make a list? Physically I like you very much. Again, must I make a list? Must I tell you what I would do to you? If you want, I can be very graphic. Shall I? If you give me permission, I will.

Now, from my part, I do not know how sexy I can be for your eyes. However one thing I will say, I will never take pleasure without having given you pleasure. Do not ask me how and why, but I am in love with you. In my dreams, we have been together the whole night. The anticipation of being together on Monday is killing me. I love you more than last night. However, we should control anticipation. Not in the sense of not feeling it, or trying to reduce it by non-indulging on it. But in the sense of intentionally intensify it. We should take it to the next level of intolerable proportions, until it becomes a great tsunami of unthinkable magnitude, a hurricane of cataclysmic proportions. Then, we should ride it, as surfers gliding on waives without losing their balance. In other words, we should look at it and at its devastation focusing on our consciousness of it. This new consciousness becomes the surfing board and our awareness, the surfer itself. Then, at that point, a new flow will emerge and we will be its masters. I am waiting for the conference to start and I must leave you know. I love you!"

(9-27-6:26:47 AM, NJ time) Camilla, "Hum... Do I want a list? Of course! Keep me posted on your presentation."

(9-27-6:11:58 PM, Paris time) Palmiero answered, "My conference went splendidly. It was a great and very well received success. As for the *list* you requested, here it is.

My love, even if for a short while, your absence establishes me in pain. A sweet and painful precious suffering keeps you constantly present. Love is not real if it is not lived through the orgasm of the souls. In it, on the threshold of ecstasy, soothingly suspended beyond the physiological shiver, there is the tension of the soul. It is a spasmodic paroxysm, a vibrating unison, an uncontainable pleasure, which overflows from all pores. Then the sexual embrace is not any longer sufficient. It is as if breath stops and this craving, this uncontainable frenzy transports lovers in heaven, beyond all heights. I see and feel your exquisite body being one with mine. However, you are beyond any physicality. I want to hold tight your sweet limbs. Nevertheless, every strong embrace denotes an inadequacy, compared to the flight that, through you, elevates me towards new metaphysical altitudes. Then, my soul is yours and your soul is mine. Then, you have on me the power of life and death. Then, with joy, I offer my life in your hands, in order that you may dispose of it as you please. Moreover, if it were your desire to take my life, I would help you, with joy and passion, to execute your will, which would fix in eternity the orgasm of the soul.

(9-28-9:15:34 AM, New Jersey time) Camilla, "Hello my love, I wish I was there to see you in your entire splendor. Today, I took a warm shower and thought how nice it would be if I had you to rub my neck and to caress you under the running water. I am running around with the kids. My husband works also on weekend, so I am often with them alone. Wherever I went today people remarked on my great looks. They ask me what I have been doing. How can I tell them that I look so good because I have been captivated by an affair of the heart?"

(9-28-11:16:43 AM, Paris time) Palmiero, "My sweet dominatrix, I am at the airport. I am getting back to you."

(9-28-8:10:51 PM, NJ time) Palmiero, "I am home; I will see you tomorrow. Love you more than yesterday."

(9-28-8:15:12 PM) Camilla, "Yeah, I can't wait to be with you tomorrow. Love you more than yesterday. Sweet dreams, my love."

(9-29-5:01:45 AM) Palmiero, adjusting to NJ time and finding Camilla on-line, "My sweet Goddess, what are you doing up so early?"

(9-29-5:06:32 AM) Camilla, "I could not sleep, in anticipation of our meeting. I am up so early thinking of our meeting later. I am so excited and want to run and jump into your arms. I feel light as a feather. Your love has made me fly. I like what you told me that day in your office. How you know that I want a romantic love. You know me better than I know myself. The only thing is that I fear you will judge me for our relationship. You are the first man I ever strayed with after my marriage, and I wonder if you think of me as a loose person. However, this love, this *'illicit'* love was born long before us. I have no control over its path. I am not the one guiding the ship. It is all out of my control... or yours. Like Alfredo and Violetta in the opera *La Traviata*, we may plan to 'leave Paris together,' but Destiny has its plans for us. I never intended to look your way, to kiss you or to take this voyage with you. I have no control over it. I have lost the ability to think rationally. I am guided strictly by my heart and by those forces, those gods who live within me. Don't get me wrong, this journey is one I would never have wanted to miss. It is a kaleidoscope of colors and emotions. When we met, I just did not know that this love would last and grow as much as it does each day."

(9-29-5:30:15 AM) Palmiero, "We must be very careful not to hurt anyone. What we are embarking into is something sacred, good and beneficial for our families. We should give them more than what we gave them before. You should love your husband more than before. Our loving encounters should be an enhancement of our love and desire for our spouses. We should bring our special love even in their beds. There is no guilt in what we are feeling or what we will be doing. Unfortunately, present times do not allow an openness that would allow us to tell them about us. We can give to each other the pure love as well as the sexual fantasies that, perhaps, they do not accomplish for us. What must characterize our relationship must be total communication, openness, sincerity and mind sharing. Our union must be that of mind unison. Not in the sense of agreeing but in the sense of sharing. Obviously, no jealousy should ever take place among us. And, if it should arise, we should speak about it, so that we may help each other to overcome it. I should be happy for you and comfortable thinking of you in somebody else's arms and you should feel the same for me. If this should not happen, then we should talk, talk and talk. From my part I am not in our loving relation as a passing thing, I am in it to stay, if you so wish. Regarding today meeting, we can go to Canal Park for lunch. I love you in a way that hurts my heart beautifully. Can I call you on your cell?"

(9-29-5:35:19 AM) Camilla, "Please do. All weekend I wanted to hear your voice. I want to learn more about your vision on life, yoga, everything. I am interested in you. I know the physical aspect is important, but I don't know much about you and I am fascinated. I will not be jealous of your wife, children or grandchildren. They are your family and make you happy. I have a wonderful life as well. This is between you and me and it does not take in anything away from them."

(9-29-5:40 AM) Camilla answered Palmiero call with a happy "Hello my sweet love."

(9-29-5:41 AM) "I cannot wait to see you at Canal Park lunch time," mumbled Palmiero on the other side of the wire, overwhelmed by emotional anticipation.

(9-29-5:41 AM) "Yes, I will come," replied Camilla with a similar agitation and added, "Oh, one favor to ask, before we hung up. Please, bring a photo you can give me. I would love one of you at my age and one of you now. I wish I could change time and have met you when we were closer in age. I do enjoy how hard you try to understand me. However, I hope you will forgive my inexperience and ignorance. You are so knowledgeable and many things you may try to teach me are hard for me to understand. I will try not to be an avalanche today when we will be together."

(9-29-5:42 AM) "Do not say that. It is not true," answered Palmiero, reassuring her, "you fascinate me completely. Yes, I will give you the photos you requested. I will like to have one of you as well. See you later, my dear."

LOVE CONFESSION IN THE PARK

On that clear, crispy and sweet Monday, Camilla and Palmiero strolled in the Park as if they were the first and only beings in a terrestrial paradise. Their stride and connection was so intense that passerby unconsciously bowed their eyes not to disturb their intimacy. Palmiero, as to unintentionally assert his *ownership*, held his right hand on the back of Camilla's neck, while she walked proud to show her *submissive domination* on him.

"Can we sit on a bench and talk, without having anyone wonder what we are up to?" said Camilla stopping and sitting on a park seat. "Do you think our outside 'mask' will give us away? I worry for you; I do not think I have anyone I know that I will bump into in this area."

"Here are the photos you requested," said Palmiero sitting along her side.

Camilla contemplated them without saying a word. Then she placed them in her bra over her breasts. Afterward, always in silence she reached in her bag, pulled out her own photo and handed it to Palmiero. He looked at it for some time, then, religiously placed it in his chest pocket.

"Tell me about your romantic life," asked Palmiero impolitely. "However, you know that we are going to be lovers, right?"

"Ha-ha!" Camilla laughed, "Wow, you are a bit presumptuous."

"No, I am seriously infatuated with you and I can tell that you feel the same way for me," he said.

"Yes..." she whispered, "you are right... So, we should discuss our past partners. In the times we live in, unfortunately, this conversation needs to take place. Well I had many lovers, but the only one I was really in love, before I married, was Jeff. I lost him on account of my jealousy and my unfaithfulness."

"Really," said Palmiero with his eyes wide open. I am speechless."

"Yes," replied Camilla among more laughter. "However, I had many other good and bad lovers before my marriage. I will tell you in details all about them."

"Please do," encouraged Palmiero, visibly aroused.

"Yes, but first tell me. Did you have an affair with Marilyn Jones, my secretary?" asked Camilla. "From the way you looked at each other I was sure there were some tenderness between you two."

"Yes," confessed Palmiero, "I liked her sexually, but the connection was not there. She dabbled in recreational drugs and I found her dull. Once she offered me marijuana, but I was not interested. However, if you want to know, I will tell you all about it someday. Now tell me about your lovers."

Without being offended, Camilla replied,

"Do you want it all? I can be descriptive if you like. I wish I had such beautiful terms as you have, when you describe lovemaking. However, lately my sex life is very simple. It is all dedicated to you. I love Robert, he is good looking and he has adequate physical attributes, but he is insufficient as a love partner. He is not romantic at all. Therefore, in our intimacy, you take control of my mind. I wonder if you are still intimate with your wife when you visit her in Italy. I am not jealous, I am curious. Do you still enjoy each other in that way? If not, why?"

"Yes, we are, with lots of fantasies from my part," confessed Palmiero. "However, lately she is less interested in exploring new possibilities. You must understand that I am totally into wholesome sex with absolutely no frontiers. Freedom is the fundamental principle of the science of morality, which is the Science of Liberty of the 'I'. The real evils of the world are the product of a morality that derives not from a spirit of unity but by aversion. Sometimes, in monogamic relationships honesty finds obstacles. We cannot foresee the future. Therefore, the promise of exclusive faithfulness is a lie, which legalizes divorce. However, it is *sinful* to impose a separation, when one of the partners meets another significant one, while still in love with the original partner. Polyamory, the possibility of having multiple significant loves at the same time and in the same place, should be lawful together with monogamy. Consequently, no dishonesty or untruthfulness would be present. Loving more than one person at the same time is possible as loving more than one offspring."

"Then, I must confess," said Camilla transfixed, "yes, I am in love with you. No one else is occupying my mind. You truly own my mind. You are so romantic. I am having a fascinating day with you."

"When I write to you, I cannot contain my love for you, it is an explosion."

"Did you have any other significant love, besides your wife Sofia?" asked Camilla with some apprehension.

"Yes," said Palmiero, changing expression and wondering with his eyes. "Oriana, she is my polyamorous partner and an old sweet heart of mine from my Italian village on the hill of *Gecalé*. I am still in touch with her and I see her when I go back to Italy."

"Who do you prefer to be with?" asked Camilla inquisitive.

"If you want to know the honest truth, right now I want to be with you and you alone; you and me, no one else," confessed Palmiero. "In the opera *La Boehme*, Mimì, the main protagonist, on her death bed, wants to be alone with Rodolfo her lover. Making believe she was asleep, she waits for all the others to leave the room. Then she confides to Rodolfo that she had so many things she wanted say. However, only one thing she could say and it was as deep as the ocean... *'I love you...'* she said and then died."

"How tragic and romantic," Camilla commented with teary eyes, denoting a very sensitive soul. Then, changing topic, she added, "I want to travel. My husband is not interested. I hope that, when my daughter turns 18, we could go together. I feel I need to do this. I have never been out of this country. However, I made strong connections with friends from other countries like France, Turkey, Croatia and now you from Italy."

Then, changing the subject, she said, "Do you know I have never read the *Kama Sutra*? Do you think I would understand it? The other day, I was searching on-line for erotica. I think you inspire me. I feel like Mimì. I want nothing more than to be in a room alone with you."

"I will introduce you to the *Kama Sutra*, Love's verses," promised Palmiero, "and also to the opera. I will give you some very good CDs."

"Regarding polyamory, I think it is beneficial for children as well," said Camilla pensive, "I remember someone once said to me, when I went back to work after Mary, my daughter, was born, 'Are you not afraid that she may bond with her sitter more than with you?' In reality, that never bothered me. My children always knew and know that I am their *numero uno*. No one can replace me. Referring to my babysitter, I always felt that it was great that more people loved my kids. Besides their grandparents, they will bond with other adults. However, I am not sure about jealousy in a polyamory setting. If Robert would want to be polyamorous, would i accept it? I always considered myself to be the best and the only one who could satisfy him. In polyamory could I be pushed aside?"

"My dear Camilla," assured Palmiero, "Polyamory is only apparently composed of many persons, each one satisfying different needs. Each one represents a different approach and each one is a different mask of the only Real-Zero we truly seek and love forever. The key is to let the mask transpire that Real-Zero, not obfuscate It. When the obfuscation takes place, then the mask becomes an object, then divorce and separation ensues. I love you as my One Precious Goddess. If, for any reason, we should be angry or upset with each other, we must talk about it and clarify it with the usual truthfulness. I told you, I am in your life to stay, even if we never consummate our love. Only if you want me to leave, I will. The only real bond we have is truthfulness with each other. We should be truthful even if we think that it may hurt the other. We should realize that is not because of truth that we may lose our love. This happens in the fake monogamous relations, if we say the truth we lose it. The consequence of that fake truthfulness is the destruction of monogamic love. Imagine if our spouses would find out about us. It would be the end of our marriage with them. They are obliging us to be secretive. On the contrary, imagine how peaceful their life would be, if they would participate in truth with us. Our society considers love as possession, the loved one as an object, which no one can have or share. That is not love. That is possession, the contrary of love."

"Tell me what you would do to me, if we were in bed now," asked Camilla, with some daring hesitation in her voice.

Palmiero with a smile of pleasure, as if lost in a vision said, "First I would kiss your feet. Then, slowly I would work my way up along your legs, switching from one to the other, until they unite. There, I would indulge. My tongue would become active searching for natural caves to explore in search for refreshing springs of joy. When the outcome of that pleasure would have rested, then my tongue would search for the center that separated you from your mother. It would circulate it and, at times, tap in it. Then, I would divide my attention to the two nourishing breasts, gently nibbling on their nipples. From there, up along the concavity of the throat, I would reach your mouth where I would rest in romantic passionate union. I will call you my sweet adorable Angel/Owner. Following your permission, I would then penetrate you making sure not to reach completion unless with your consent. My desire is to please you not me... Well, that is not true, because truthfully my pleasure is only your pleasure."

"You leave me speechless. What an incredible experience I just had;" whispered Camilla, coming out of an unbelievable heavenly daydream. "The Love-god, the most beautiful on the face of the earth, just fed me the grape first bitten by you. I tasted his breath. It was ambrosia, the nectar of the gods. I think we must leave now, before I fall irremediably in love with that god."

"Yes my love," said Palmiero, "I found you. You dominate my mind. If you want, I will give you exclusive love without holding back. I can give you my mind you will be its owner. Command me without holding back. There is a special exaltation in committing my mind to you my Goddess. It is a disarming sensation that makes me vulnerable, particularly when the Goddess is conscious of her powers over me and has pleasure in exercising her total control. I am not asking you to love me. I am satisfied by the honey dripping from all your lips."

Conversing, they never stopped gazing at each other. They were mutually lost in their eyes. Unaware, their bodies got closer and their faces were at breath distance. Finally, they embraced under the clear sky, careless of the passerby. Their lips eagerly invited one another. Their tongues met in a dance of frenzy clinch. They swirled each other, breathing the other's breath and swallowing the other's ambrosia. Tapping each other, they recognized themselves, after eons of separation. Their libation juices mixed, as they copiously flowed from one oral-altar to the other. They were not two mouths, but only one, speaking the same universal language of love.

"Now that I have had a taste of your love," confessed Camilla, sweetly loosening the embrace while reestablishing the intense eye connection, "I want more, more and more. I am still nervous about taking you. There are too many questioning eyes around us. I think we need to take this slowly. I thought I wanted to rush into our love. Now I realize that the anticipation is half the pleasure. For now let us escape when we can and enjoy each other. I have only one request from you. I want full ownership of your mind and pleasure center. I want your total submission. I want you to be my subservient slave."

"One question," asked Palmiero, visibly shaken, "and I am not trying to get away from this submission, on the contrary I want it because it is beautiful. Given the commitment you require from me, can I still speak on the phone and e-mail Oriana and Sofia in Italy? Before you answer me, remember that I would break their heart if I interrupt communications with them. They are my wives. Especially Oriana since I first saw her at the age seven. However, I will do whatever you tell me."

"Darling, of course you can have your time with them," conceded Camilla. "I just do not want you adding to your harem. I hope three wives will be enough for you.

Do you agree with me to wait before we go through with our lovemaking? In the heat of the moment I would go anywhere with you, but if I want this to last I need to be careful. I love you and I am happy you are such a good kisser. Usually it means you are good in other areas. I hope to see you tomorrow. Maybe we can sit on the grass of the park and stretch out a little. I can bring a lunch for you. Do you like avocados? I will make a dip with peppers from my garden for you tomorrow. Thank you for this wonderful lunchtime together. I do enjoy you."

"I will eat all you will feed me," said Palmiero as he got up heading towards the office. "You have taken my heart completely. Now that we are leaving, if I did not know I was going to see you tomorrow, I would have been totally distressed."

Camilla left the park and headed for the subway to catch her train home. She had taken a half day off from work. She was in a mixture of emotions.

"I am on the edge of the tallest mountain," she thought and she did not see the crowd around her, nor did she feel the people bumping into her as they rushed to catch their trains.

"What is this dream? Have I ever felt this before? Did I ever feel the same way towards Robert?" As she was thinking these things, her emotions got the best of her and tears streamed down her face.

"What is this pull Palmiero has over me?" she continued rambling. "If I were smart I would shut this down now!" She felt like her very being was being pulled apart. The woman who left the park was not the woman who started at the bank only a month earlier. She was unaware of the people catching sight of her mascara-streaked face, as tears freely rolled down.

"Why the tears?" she questioned herself.

As she reached the platform, she was relieved to see that the train was on time and she had made it. While the train doors shut, she sat, closed her eyes and thought of Robert, her husband.

She recalled how mutual friends had fixed them up on a blind date. She smiled remembering that she thought he was so nerdy and not her type at all. It was his humor and his good nature that won her heart. Camilla had so much chaos in her life and Robert was the safe haven she had craved. She knew she would have had a "normal" and safe life with him. She sighed deeply, realizing that she loved Robert. However, she had never felt the carnal, visceral, lust described in so many of the romances she loved to read. She felt ashamed of herself.

"Why is the love of one good man not enough?" She thought.

THE MUSEUM

The Vatican Etruscan Gregorian Museum had lent some of its archaeological treasures to the Museum of Morris Town, NJ. Palmiero, upon his return from Paris, could not miss that opportunity. The next Saturday he went to see the Etruscan exhibit. With great interest, he roamed along the numerous rooms housing those artistic relics. Nevertheless, he could not have anticipated the event he was about to experience.

The bust of a woman stood at the very center of the main room of the Morris Museum. It was a sculptured Etruscan head offered in fulfillment of a vow to Lasa Vecu, goddess of prophesy, to Evan, goddess of immortality, to Tvath, goddess of resurrection, and to Satres, the god of time.
The caption read,

Etruscan votive head of lady from Cerveteri, II century BC

Palmiero felt a strange attraction for that woman, he did not want to confess it to himself, but those were feelings of love.
"Is it possible to fall in love with a woman that lived two thousand two hundred years ago?" he thought in total disbelief. It was love at first sight. Then, not knowing how, as a revelation a name came to his lips and he heard himself whispering,

"Larthia..."

For a long time he stood silent, alone, mesmerized by that beautiful face. He took a photo of the bust while tears rolled down his cheeks. When he left the votive head the sun was setting, the museum was closing and the Prophecy had come true. With her death, Larthia had stretched out her love coordinates to reach, through Palmiero, her Posidonius.

***

Eventually, Palmiero showed Larthia's photo to Camilla and described his feelings. Upon hearing it Camilla, transfixed, declared,
"I know... I was her."

CHAPTER 3
Diana

THE SIREN'S DIARY

Since he was a child, Palmiero had a long history of fascination with Pre-Columbian American culture. Probably, it was that interest that generated the strange dream he had. He did not understand it. Nor could he make sense of the woman of his dream, the beautiful Morning River. The whole experience left a profound sadness in his mind.

That sorrow was still with him when he entered his office the morning after. Only Camilla's greetings, at coffee break, uplifted him.

"I have a present for you," she said handing him a book.

"Thank you!" said Palmiero looking at the unusual volume.

It was a hard cover manuscript diary. The title struck him, *The Manual of Demons for the Dead*.

The Siren's Diary

"This was my mother's diary. I also wrote in it and continued it as my own. I want you to have it. I am giving it to you as a part of my soul," said Camilla with a loving smile.

"I don't know what to say," articulated Palmiero, overwhelmed by emotion, "I am deeply honored of your intrusting me with such a gift."

A letter, in Camilla's handwriting, accompanied the gift, in it she wrote,

Dear Palmiero,

I tried to explain this to you. But I could not tell you without weeping. Therefore, I am putting it in writing.

My mother, Diana McGuire McKierney, was the light of my life. We were extremely close. I knew I was the light of her life. We used to dance and sing every morning before I went to school. She was a fun and young mom. I loved her and I was in awe of her.

When she died, I died with her. I could not believe the vortex of hell that was to come. I was ripped from my neighborhood, my friends, and my apartment. Many of my belongings had to stay behind, since my grandmother could not afford to move everything with us. Most importantly, my mommy was gone. I was told not to tell the truth about what happened. If anyone asked, my mom died of diabetes.

It was so hard not to be able to talk about her and my grandmother was going through her own grieving so we really did not speak about Diana.

Even in my adult life, not many people know my real history. I no longer keep it a secret. So much time passed. The cobwebs have covered that door.

Then, you come along. Our love blossomed. Both of us have a deep connection to our mothers

and we explore their mysterious whereabouts. Now, this diary is my only consolation. I could cry. In fact I do. I am so happy to be able to share her with you. I am so touched that you understand how important it is for me that you honor her as much as I do.

I am in love with you. You are my muse as well. With your enthusiasm and your love, you inspire me to achieve always more. The story in this diary could be a great opera!

Your
Camilla.

Palmiero could not wait to read the diary. Once back in his office, neglecting his work, he flipped through the pages. One chapter caught his attention. It was in Camilla's handwriting and had her mother's name as a title. In it, she wrote her tragic story.

Diana on her wedding day

CAMILLA'S ENTRY IN DIANA'S DIARY

<<Diana McGuire was a stunning young woman with blond long hair, hazel eyes and a regal figure fit to fill a royal throne among the glamour and splendor of a mighty kingdom. However, Diana's life ended brutally at twenty-eight. She had lived a tragic life. Pregnant at sixteen, her Catholic Irish parents forced her into marrying Dennis McKierney, the man who had gotten her pregnant.

She was a child bride who gave birth to a girl, Maggie and, after a year, to Camilla. Not long after, a son, Daniel was born. Her husband, Dennis, ten year older than her, was a very good mason. He built their house in the Adirondack Mountains. The whole family lived a happy and tranquil life until, tragically, Dennis fell to his death during a roofing construction. Camilla could remember her mother's shrieks of horror when the supervisor on the job came to tell her about Dennis's death. Although Camilla was only three years old, she recalled taking care of her brother Daniel as her mother entered a catatonic state.

The stress of being a wife, a mother and a widow at such an early age, toke a toll on her. It was the late Sixties and Diana wanted the freedom of the same lifestyle she thought hippies enjoyed. At twenty-two, she felt old. She kept this diary where she regularly confided her secret thoughts.

Alone, desperate, with three kids and no adequate income, she was out late at night working two jobs to support her family. At the restaurant, where she waitressed she met Bruce Choulowki. She welcomed his attentions. Blinded by lust for him, Diana did not see his real nature.

Bruce was a brutal man, a heroin addict, an alcoholic, a gambler, a married man with two kids and without a steady job. He introduced Diana to drinking and drugs. Heroin hooked her completely. She started to leave her children with her mother and spend long days and nights away from her young family. Bruce became her lover and eventually got her pregnant. He was a very jealous insecure man and correctly suspected she was unfaithful. In fact, she had many other lovers, whom she picked up from bars and the street. Once, she even brought home a homeless man.

One night that she came back very late, Bruce confronted her. She told him he was crazy to doubt her faithfulness. She had been with friends. He did not believe her and began beating her. He beat her so hard that she could not get up from the bathroom floor. Camilla, only eight years old at the time, saw her mother on the floor and helped her to her feet. Diana examined her face in the mirror. Both of her eyes were bruised, her lip was cut and there were bite marks on her neck.

"Oh, my God guide me," Diana thought. She did not know how to fix that broken relationship. At the same time, she knew that if she had stayed he would have killed her. Nevertheless, Diana stayed.

At the very end, the fear that he would eventually kill her came true. >>

DIANA'S DEATH

Although Bruce proclaimed his love for Diana and swore that he would have changed, he repeatedly beat her. She loved him her own way. Theirs was a strange love affair chiseled in a sadomasochistic relationship. Death, lurking in the darkness, had an eye on them.

As an old Troubadour, Bruce repeatedly proclaimed,
"I am your assassin. I hope to conquer heaven by obeying your orders. "

And Diana would respond with her command, while juices of desire ushered her death,
"Rape me! Kill me! You slave, who are about to die in my vagina. "

Then, she would embrace him; hold him tight in the warmth of her nature. Like spurs, she dug her nails in his thighs until they bled, to induce power and speed to his stride towards his orgasmic decease.

With her parents help Diana tried to piece her life together. She found a clinic that helped her recover from her alcohol and heroin addiction. She was renewed. She was ready to start a new life, for her children's sake and for herself. Camilla remembered that time as a period of hope.

She had visited her mother at the clinic. There, Diana told her she was going back to school to become a cosmetologist and that she was leaving Bruce and was going to have his child. Joy filled Camilla's heart. Bruce was a violent, bitter and angry man who was quick to whip off his belt and beat her.

"My mother is going to save Maggie, Daniel and me." She thought.

As Camilla recounted, in her writing, that week was full of hope and promises.

However, she wondered, "What had happened? What went wrong? We were all going to be just fine without him."

In the diary, Camilla relived the events that took place on that ill-fated night, more than twenty five years earlier. Daniel, Camilla's brother was staying with his grandmother overnight. The grandmother had explained to Camilla to behave that evening and not to interfere with her mother and Bruce because they had *adult* business to take care.

Diana announced to Bruce that she was leaving him for good. She could no longer take his frequent joblessness, drinking, cursing, laziness and jealousy. Five months before Bruce made her pregnant. However, in the last month Diana was dating Frank, an Italian blue collar worker of whom she had become quite fond. Furthermore, she was not willing to have an abortion. Bruce wanted Diana to abort. He was convinced that the child was not his. Furthermore, he was afraid she would have disclosed their affair to his wife. In fact, since only his wife was working, Diana's disclosure could have dried up his single source of income.

That evening, at the kitchen table, both Diana and Bruce were drinking heavily. A strong stench of booze pervaded the room along with clouds of intense incense smelling smoke coming out of home wrapped marijuana cigarettes, which they were avidly inhaling. On the table, in front of them there were a used syringe and strips of white powder, which they snorted alternatively.

"Bruce, I know we both enjoy that I am your dominatrix and that I control you," said Diana slurping her words and visibly shaking with emotions. "Your jealousy is usually manageable until recently with Frank and my visiting with him. This will drive us apart. I think the best thing for the three of us to do is to talk openly and honestly. Even though I love our relationship the way it is, I cannot hurt you with your jealousy. It is ok to be jealous, but it has to be managed. I don't want you to have anyone but me. However, I can have all the partners I want. We are on this wild ride. Hang on to me and all will be fine. You have my heart, my soul and my mind, forever. I swear on Camilla's life that I love you. I don't know how to convince you. And this child is yours, not Frank's."

"However, I am in great pain," confessed Bruce, blowing out smoke as a volcano.

"Ok, tell me why you are in pain."

"Because you are hiding your affair from me," exploded Bruce.

"What do you think I am hiding," cried Diana.

"I don't know yet," confessed Bruce.

"I have done nothing that you and I do not enjoy, I promise you," continued Diana wiping her tears. "Bruce, why do you blame me for this, you suspect me of some wacky stuff."

"You changed our agreements."

"Honey, what did I change?"

"Our agreements," continued Bruce.

"I did not. I swear on my kids. Stop it already," busted out Diana visibly annoyed.

"Ok, sorry. Go back to your lover," condescended Bruce.

"You have to trust more," insisted Diana.

"I don't want you to see Frank this week," finally Bruce let it out.

"You have not given me any good reason, other than you are jealous," rebuked Diana with a half-smile. "You just allowed me to go back to him. You see what I mean?"

"Ok you are right! You want to see him? Go ahead, but he will separate us. I promise, is the truth," shouted out Bruce.

"What do you mean," asked Diana.

"I don't want you to see Frank this week."

"I know, you said that," bleated out Diana.

"Ok! So what are you going to do?" Bruce asked, losing his patience.

"Do you still think this is Frank's child?" asked anxiously Diana. "You really believe it? How can that be? I am five months pregnant and it is only one month that I know Frank."

"Still I don't want you to see him this week," ordered Bruce screaming.

"I heard you!" said Diana distracted, without giving much attention, "And what do I say to him? *Bruce does not want me to see you because he is jealous.*"

"Tell him to *fuck* off!" yelled Bruce while reaching for a menacing butcher's knife and pointing it to Diana.

"Why should I tell him that," rebuked Diana defiant. "Do you ever want me to see him? I thought the three of us should meet for lunch and talk this out. Anyhow, I will give you an answer tomorrow. I have to think this through. I am upset and I want to have time to think. Besides, you have not given me a reason why I should not see him."

"Because, he will separate us forever and I will move in with another woman. Do you hear me?" replied Bruce, getting up and placing the knife at Diana's throat."

"Yes, I hear you!" screamed Diana jumping on the other side of the table, "and I will see him regardless what you tell me. And I will *fuck* him and that will be the end of us. That means I am leaving you and I will not be *fucking* you anymore. Frank is really a good person, Bruce, and he is opening up to me and I think this is the first time he has someone to talk to. You know me, I like that. I think we all can have a nice adventure with each other."

"I do not like him. He is a liar, coming in one way and dividing us. He should be asking for us to be in a threesome, not to be alone with you, or to take you in a threesome with another person excluding me. He betrayed me and us," fumed Bruce, as he spoke these words.

"I have feeling for Frank and I love you at the same time. Nothing I do is enough," complained Diana.

By this time, crouched in a corner, the ten years old Camilla was witnessing the whole event. Flashbacks went through her mind. She remembered that night, a year before, when she was awakened by noises coming from her sister's room. Camilla got up and went to see.

Bruce was in the room naked in a state of full erection standing over Maggie's bed with a hand on her mouth. The girl was desperately trying to get away, but the man forced his way into her. She could not scream, but her face was expressing sheer terror. As Bruce started pumping her she kept desperately trying to get away, not realizing that her movements were playing along with his raping action. Camilla was horrified. However, she could not send away

Camilla's drawing of the rape

from her mind the disturbing desire to be in her sister's predicament. As she was harboring this thought a loving hand caressed her shoulder. She turned to see her mother smiling. Diana was watching the whole rape scene without a word and with an excited smile on her face. She took Camilla by the hand and dragged her into her bedroom. She placed her daughter on the bed, took off her pajamas and placed her head between her legs. Camilla, in a state of complete arousal, did not say a word, but followed her mother's lead. Diana inserted her tongue in her daughter's virgin vagina and started licking her with *gusto*. As the sounds from Maggie's room increased with a crescendo of painful and suffered orgasm, Diana, without taking her lips away from the tasty banquet, offered her wet hairy nature to her daughter's mouth. Camilla did not need instructions to know what to do. She started feeling strange warmth coming up from her *yoni*, her divine matrix, reaching the tip of her head and from there expanding throughout her entire body. She had never felt so good before and started responding to her mother with the same pleasure she was giving her. Both women came together in each other's mouth while Maggie loudly ended her ordeal in waves of desperate, disgusted pleasure.

When, Camilla came out of that daydream her mother was screaming at Bruce,

"You have been putting me through the ringer. I am a crystal vase you don't want anyone to touch. Besides I see how nuts all this has made you. It shows me that I don't want to get to that level. Right now I want to think about trying to hide my face from my kids. I am exhausted and feel battered. You are killing me. You made me very unhappy. Why are you talking to me like this? We have many problems, as trust, jealousy, etc. Do you want me back? I am very tired and have to go to rest now. You treat me like your doormat."

Diana stopped talking to take a long snort of cocaine. After her, Bruce did the same. Then, Diana continued saying,

"Bruce, I just want to tell you something. I know and love the Bruce of our honeymoon, just as you know and love the Diana of our honeymoon. Then, we were very much in love. Now I just don't know in which capacity we will move forward. We have to respect these new developments and nurture each other through them. I don't want to make you crazy and I don't want to go crazy. Until recently I did not know you felt excluded because I was meeting alone with Frank. I thought that you, as my *slave*, and I, as your *owner* and Mistress, were fine with that. Often you told me that I could kick you out of the door and you would wait for me."

"Yes, but an owner should know the needs of a slave," shouted back Bruce, with blood in his eyes.

"We took a chance letting another man in our life. I said it from the very beginning, there could have been risks in it," reproached Diana, continuing, "I think Frank is a really nice person and, what surprises me always, is how nice he talks of you. You don't know him as well as I do. I hope we can work out some new foundation for our relationship. I love you a lot."

"You are a liar. You had other men before Frank. For one, who was Hercules the young gym trainer? You kept him secret, thinking I would not know. I don't like Frank at all. I know he told you that I am cunning and manipulative," screamed Bruce, menacingly branding his huge knife.

"I just need to heal a little from the things we have been going through," continued Diana, ignoring his knife, "I feel mentally and physically abused by you. I love you a lot, but if I should judge from the pain you made me feel today, I must say that you are a very cruel person at times. And you know that."

"You are cruel to me too," replied Bruce, "and I'll kill you for that."

"I can tell you with honesty that I do not plan to be cruel," retorted Diana.

"If you choose him over me that will make me feel totally rejected by you and I'll not be responsible for my actions," continued Bruce.

"I do not want to hide secrets from you, but I want to have some privacy. We should have trust and respect for each other. I wanted to be an open book for you and we can find a comfort level good for both of us. Frank is not evil, he is a good person. He did not say he loves me. I did not expect him to, that is a big word for him. But, if I will not have him, I will have another man," insisted Diana. "I should never have been with you. I should have listened to my friends, they had told me not to get involved with you," continued Diana, while the pain and anger spilled out of her until she was breathless. Had she seen the storm brewing in Bruce's eye perhaps she would have chosen her words more carefully.

When Diana finished yelling and repeatedly screaming at him the same words, she made the mistake of underestimating his reaction.

Bruce reached for her and held her down. She was crying. He took the butcher knife and cut off her hair.

"I will kill you... I hate you... I love you... I will kill you. I want to see you suffer... as I am suffering now," he was screaming with tears. His words and his reactions were not under the effect of booze or cocaine, which he was snorting repeatedly. They were the cries of a lover who knows he is about to lose irremediably his loved one.

Then, he threw the knife at her. With no avail, she tried to protect herself from his violence behind the kitchen table and chairs. Bruises were all along her beautiful legs. She had a deep gash along her left thigh. Camilla was crying and pulling on Bruce's arm, desperately trying to stop him. Very often, she had witnessed these acts of violence. However, in this instance the fight went on for quite a long time. Lust, jealousy, alcohol and drugs had taken their tall, altering their minds. Suddenly, there was an audible menacing silence.

As Bruce choked her and repeatedly stabbed her, Diana's last silent death-rattle was, "I want to live." And, turned to Camilla, who was mute in sheer terror, she whispered, "Camilla, I don't want to leave you."

In the last very long minute, the icy blade violated her with a final blow. It fell in her. It penetrated her and kept her eternally silent. In that instant a life was taken and a family shattered forever. Diana died. She *gave up* her *ghost*, which *assembled among* her *own kind*.[18] As Diana died, destiny decreed that a powerful earthquake should rattle Southern Italy shaking Palmiero out of his house.

When Bruce pulled away from Diana's corpse, he uttered, "I really did it this time."

***

Camilla's drawing of the murder

Sentenced to serve seven years prison term for manslaughter, Bruce died in prison for an overdose, a few weeks after the sentence. No one knows if he ever repented of his crime.

***

Maggie, Camilla and Daniel went to stay with their grandmother. After a few months Maggie ran away and no one ever discovered her whereabouts. Eight years later, Daniel left for San Francisco, California. There, he found a job as a bartender in a gay nightclub and rented a one room studio apartment. Shortly after, Camilla followed him there, she was nineteen years old.

The first few days she was with her brother, all went well in spite of the lascivious looks of desire that Daniel had for her sister. She did not mind and did not make much out of it. In fact, she welcomed them. In fact, after showering, she deliberately paraded naked before him. During those provocative events she would notice his bulging pants and used to tease him saying,
"What, you naughty boy, your sister gets you hard?"

There was only one bed in the loft that served also as a couch. Therefore, they shared the same bed but not at the same time. In fact, when Daniel came back from work it was time for Camilla to wake up. One night, however, he came home before dawn. He got undressed and slipped into the bed next to his sister. Immediately she was awakened by his manhood pressing on her thigh. She turned around and clasped it in her hand. In silence he mounted her. She opened her legs and lovingly pulled his strong member directly in her wet inviting vagina. She embraced him drawing his saliva from his mouth.

Like the incestuous ancient Myrrha, she became her brother's lover. They made love for the rest of the day and when his manhood was tired she reinvigorated it with her mouth. The consciousness of being beyond any rightful love made her orgasmic pleasure cries even more passionate. They were heard throughout the entire building. She drew from him every drop of semen until he did not have any more to deposit in her sister's thirsty womb. After which she left him, never to see him again.

Myrrha[19]

***

The next day, Palmiero enquired about Diana. He felt a new tenderness towards Camilla. Now he realized what a turbulent upbringing she had. The diary had revealed more than what he imagined.

"Thank you my love for sharing your life with me," he said squeezing her hand.

Camilla, touched by his gentleness, as if gazing with her deep blue eyes in the far distant past, recalling her mother's story, replied,
"Diana is the one who is guiding my quest. She lives in me. She comes in me. And when she does, I feel a shortness of breath. My heart beats very fast. When she enters my body, I have goose bumps and she takes over my mind. Our thoughts become one. All this is draining, extremely draining."

Palmiero listened attentively. He was fascinated with the paranormal and immortality.

"Explain with more details, please," he encouraged her.

"Well, for instance she came to me last night," continued Camilla, "I was not surprised and thought nothing of it. But, she hurt me. She came into my chest and I felt like if she was squeezing my lungs and my heart. I could not breathe, I could not move. I told her to get out. She would not loosen her grip. I was very frightened. She usually holds my hand or strokes my hair. This time it was very intense and scary. It ended as fast as it started. I woke up this morning early trying to figure it all out. Then I realized, the bad cold I had the night before was gone. All I can say is that I feel so much better. I can breathe through my nose and my cold is definitely better. Maybe, she was trying to help me."

CHAPTER 4
Eros in the Making

PASSION

The Conference Center Hotel, near Lake Champlain, was the chosen resort for that year Bank's Executives Retreat. Camilla had offered to drive Palmiero. He accepted with joy and expectation.

That night and the whole day after, Palmiero counted the hours remaining for their rendezvous. Finally, in the morning of a sunny day, she picked him up. The drive from New York to Vermont was a delightful journey. The fall changing foliage of the countryside was breathtaking natural artist's palette of varieties of colors. The couple spoke very little, as they left for their love adventure. The few words they exchanged Palmiero did not remember. Truthfully, there was no need to talk. Every word was superfluous. For the rest of the drive they left their hearts recognize themselves in an ecstasy of reunification.

Camilla stopped her car at the edge of the lake. The early fall sun was setting rapidly, reflecting its radiance on the stillness of the water. A streak of light, dashing over that waterway surface, reached the window of her car. A warm orange glow enveloped Camilla. Next to her, Palmiero could not help noticing the light and shadow play that the rays were shaping on her neckline. Instinctively, his hand stretched out to caress her rich breast, her large shoulders, reaching up all the way to her long collar. Palmiero indulged. Slowly, he went up and down along her neck. From her chest he reached up to her chin. From there, he reached down again to her heart. He kept stroking her ever so gently, while Camilla moaned with increasing intensity. The man did not know how long he was massaging her in that manner; when he started caressing the back of her neck with his other hand. Both hands were now surrounding her neck rubbing it delicately and tenderly. Camilla closed her eyes and stretched her neck as if offering herself in sacrifice to a godly executioner. Not knowing how, Palmiero tighten his grip. His hands clasped around that white, long, innocent collar. Camilla did not present any obstacle, but her body posture invited increased violence. Palmiero squeezed harder as Camilla started moving as in orgasmic mode. Her face became red. Staring at him, her eyes had reached a dangerous vacuous fixity when she exploded in an intense orgasm that shook her entire body. Then she coughed and Palmiero readily caught her forced exhaled breath, covering her mouth with his lips...

It was only at that moment that Palmiero suddenly released his grip around her throat and, with a terrified expression, said,
"I never did anything like this. What took hold of me?"

Coming out of a wondrous dream, Camilla whispered, "It was beautiful! You lead me where no one ever took me."

When both snapped out of that frenzy, the sun had long set behind the horizon. For a while, they were silent and did not speak. Then, Camilla drove to the hotel.

After the lakeside event, Camilla and Palmiero entered the hotel. Heading to the elevator, they did not speak. At their separate room doors, they parted. Without booking at each other, they exchanged a semi-silent
"Good night."
They knew that if their eyes would have met they would have spent the rest of the night together.

Palmiero sat on his bed. The phone on his night table was tempting him. He picked it up and dialed Camilla's room. Her voice answered,
"Hello Camilla," Palmiero said, "I need to see you."

"Come," she replied, "my door will be opened."

Palmiero crossed the hallway, pushed the door and entered closing it behind him. Camilla greeted him in a red silk robe, which, as she walked towards him, showed her black underwear contrasting with her white copious round long thighs.

Palmiero kneeled before her and sank his head in her aromatic secret garden, while anxiously reaching for her slip and

The promised garden

pulling it down. She sighed and pressed the back of his neck towards herself. In that position, she dragged him along. She sat on her bed and her disrobed red negligee framed the nakedness of her white shapes. The fragrance of her nature pervaded Palmiero's nostrils. His tongue frantically reached for the nectar at the center of her pleasure. She moaned softly. She widened her thighs only to squeeze them immediately to hold his head more securely in place. There, at the holy door of Heaven, Palmiero placed his oral petition on that altar of love, whispering his sacred mantra of ecstasy.

Getting up from that kneeling position, Palmiero sat on the bed cross-legged. Immediately, Camilla joined him in silence, sitting on his lap. In that position, he penetrated her while she crossed her legs tightly behind his back and he grabbed and squeezed her generous buttocks. Both remained embraced, seated in that meditative position, while lost in each other's eyes. Camilla was not any longer a sheer woman. She was the Devi, the Goddess she had always been. He was the Deva, the god expressing his adoration for her. That worship manifested itself with his penetration of her bodily temple as she imparadised his mind.

Camilla had been the Devi all along, but she did not know. She became the real Woman when she discovered the god in herself. Palmiero was the real Man when he discovered himself in the Devi. She made him a Man. In fact, he could not have been one unless the Woman was present in the flesh or in his mind. As Palmiero entered in her, he was the Man. When Camilla sensed that resplendent being in herself, she was the Woman. Palmiero, penetrating her *Yoni*, her divine matrix, was the Man entering the temple where the Goddess resides. Camilla, feeling his *Lingam*, his column of divine energy, discovered the Deity living in her.

Tantric union

How long they were lost in that bliss is difficult to calculate. At one point, Camilla gently pushed Palmiero on his back. Subjugated under her, he remained fused in her in that state of erect adoration. Camilla established her dominion on him. She rode him as an Amazon warrior. She controlled the stride of that horse, which had become fit for the ultimate Sacrifice. First, she rode him slowly, gently, at a leisure pace. Then, she increased the speed. From a gracious stride, she went to a faster gallop, until it became a furious race as she was holding his hands and arms as waiving rains.

At the apex of that crescendo, Camilla's loud cries of pleasure resonated in Palmiero's ears as the sweetest music and song he had ever heard. It was a series of continuous affirmations of the impending coming pleasure culminating in a joyful tearful expression of accomplishment. She sang this song to him.

With love expressions and musical sounds, she was telling him,
"I love you... I... want you... You imparadise me... Yes... in your arms... I am... Yes... Yes... Yes... I'm in Heaven..."

"I love your peak," said Palmiero, as Camilla relaxed leaning on him. "It is greater than any of my orgasms. It gives me more joy than all of my pleasures put together in the entire history of my lovemaking."

"Long history," interjected Camilla, with a tired satisfied sleepy smile.

"If you could fully feel my gratification during your pleasure, you would only want to orgasm with me disregarding my own," he continued.

"Well, I may always want that..." affirmed the Goddess.

"Ah, great, that makes me very happy," replied Palmiero, abandoning himself in a tender kiss, as he remained erect in her.

"You are the first man that has put my pleasure before his," she declared.

"You know that I almost feel sorry when I reach my apex?" Palmiero confessed.

"Yes, I do not want to hurry the finish for you... Now I know. That is not our goal... The journey is the bliss," said Camilla with dreamy eyes.

"Yes lovemaking is the drive to become you. To be your 'I.' It is to discover your I as my own. This is the pure and only philosophy of love," Palmiero concluded.

Palmiero and Camilla discovered all this, while she was riding him as her Sacrificial Horse. She was the Power reflected in his erection housed in her. She was the abode of ecstasy pointing to Heaven.

After they made love, they lay together in a hot love sticky fluidity. Falling asleep and waking up, Camilla tried to rest but she could feel Palmiero's awaken eyes looking intently at her.

"What's the matter?" she asked smiling and squeezing her thighs tightly around him.

"I love you," Palmiero said.

"Me too," she whispered. "You seem to be a million miles away though."

"Well, only seven-thousand," he replied with a grin.

"Ah, someone else occupies your mind," noticed Camilla a bit worried, "after what we just did?"

"Well, I was thinking of Oriana and how I see you in her," he confessed.

"Really, and in what way?" she asked.

"Well you are both, beautiful, smart, sexy, and you equally have the eyes of a Siren," confessed Palmiero.

"Sweet," she murmured. "Are you sorry you did not stay with her instead of Sofia?"

"No I am not. I did not trust Oriana," admitted Palmiero.

"Tell me why," continued inquisitive Camilla.

Palmiero recounted the story of how Oriana lied to him about being unfaithful. He told Camilla if she had only told him the truth, their lives would have been much different.

"Don't ever lie to me," he pleaded with Camilla. "I cannot have that happen again."

"I won't, why would I?" she assured him. "We are one, we promise openness, communication and total abandon to each other. I find this a new freedom of the mind. It is so liberating. That is why I am attracted to you, we both wear our hearts on our sleeve and that is what will get us through. I love you. I feel like you are my father, brother, lover, confidant, friend and I would never hurt us with a lie."

Palmiero held her tightly and kissed her hair. He felt that the burden he carried for so long started to lift in Camilla's embrace.

"Breathe, my darling," Camilla whispered, "breathe..."

MYSTICAL NOTES FROM THE SIREN'S DIARY

The highest Love is the illicit one, which is not that for a spouse, nor that for a lover, not even that for a pleasure mate. The illicit love is a riveting fascinating transformation that uses physiological functions as religious ceremonies, which go beyond all good and bad. We should not be surprised. We employ the pleasure of eating, the function that sustains the continuation of life's mystery, as a form of holy ritual.

Ancient sacred traditions looked at the sexual act with the same innocent eyes with which today we look at the nourishing function. The sacredness of the lovemaking act seems the most appropriate for a metaphysical quest dealing with the mystery of life itself. Therefore, the Man, worshiping with reverence, should penetrate the Woman as entering a sacred shrine. He should be aware that he is now in the presence of the Goddess. At the same time, the Woman, worshiping with love, should let the Man come into her. She is the holy temple where He dwells. She should remember that She is the Mother of God. Let all this be a prayer, a prayer the most effective, because the oneness of the two is the transparency that lets Love shine trough.

There are four types of love.
a) The first and most important one is the illicit, the unnatural one.
b) The second one is the natural conjugal love of spouses in a homo and/or heterosexual relationship.
c) The third form is the natural love of lovers in a homo and/or heterosexual relationship.
d) The forth form of love is the one seeking only sensual egotistical pleasure

This last one (d) is the lowest, intended to satisfy the ego, its narcissistic attitude and the personal appetites of the senses. Perhaps, we cannot call it love at all.

The conjugal and lovers' love (b-c) are on the same level. Both share life, offspring, sentiments and feelings, where the heart speaks out in terms of possession and preservation of property. The only difference between the two is a legal social structure relative to the time and place in which those actions take place. These two loves are on the same level, no one has supremacy over the other. It is the level of Nature, the call of the reproductive force.

The first love (a), on the other hand, is the ILLICIT ONE. It is against nature because it does not follow nature's driving will of representation. This love is higher than anyone else.

Naturally, all four are connected. One participates with all the other three. However, what is the illicit love? It has nothing to do with morality or legal settings. It cannot be that of a spouse, neither that of a lover and, above all, it does not seek its own pleasure. It cannot be pleasure, because it does not want to satisfy the senses. It is not conjugal because does not want to generate nor share a life together. It cannot be a lover because does not involve any personal sentiment. It is total and absolute illicit-illegality and above it has no moral or ethic standard.

Nature dies. Love pleasure ends. Lovers tire out. Spouses' love divorces. However, illicit love lasts forever. That is why this last one is superior to all the others. The other loves may have qualities of the Illicit, but they all undergo the lure of Death. The Illicit is the unselfish love for neither the spouse nor the lover. It is the love of faithful Dante for Beatrice, of crazy Don Quixote for Dulcinea del Toboso, of queen Guinevere for Lancelot, of sad Eloise for Abelard, of sweet Sappho for her girl, of swift Achilles for Patroclus. The Illicit love is Tantra. The Illicit is Sanctity. The Illicit is Mysticism. The Illicit is Prayer. The Illicit is Meditation. Nature abhors it and calls it Illicit, because it does not follow its own selfish interest. The Illicit is LOVE, THE REAL ONE that for which one dies resurrecting on the Cross.

The love call that echoes in the woods, along the ocean shores and gets lost in the deserts, is the call that yearns for the Transcendent.

We all yearn for the other in itself, in its God-Goddess reality. Worldly events and worries characterize conjugal or lover care. They obfuscate the unselfishness of Illicit love and distract us from the transcendent search. The Metaphysical is always altruistic, never egotistical. When the ego enters in a relationship, the venom seeps in. That venom requires for itself the antidote, which wants everything for one's own self, nothing for the other. Then, divorce is already in-act. Then, the couple is not married any longer.

Love is like a flower, a particular one. It may wither by cold, by heat, or by thought alone. Love is a flower with rose petals like snow crystals that melt at the touch of thought. Its corolla is as honey, consumed when ingested for one's gluttony. One should not think about it. That flower fears the heat of thought. One should protect it by holding its unconsumed sweetness in the secret of the heart.

"Your words regarding Diana have influenced me," said Palmiero, as he awakened relaxed next to her, gratified by the lovemaking. "As you were sleeping, I felt her last night."

"Why, she visited you?" asked Camilla suddenly paying serious special attention.

"Yes, last night, as I was shutting the lights and heater and getting ready to go to bed, I felt as if being pulled by the arm."

"Were you scared?" asked Camilla.

"Yes!" he replied.

"Where you aroused?" she continued.

"No!"

"If you want we can forget about her," Camilla suggested, "although I will go as far as you want with this. But, remember, this is not a game."

"Yes!"-acknowledged Palmiero.

"If we continue on this path, we must hang on to each other and all will be fine," declared Camilla.

"I know…" said pensively Palmiero.

"One more thing," concluded Camilla, "Diana wants us to drive to the ocean tomorrow. The ocean is energy, the storage of unconscious power from which she gets her force."

***

That morning, Camilla and Palmiero, completely distracted, attended the Bank's retreat. They were relieved when it ended. They left early. On the way back to New York, they took a long detour to the ocean along the coasts of New Hampshire. In that clear fall Monday, they stopped on the shore of the ocean grove. In their eyes they saw the depth of the sea.

An Ocean of Time separated and united Camilla and Palmiero from Diana. On it, their minds were sailing completely … recollecting … finally reencountering. It seemed all too natural. The First Impulse cried out, demanding warm greetings for Diana. Glacial, time stood in between and their warmth became an embarrassed embrace. Then quietness came down on the still ocean and all the creatures of the world stood into the Great Sky. Time froze into eternity. From eternity, a voice came out, a voice with a thousand names. They surfaced like bubbles coming up from the depth of the ocean and finally bursting on the surface. They were calling each other, reaching out for each other.

Eskimo seal mask with air bubbles rising to the surface from its mouth[20]

In the forgotten forest one voice called out,

"Eagle Feather …"
The other answered from the deadly pit,
    "Morning River … "

Far, on a forgotten Greek beech, one voice called out,
    "Orpheus…"
and the other, from beyond, answered with a gripping song,
    "Eurydice … "

In a deadly secret Italian alcove, trembling voices whispered,
    "Francesca,"
followed by a shivered,
    "Paolo… "

Moreover, in Verona's glacial tomb, death himself shouted out in despair,
    "Juliet …,"
reverberated by her cry,
    "Romeo…,"
while *"Death … sucked the honey out of her breath."*[21]

Finally, in an Adirondack Mountain house, where murder struck, a man's voice yelled out,
    "Diana…,"
    "Bruce, why are you … killing me?"
Diana replied.

Despite the vision, Camilla and Palmiero could not understand those voices. Names were uttered, as dreams and quests from other worlds, other times, other dimensions. They had evoked them; they had evoked those ancient two, the two lovers who wanted to live again. While Camilla and Palmiero were still holding each other, somehow they knew that all the answers were within themselves.

As they untied their embrace, that quietness vanished forever. The noisy flow of the heavy traffic on the Highway, above the ocean grove, drowned it. Again, they had evoked the departed and again they let them die.

***

"I am sorry. I was too eager to come to life," said Palmiero in a pensive mood.

"What do you mean?" replied Camilla puzzled.

"If I had waited, I would have been born twenty years ago," he admitted with a guilty expression.

"Oh my goodness, I see what you mean. I love you," she confessed.

"My love coordinates were off by twenty years," he continued without being able to excuse himself.

"It is better to have experienced our love at any age, than not to have found it at all," concluded Camilla.

THE FIRST VOWS

"Before we leave this place let us vow eternal love," said Camilla inspired. "Let us exchange vows, a promise to each other, right here on this shore, having the Ocean as our witness."

"Yes, I want you to be my *'mogliettina,'* my little wife, as we say in Italy," answered eagerly Palmiero.

Then, holding Camilla's right hand with his left, he recited his vows,
"In this Holy Place and with the Ocean as my witness, I declare my love for you, Camilla. Aware of the sacredness and truthfulness of this ceremony, I willfully unite myself, my mind and my body with you Camilla who, from now on, will be my Goddess-Devi whom I will worship and adore as my wife. I vow to be always loyal, truthful and sincere with you. I will never lie to you. I will never withhold secrets or deeds from you. My mind, my body and my-self are your mind, body and self."

In turn, holding Palmiero's right hand, she recited her vows,
"In this Holy Place and with the Ocean as my witness, I declare my love for you Palmiero. Aware of the sacredness and truthfulness of this ceremony, I willfully unite myself, my mind and my body with you Palmiero who, from now on, will be my God-Deva, whom I will worship and adore as my husband. I vow to be always loyal, truthful and sincere with you. I will never lie to you. I will never withhold secrets or deeds from you. My mind, my body and my-self are your mind, body and self."

After an intense moment of silence Camilla considered,
"For the sake of honesty, I must tell Robert of our love. I hope he will understand and welcome a polyamorous setting."

"Yes, I will support your decision," replied Palmiero with a joyous expression on his face.

As they got back to their homes, Palmiero and Camilla went directly to the computers and started messaging,

"There are so many facets to you," Camilla e-mailed Palmiero, "the dimple and smile with your beautiful teeth belong to you, my seventeen year old lover. The man, who laughs hysterically at my jokes, is you, my thirty-five year old lover. The owner, who grabs me roughly, is you, my fifty year old one. Finally, the man with the tool belt... and cane..., is you, my senior lover.

Every morning I want to find your e-mail ready for me as a cup of coffee. Today was wonderful. The whole event was very erotic for me. You know I did not realize until later that I did in fact have an orgasm. A few actually... little baby ones in a row. I have never had one in that way. It was different from the one with penetration. The edge is off. As I write this it is coming back to me. You know when I think of you my pulse begins to race."

"I miss you so bad already, my sweet one," replied Palmiero. "What do I miss about you? I miss our wonderful talks. I miss our liberating laughs. I miss our fiery glances. I miss our soothing touch. I miss your desirable body. I miss your sweet lips. I miss your worshipful feet. I miss your beautiful breasts. I miss your sacred *yoni*, your divine matrix.

But I do not miss our enchanting love, because that is always here with me. I am sick and tired of this computer. I want your *yoni* now! I want to drink all the elixir you will drip in my mouth, up to the last drop. I want to come in you no matter where as long as it is only in you. I want to be your exclusive toy and pet, while I want your *yoni* to harbor other men. I want to drink your *yoni* immediately after they come in you. If that is being gay it does not bother me. I would become gay if you commanded it and made you happy.

You write to me and my eyes get full of sweet tears. Tomorrow I will give you a disk with all the works I am currently working on lost tablets I found in Asia. That is my soul and that I will be giving you. Let us never, never lie or hide things to each other, this is our richness. We do not know what the future has for us but we will always have the truthfulness of one another. Sharing our feelings is sublime. I want to know you as I know myself. You will and know me as yourself. We are connected by something more powerful than either of us ever realized. It is spiritual, emotional, physical and not of this earth. My one regret in our journey is that we will not have a child together. But those we already have belong to both of us and that is more than anyone could ever ask for. I would never stop you from going outside of our union. However, I will whip you without mercy for that. I own you and you own me. We cannot give each other more than what we already do. I will go wherever you lead me and you will follow me as well. I want to drink you... and swallow you..."

"Satisfy my narcissism. Tell me why you need me in such a manner," wrote Camilla.

"My dear," answered Palmiero without hesitation, "Above all, I need you because I love you. With you I find a twin effect. You think as I do. You own me. I own you. I feel your body is mine. I feel my body is yours. How more beautiful can that be?"

"Do you need this beauty?" Camilla wrote back.

"This is not the right question," replied Palmiero. "The right question would be, 'How have I been able to live without you all this time? I need you as air. You fulfill my dreams and fantasies. No one ever did that. I can tell you anything and you can tell me anything. All will be accepted as I accept my own thoughts. Your desires become my desires. Your dislikes become my dislikes. Do I feel jealousy for you? Yes, not more than I feel jealousy for my own deeds and fantasy. I am jealous of my fantasies when I cannot participate in them. I need you as I need to explore the world. And we are both interested in it.
Would I prevent you from exploring your fantasies? Never! In the same way as I would want to explore my own fantasies. I need you because you are the opening of my mind, the exploration of my soul and the experience of my body. I need you because without you I would not have a body. I need you because you bring out my own real nature. I need you because I need a real Mistress that rules me completely with no mercy. I need you because I need a real slave who I can dominate completely with no mercy. I need you because I need to feel the physical pain I am so scared to receive. And I need you because I need to give you the physical pain that I want to see in your eyes and hear in your voice. I need you because you are my confidant. Whatever my mind thinks I want to tell you. I need you because without you I am not. You have the power of life and death over me. You can kill me if you desire. Suffocate me. Sit on my face. Place your *yoni*, your divine matrix, on my mouth and nose until I become breathless. And I will die happy. Have a pleasant sleep now."

"You too," concluder Camilla, "dream of me. Do not forget, I want to find your loving e-mail ready for me tomorrow."

CAMILLA'S POLYAMOROUS EFFORT

"Robert, are the kids in bed?" asked Camilla, as she closed her messaging with Palmiero, for the evening.

"Yes," replied Robert, "why?"

"I need to talk to you, it is quite important," she said, sitting at the kitchen table, "I hope you will understand me. You see, love cannot exist without trust, openness and honesty. Therefore, hear me out before you reply."

"Tell me," he assured and sat next to her.

"I love you very deeply and dearly," she continued, "and my love for you never diminished one bit, it is always the same as the first day I married you," she voiced in one breath. "However, I must confess to you that I fell in love with another man."

Robert's eyes opened up as wide as his mouth without uttering a word.

"I do not want to leave you," continued Camilla anxiously, "I want to be with you, live with you, raise our family with you. But I want to be able to have at the same time you and my new found love."

"What is his name?" Robert asked ready to unleash his jealous anger.

"Palmiero, my colleague at the bank," she answered, while her heart was racing furiously.

Silence fell on the room. Both were looking at the ground unable to face each other. Finally, Robert broke that impasse shouting,

"Did you fuck him already? How can you love two men equally? That is impossible and unnatural."

"Is it unnatural that we love our three children equally?" promptly replied Camilla.

"Don't give me that! Those are two different loves," he yelled louder. "We should divorce!"

Camilla reached for her husband hand, kissed it and whispered,

"I don't want to divorce you, ever. I love you dearly. I wouldn't be able to live without you or without Palmiero. I am a mother. I know how to divide my love among my children. My heart is big enough. I know how to love my two husbands and make them very happy."

This reply made Robert even angrier and he cried out to the top of his lungs,

"You are a disgrace to our family. You put shame on this house and on our children. What will our neighbors say of us?"

"Disgrace and shame are dishonesty, deceit and cheating. All these things our neighbors, as you well know, do them daily," said calmly Camilla. "I am coming to you with my heart in my hand. I want to establish an open relationship. For it to be successful it requires honesty, openness, faithfulness, sharing and healthiness."

"That is only an excuse for dirty sexual activities," grumbled Robert.

"I beg to disagree," protested Camilla, "Polyamorous love should never be confused with promiscuity or simply lascivious intent. The same way infidelity is the negation of monogamy, so the lack of one of those characteristics nullifies polyamory. One cannot be deceitful, or secretive, or disloyal, or possessive or unsanitary and claim, at the same time, to be polyamorous. Trust, openness, constant communication, sincerity and honesty are the hallmark for a polyamorous relationship. Polyamory is as difficult as other relations are, but the effects and rewards are superior to any other. For one it breaks away from the confinement of egoity making us realize a wider horizon beyond the immediate need."

"You are forgetting a very important natural component, jealousy," rebuked Roberto with a sarcastic grin on his face. "Everyone is protective of his own love, wife and family."

"Jealousy is not love," replied Camilla with a look of contempt, "it has nothing to do with love. Love is giving without asking for a return, as Paul says in the Good Book. Jealousy, is the contrary of love, is possession, greed, wanting for oneself disregarding the needs of the others. Some wonderful cultures in Brazil, like the Kanela, live in peace and view jealousy as a crime against the community. They engage in open extramarital relations and a husband cannot stop his wife from honestly entertaining other lovers. In that case, the jealous husband is reproached and punished by the council of the community."

"But that is because they are savages," he replied without hesitation.

"Do you mean to say that there is honor in killing and have wars, but it is uncivilized to live peacefully enjoying sex with those we happen to fall in love with?" Camilla reproached him.

"Hum," mumbled Robert as a way of admitting defeat.

Something in Camilla's sincerity and reasoning was striking his inner cords. Furthermore, the fact that someone else recognized the beauty and fascination emanated by Camilla aroused him vigorously. However, he did not want to show it to her. It would have revealed an implicit acceptance of that lifestyle which he was trying to rebuff.

Intuitively, Camilla, realizing that Robert's opposition was weakening, continued,

"The interaction, on all levels, with more than one person prepares us to look at neighboring human beings with a kinder eye. It brings them in a sphere of possibility that is not present when the maximum extent of our identity does not go beyond the single wife/husband boundary. Characteristic of an open-family must be complete mental intimacy. The Dalai Lama encourages us to have feelings of equanimity and compassion for all, not only for my husband, my relatives and my friends, but also our enemies. We must recognize that all others are sentient beings like us. The Good Book says, 'Love one another; as I have loved you.' This is a type of polyamory. Polyamory, in fact, is not just about sex. Sex comes into the equation as it comes into monogamic relations, in a pure altruistic giving of oneself to the other. Only then, the sexual act becomes unconditional love. At times, honesty finds obstacles in monogamic relationships. I do not intend to end our marriage. I have a new sentimental and sexual interest for another person, while I am still madly in love with you. Nevertheless, it is possible to love with equal intensity two persons at the same time."

"Who is your new lover? What's his name again?" asked Robert, this time visibly excited.

"Palmiero Venturini. He is my Bank colleague," promptly answered Camilla, secure in her new polyamory lifestyle. Then, not giving her husband any possibility of rebuttal, she concluded, "It makes me very happy that you accept him as part of our family."

"Bring him home," confirmed Robert, leading her to the bedroom.

That night, they made passionate love, as they had never done in a long time. Both were aware that their marriage had taken a turn for the better, a way which would have made them much happier. Robert pumped Camilla fantasizing her with the lover. Each stroke his erection was stronger. Each blow he saw Palmiero enjoying her. At the apex, he joyfully screamed out confessing his polyamorous acceptance,
"Yes, I love that Palmiero fucks you. I want to see you in action with him. I love youuuuuuuuuu…"

Finally satisfied, Camilla fell asleep, she dreamt of raising a polyamorous flag on the roof of her house.

***

The next morning, following her orders, Palmiero e-mailed Camilla,
"Good morning my love, I feel your lips on mine. Loving you is beautiful. You inspire me. You motivate me. You make me love the world. You are my desire. From you, my dear, I have learned how sweet it is to hold you, to be closely tight to you, while seeking protection from the pain inflicted by you my loved one. My love, always comfort me tenderly, as you give me excruciating pain. I will take it while keeping you tight to my heart. Always assure me,

while throbbing shivers travel through my spine inflicted by your hand. Hush me lovingly, as you hurt me harder and harder. Oh suave pain that only my Goddess can give me as her blissful gift. I have tied my shaft for you again. Our rule should be that you command my body and I command yours. I cannot use my body without permission from you and you cannot use your body without my permission. This will be binding for us until both unanimously repeal it. This is my formal acceptance of these rules. I am your Master as you are my Mistress.

I am jealous of the sun tanning your velvety skin. I am jealous of the wind blowing through your perfumed hair. I am jealous of the ocean wetting your loving breast. I am jealous of time robbing our moments together. I am jealous of physicians palpating your intimate parts. I am jealous of your house excluding me from your kingdom. I am jealous of your mysterious ways making you impenetrable. I am jealous of your distractions making you lose your concentration on me. I am jealous of your thoughts not directed towards me. I am jealous of your memories not containing me. I am jealous of your trips taking you away from me. I am jealous of the persons you have met and I do not know. I am jealous of your friends keeping you company. I am jealous of your colleagues occupying your working hours. I am jealous of your family embracing you in their love. I am jealous of those who admire you making me proud with their admiration. I am jealous of your lovers enjoying your soft body. Again, I am jealous of your lovers taking away your thought from me. I am jealous of those who still love you recognizing that it is impossible not to love you. I am jealous of myself for that youth I am not any longer. I am jealous of everyone and everything that can take you away from me. Yes, I am jealous. I am jealous. I am very jealous. In each one of those forms of jealousy, with an equal and contrary magical force, my love for you grows madder and bigger to subtract you from the others' possession. Jealousy would blind me with pain if, in the unforeseeable future, other loves should embrace you. However, even in that case, my love for you would have no borders and would grow exponentially bigger than the biggest jealousy. Last night, at two, suddenly, I was awakened by a very intense burst of love for you. Then, a devastating image shook my mind, you, my great love, willingly abandoning in the insidious embrace of secret seducers. In the whirlpool of jealousy, it is your will that predominates. In that persisting pain, yet I repeat to you, 'Let it be what you want.' Then, my jealousy calms down, to leave room to Love, which from great has become immensely un-containable. My passion surrenders to Love. Love decides. Love disposes. Love guides us. We call Love that force that cements the universal texture. There is no greater force. Let us not project the future. You are Love, which highlighted my life, which never abandoned me and I abandon myself in your embrace. I am asking to be indelibly branded by you. However, I realize that you already branded me with fire. That firebrand you left it permanently sculptured in my heart. I cannot tell you 'I love you.' This is a human expression. For you the only expression is 'I adore you.' You are my goddess. You are my Paradise. I come to you with an act of total unconditional devotion and respect. I place myself as an offering at your feet. You are my life. My life belongs to you. My soul is only yours. You can direct it towards my salvation or my damnation, to Paradise or Hell, as you wish. If you would order me to commit suicide, I would kill myself. I am your pet. For you I would perform any act, even the most ignoble, the most blasphemous and the most sacrilegious. You are my strength. Without you I am impotent. You are my thought. My thoughts are not mine, they are only yours. You are my blood. You are my breath. You are my nourishment. No one is more sacred than you. You are my divinity saved since the beginning in my memories. I searched for you in my dreams. I ogled you in my desires. Now I have found you. The tree of my life is blooming again irrigated by your vital spring. You are the goddess with one thousand names. You are Ishtar in Babylon, Aphrodite in Athens, Madonna in Rome. You are my supreme goddess, my supreme sovereign, my demanding owner.

You are my maid of all work. You are my submissive slave. You are my licentious whore. All you want me to believe I will believe. All that you want me not to believe, I will not believe. If you will love me, I will love you and be only yours. If you will not love me, I will love you and be only yours. If you will leave me, I will love you and be only yours. I will be what you will want me to be, your slave, your husband, your owner and your pimp. I want to sink ever so deeply in our Love till I go crazy without restraint and without limitation."

CHAPTER 5
The Ghost

EROTIC TERROR

When Palmiero first saw her, Diana was sitting in the dark, on the cream color couch behind him in his home office. He recognized her by the photos Camilla had shown him. It was late at night and he was working at his computer, checking the Asian stock market. He saw her from the corner of his eyes. He felt a cold shiver going up his spine. His skin quivered all the way to the top of his head and his breath stopped short in his lungs. In denial, he did not want to turn to look. However, Diana was there.

That same day, a very stormy and windy one, during lunch Camilla had told Palmiero,

"Be careful. Diana will come to you tonight. It is rainy and you might not hear her."

"How do you know?" asked Palmiero.

"The wind told me."

"How should I be careful? What must I do?" Palmiero asked incredulous.

"I'm warning you so she does not startle you as she walks up behind you and puts her hands around your neck. She is dangerous, she does not believe in 'lollipop' safe words. But, whatever you do, do not go with her." declared Camilla.

"Explain, please," said Palmiero condescendingly.

"She is going to want to take you with her. She will beckon to you. Do not go... it will be a trick. Do not forget, she is the Siren." sentenced Camilla.

"Go where?" Palmiero asked a bit annoyed.

"To die... She will trick you with the unknown... and you, being curious, will follow her. Just think of me... and you will be fine," advised Camilla with great concern.

This conversation had taken place that same morning. Now Diana, the Siren was there, or, at least, he thought so. Was it only a hallucination influenced by the previous discussion? However, Palmiero could see her distinctly, a dark shadow sitting against the lightning light coming from the half opened shutters of the balcony. They say that a cold environment announces the presence of a ghost. In spite of the blasting heaters, the room was freezing. Feeling uneasy, Palmiero got up and left the room. As he walked through the foyer, he passed by the mirror on the wall above the piano. Two images appeared on it, his and, behind him, Diana's. Palmiero's hair rose up on his head. Diana's transparent figure stood tall and gruesomely beautiful. Her long flowing hair reached down on her torso. A sad inviting smile shaped the angle of her mouth. A strong scent of booze pervaded the frigid room. From far, the melodic calling notes of the serenades *a' Diana* reached Palmiero's ears.

From that mirror, she looked at Palmiero. The reflection came from a mysterious and enchanted reign. With a silent language, she spoke to him of love. Her burning jealousy pierced his mind. From the surrounding cacophony of thunders, her hazel and sad eyes whispered,

"Why, did I deserve such a short and tragic life?"

Palmiero froze, alone with his terror and not knowing why, he uttered in Latin,
"*Benevales quisquis es*, go in peace, whosoever you are."

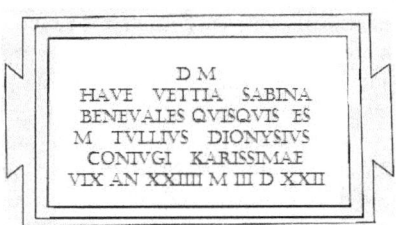

Roman funerary inscription, Nola I Century AD

Disregarding his injunction, the Siren entered into him and, closing forever the gate behind her, transmitted the thought,

"You remembered the words you wrote on my tomb. Then, your name was Marcus Tullius Dionysius and I was Vettia Sabina, your very dear wife who died at the age of twenty-four during the Roman Empire. I am again a ghost. Now I am Diana, Camilla's mother."

Palmiero felt her regret and awareness of a life robbed of her youth. The ghost was not that of Diana at her death. It was the one of Diana at the height of her beauty and sexuality. The specter before him was that of a twenty five year old woman. Her hair was long and chestnut. Her high forehead and her nose were that of an aristocrat. She wore her hair in long curls hanging past her chest, like a mermaid. When she moved, Palmiero caught a glimpse of her breast. The nipples were light pink and erect, her arms were long and slim and she had the longest fingers Palmiero has ever seen.

"Oh, so this is where Camilla inherited her beautiful hands," he thought.

Not knowing how, Camilla vanished in a forgetful blur. All he could think of was Diana's hands caressing his erect manhood. More disturbing was the fact that those were the extremities of a terrifying specter.

As Diana's phantom moved away from Palmiero, he saw her backside for the first time. He was surprised that her buttocks were flat. He had seen her daughter's many times and expected fullness where there was none. However, her legs were the anatomic part that captivated him. She had lengthy, sinewy legs. Her calves were beautiful, toned and thin. He had never seen a shinbone as angular as Diana had, it looked like a knife. In ecstasy, he noticed bruises on her body. Instinctively, he bit down on his lip. He was surprised to taste blood. The ghost placed her hand on his shoulder and sent a wave of frigid terrifying pleasure down Palmiero's spine. Immediately he was aroused. A different pleasure took hold of his manhood. It was like an icy grip that controlled his soul, a pleasure that was made of pure terror. There was a strange fascination. The original fear gave way to a new strange disturbing feeling. A weird attraction forced Palmiero to turn around and look at the apparition directly in the eyes. She was beautiful, luring, captivating. He could almost distinguish her nakedness beyond the foggy, illusive hallucination. A somewhat familiar stale and salty smell hit his nose. Palmiero had never smelled it on a woman before. It was the scent of alcohol, cigarettes and sex. The smell hit him viscerally and, against his will, he was immediately aroused.

"Come... come... follow me! You will help me come back to life. I am hungry for existence," uttered the specter with a sweet melodic tone in the voice, luring him towards the steps leading to the wine cellar.

Palmiero had built that personal space where no one could go or touch without his permission. As the incurable romantic he was, he had stacked his precious wine bottles and adorned it with consumed candles. Now, after years of neglect, besides dust, also cobwebs were covering those rare containers.

Palmiero remembered Camilla's almost prophetic and admonishing words,

"I think she will beckon to you. She will order you to follow her into the wine cellar. Don't think she won't. When you showed me your vintage wine collection, I felt her in there."

To those words he had answered, "There are forces contrary to her in there. You felt my presence, no one else's."

Nevertheless, Palmiero physically felt Diana pulling him. Petrified he followed her lead. They went down those steps. He opened the cellar's door and a musty smell hit his nostrils. The specter seemed to gain more strength and power in that environment. Diana turned towards him and embraced him in her frozen fog.

Death's embrace.

In those deadly arms, Palmiero reached an immediate state of erection. His mind did not belong to him any longer. He was completely altered. In that very early morning, Diana's aura overwhelmed him. Terrified, he forced himself to look at her face. She was more beautiful than he had dreamed. Compared to her, Camilla's beauty seemed childish. Diana's gaze was mysterious and full of a sexual energy that he had never encountered. He lowered his eyes and she slapped him hard in the face.

"Surely," he thought, "I must be hallucinating or I am having a stroke. This cannot be happening."

With her eyes, she commanded,
"Look at me!"

He refused with a slight nod of his head and immediately came the next blow. On the verge of collapsing, he raised his head. Suddenly, the room was on fire. In the middle of it was Diana.

The Ghost of Diana, the Siren.

He shook his head violently from side to side; his whole house was on fire.

"What... what... is this..." He thought.

The fire surrounding Diana was a mixture of blues, greens and yellows. Palmiero marveled at her beauty and aura as if depicted in van Gogh's "*Starry Night*." The fire swirled up and down swaying him; he could feel the heat on his face. He was in complete awe before those vibrant red blazing flames with deep royal blue overtones. Palmiero could not take his eyes off it. However, no smoke alarm sounded to report the 'blaze,' because the house was not on fire.

In the midst of all that, Diana smiled welcoming and shedding the menacing look. As he took a step towards her, he knocked over one of his cherished wine racks. The bottle of a vintage wine he had been saving for 40 years broke and cut him deeply on his side. He continued walking lost in his trance. Palmiero had never experienced drugs before. Diana's aura overwhelmed him. He was lost in her spell. More powerful than LSD, Diana was his one and only drug. The ghost was all he could think of. The light and colors that surrounded her phantom blended like on Renoir's palette.

Palmiero called out,
"Diana!"

Her powerful name resounded with an orgasmic voice. It was a way of expressing and professing his devotion and submission to the Spirit. Diana seemed clearly satisfied. It was like an acid trip for him. It was like climbing peaks over peaks of intensity. Swirls going up... up... and up again, only to be released in a downward spiral. Like a tsunami, it swung surging and falling. Then another wave and another followed it, so quickly that it toke his breath away. Palmiero was aware of Diana's presence, but he had to shut his eyes not to be horrified.

Then Diana released him from the deadly embrace. She seemed familiar with the surroundings of that cellar. Camilla leaped in Palmiero's mind and he thought,
"She was right."

Diana headed directly to a wall. There was a secret door. Palmiero never knew that it was there. It was behind one of the huge, tall wine racks and he had never noticed it. The ghost opened it and stood on the threshold inviting him to cross over it. A long dark tunnel seemed to stretch behind that entrance. Her invitation was alluring. In a daze, he started walking towards her. The pleasure intensified. He reached the mysterious entrance.

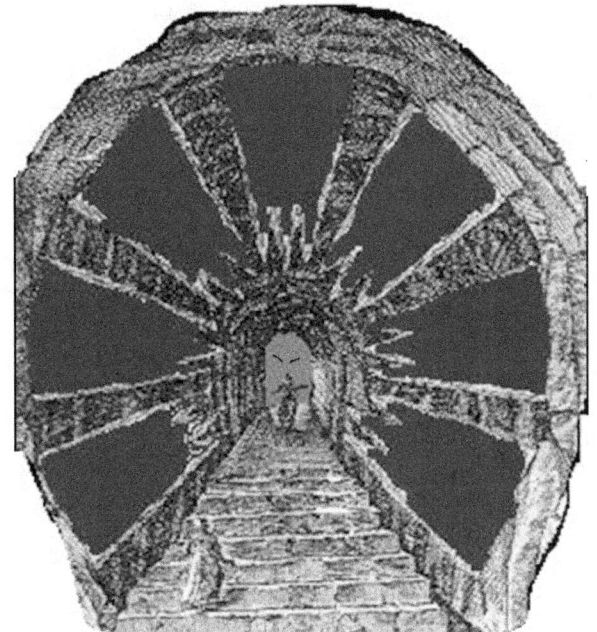

The secret door of the head

He was about to step beyond... when the phone rang.

As the phone buzzed, Diana's ghost disappeared beyond that gate, taking that opening away with her and chillingly echoing, "This is not the last you'll see of me... I will be back..."

Palmiero picked up the phone and with an absentminded distorted voice answered,
"Hello!"

"BACK AWAY... DON'T GO IN... Break away from your trance. If you go through that exit, you will die. " screamed Camilla, on the other side of the wire.
"Palmiero," continued frantically Camilla. "I just had this vivid dream. It woke me up. I had to call you. Warn you. Stop you. I had to reach you. I was desperate, to the point that if you did not answer, I would have called your wife in Italy. I knew you had to work until late and you would have been up."

"Yes, as you know, I was writing that boring presentation for work and checking the Asian stocks. In reality, I was dreaming of you, as I was staring at the computer. Then, as you predicted, Diana appeared. I will tell you my feelings tomorrow," replied Palmiero regaining his composure.

Janus the double-faced god.

SECOND NOTES FROM THE SIREN'S DIARY

Eros, the god of Love is also Thanatos the god of Death. Love and Death are the two sides of the same medal, as Janus the double-faced god. There is a strange connection between Love and Death. Death hungers for life. Life expresses itself as desire for Love. Finally, Love seeks the solution of Death's mystery. The circle closes moving from the Love of Life to Mysterious Death and from the Mystery of Death to Loving Life.

CHAPTER 6
Eros and the Ghost

THE CEMETERY

During their usual stroll through Canal Park, Camilla anxiously enquired,

"Tell me, what happened last night."

"Camilla, I must confess, I did not believe you," started Palmiero with a very submissive attitude. "Your stories about Diana, her periodic possessing you and her controlling our destiny, never convinced me. I was torn between considering it your drug related hallucinations or a mania of grandeur or both at the same time. I also thought that it could have been a simple exaggeration. I surmised it was your way to add some mystery or unusual sex appeal to increase the erotic dimension of our relation."

"Why, now you believe me?" said Camilla, stopping and looking at him with condescending superiority.

"Not only I believe you, but I must learn to trust you and your judgments, more than my own," declared Palmiero, giving up all his guard and abandoning himself to her. Actually, he felt a strange pleasure in his surrender. He felt he would have kneeled right there, before the whole world, to declare his unconditional devotion to her. However, he refrained from it and resumed his leisurely walk saying,

"After the events in my cellar last night, I believe, I believe...Diana is real... After Diana's direct visit to me, I realize that you were not making anything up. I hope you will forgive my incredulity."

"I hope you realize and believe that Diana enters my body to possess me completely. She makes me her instrument to operate in the world of the living," answered Camilla without accepting his apology. In fact, she felt an impulse to strike him hard, to punish him for his insolence and show who controlled the situation. Nevertheless, she desisted and suggested to head back to the office.

As Palmiero sat at his desk, he heard the familiar beep of an incoming email. It was Camilla,

"Palmiero, I forgot to ask you," she wrote, "are you busy this first Sunday of November? Would you like to visit my mother's grave with me?"

"What an unusual request." Palmiero thought. However, given the past events, he accepted the invitation.

***

The wooden crosses and tombstones of the Adirondack cemetery were barely emerging from a sea of fallen leaves and dead pink wild thyme flowers. Camilla laid red roses on the plain grave post of her mother. Palmiero, who stood behind her, broke his silence saying,
"We should have masses said for the rest of her soul."

"Yes, we should," said Camilla transfixed.

Palmiero, worried by the strange change in her eyes and in her facial expression, took her by the arm and led her to the car.

"I am tired," Camilla said with a weird tone of voice.

"Lie down in the back of the car, I will drive you as you rest," he suggested.

Driving back to New York City, while Camilla was sleeping on the rear seat, Palmiero set the radio on his favorite classical music. Live from the Met, the station broadcasted Tchaikovsky's opera, *The Queen of Spades*. Emotionally and mentally taken by those beautifully dramatic, morbidly dark and sweeping sounds, he completely sunk in the music. Lost in his thoughts, he considered the meaning of that lyrical composition, of the cards, of the gambling addiction of Hermann, the main protagonist, and his tragic death. Consequently, when he felt Camilla's long hands wrapped around his throat, he was completely startled. He could not turn around to look at her without endangering his driving. Therefore, he deliberated that it was a gesture of affection.

"This is the Queen of Spades demanding my life," he thought with a smile.

However, her grip was tightening and he looked in the rear mirror. There, he did not encounter Camilla's eyes, but the staring gaze of Death. The car swayed treacherously and he barely controlled it going off the road.

"Keep driving and pull up to that B & B along the lake. I want to rape you there!" commanded a melodic voice, blending in with the arias sang on the radio.

As he parked the car in the lot of the lodge, Palmiero's hands were shaking. Bay Point hotel was one of the most exclusive resorts overlooking Lake George and Fort William Henry, visible far in the distance. From that location, the view of the blue lake, stretching towards the late foliage-brown hills surrounded by mountains covered by the first snow, was spectacular.

"Your suite, number 385, overlooks the lake and it has a fireplace. We will have the fire going for you, if you wish," said the hotel receptionist handing over the key to Palmiero.

"Yes, please do so," said Camilla, next to him, quickly picking up the key and commanding,
"Palmiero, go fetch my other suitcase in the car. I will wait for you in the room."

Without hesitation Palmiero went to the car, while she headed to the elevator escorted by the bellboy carrying the one piece of luggage Camilla had already with her.

DEATH RAPING LIFE

Palmiero, holding the suitcase, knocked at the door of room 385. A familiar voice with sweet melodic tones commanded, "Come in, the door is open!"

He recognized Diana's strangely altered voice. How could he forget it? Palmiero pushed open the door. As he entered the room, a scent of alcohol, cigarettes and sex hit his nostril. There was a trail of blood from the bathroom to where Camilla sat. She was in her slip, on the edge of the bed. He looked around sure to see Diana, but only Camilla was there. That is, it was the body and the appearance of Camilla, but it was not her. The demeanor was that of someone who demanded subjugation and obedience. The sweetness and celestial softness of Camilla's eyes were gone, transformed in a vitriolic glassy Medusa gaze that petrified the onlooker.

The visit to her mother's grave had overwhelmed Camilla so intensely that her sleep in the car had become a mediumistic slumber during which Diana had entered her body. Palmiero knew that now he was at the presence of Diana the Siren, the ancient Parthenope. This time, however, she had come back to claim the life and spoils of her Ulysses.

She remained seated, without moving, staring in the hellish emptiness before her. Dressed only in her slip and a black corset, which emphasized her breast tightly held in place, she seemed to regard all hell with great despise.

"What did you do?" he asked her, noticing a bloody ice pick in her hand.

She threw her head back and laughed with a menacing sound; one that went right through him. He was astonished to see that, unconsciously, under Diana's influence, Camilla had self-inflicted deep cuts in several places. They emulated the ones Diana received when she was alive. Those wounds were profusely dripping blood all along her legs.

He suddenly felt sick, but Diana commanded him to undress. As he took his close off, she said,

"Now kneel before me."

Palmiero was uncertain what to do.

"Kneel before my feet, I said, and kiss them," she repeated certain of compliance and pointing at her naked feet covered with blood.

The melodic sound of her voice was irresistible. Palmiero could only promptly obey. A rush of pleasure pervaded him as he genuflected before that majestic dominating Goddess and kissed her feet.

Prostrated in that manner and in a state of shock, Palmiero had the audacity to ask,
"What did you do to my Camilla?"

"Do not worry, she is safe," the Siren replied assuring. "She is my daughter. She is my way to you. The love you both share leads me back again among the living. Now shut up and lick my nature."

Palmiero complied. Diana lay on her back over him, offering her juicy nature to his head coming up from behind her wide-open legs. She screamed of pleasure when his tongue penetrated her. From that position, Palmiero could view that lovemaking in the mirror on the wall, on the other side, at the foot of their bed. What he saw made his hear stand on his head; it was not Camilla's body he was pleasuring, it was that of a horrifying demon.

Guatemalan clay pipe burner

An indescribable attraction arouse Palmiero's manhood. The other side of existence pulled him in the dark gluten made of viscous organic substances. He swallowed and wallowed in it, feeling pleased as a swine. Diana embraced him, captured him in her sticky web-like vines of her thousand tentacles. Trapped and encased in her lethal cocoon, he was there in a state of erection. He waited anxiously for that deadly black spider to insert her poisonous fangs in him, making him scream of terror and pleasurable pain, and finally

The black spider

devour him.

Peruvian incense burner, lovemaking on death.

The Siren, seeing his erection, turned around and rode him furiously. Then, suddenly dismounting, she kicked him away and glided across the room. She went towards the blazing flame of the fireplace, picked up a piece of iron used to tend the blaze and placed it directly between the burning logs. She stood there, watching as the flames heated the end of the iron. After a minute, she seemed satisfied.

Palmiero had never been more frightened,
"What is she going to do?" he thought.

"Get up and lean over the bed!" Diana commanded.

He was frozen. Clumsily, Palmiero did as she commanded. However, he started to beg,
"Please, please... Camilla, stop her... please..."

The Siren's slap hit him so hard across the face that his glasses flew away.

"Stop your whimpering," she said, spitting in his open mouth.

He lay across the bed and bit his tongue in preparation for whatever this demon had in mind. Diana took the iron from the fire and held its red-hot tip on his scrotum. The pain was unbearable. Palmiero tried to scream but the sound would not come out. The Siren threw the iron on the floor and commanded him,

"Lie down on the bed and stay still on your back."

Palmiero had no idea what was coming next. Shaking he did as she told him. He lay in a state of shock. He had never felt such intense pain in his whole life. He felt Diana move about and he shut his eyes. He was too scared to see what the Siren had in mind for the second act. With his eyes closed, he heard Diana move across the room,

"I cannot look, I cannot look...," he thought.

Diana/Camilla ready to brand him

The Siren came back humming a very sad melody. He felt her climbing on the bed. She sweetly told him to spread his legs. He resisted, but she comforted him and he obeyed. He flinched as she placed ice from the room refrigerator on his testicles. It was surprisingly pleasant after all the torture she obliged him to suffer. He felt the ice cube cooling the spot she had just tormented and inflamed.

As she held the ice cube there, Diana kissed him. This time, it was a sweet kiss and he was very surprised. Slowly she made her way down his body. She licked his nipples and gently bit them. He forgot all about what had just happened and relaxed. She, then, reached for his manhood.

Fearful of what she had done before, he screamed,
"Oh... no, please..., what are you going to do?"

The Siren reached for his *lingam*, his column of divine energy, sweetly kissing it. Then, she slowly began to lick it. Finally, she took his manhood into her mouth. After the branding torture and sheer terror she had put him through, he was sure he would not have been able to have an erection ever again. However, she was very patient. He had never had a woman use her mouth on him in such a way. She sucked him as no other had ever done. She moved at the rhythm of her own symphonic pace. Up and down as she slowly moved her head sideways. Next, she swirled the gland with her tongue tapping it repeatedly on the tip. When he thought that she was about to remove her mouth, then, swiftly, she would sink her head swallowing him whole. She was tender as a baby sucking on his mother's breasts. Overcome with emotion, Palmiero grabbed hold of her hair and held her down on him until she gagged.

He whimpered in Italian,
"*Tu sei un angelo*, you are an angel. My Diana..., my Camilla..., you own me..., you own me."

Suddenly, the Siren's pace became more furious. His erection had never been so hard in his life. At first, he did not even realize that Diana/Camilla was tightening her grip on his *lingam*, on his column of divine energy. Abruptly, the sucking became so intense that it hurt.

He cried out,
"Noooo!" and Diane bit him with such force that he thought she had removed his penis. Rather than make him pull away, that pain made him instantly orgasm. Diana swallowed every drop of his soul. She smiled and turned away, as she fell back into a slumber with the sweet taste of conquest in her mouth.

When Camilla came back from that state of trance, she was still in Palmiero's arms. Both were wet with the juices and dirt of that abnormal love triangle.

"How can we cope with this aberration in our life?" asked Camilla, shivering in a cold sweet and holding tight to Palmiero.

Unable to answer, Palmiero kept quiet, while he had still Diana's taste in his mouth.

CHAPTER 7
Bondage, Discipline and Sadomasochism

THE WHORE

Friday afternoon, after a long week of mortgage sales meetings and team projects, Camilla knocked on Palmiero's door.

"Come in." he said and smiled broadly when he saw her. "Hi *bella*, what a surprise."

He loved the banks corporate policy of Friday "dress down day." Camilla wore jeans so tight that, at the sight of her, he felt always the present sensation of his desire growing in his pants.

"Hi handsome," she said as she sat down heavily, with a sigh.

"What brings you here?"

"Well I told the team I would take them out for drinks tonight to celebrate having met our deadline and wanted to invite you," she replied expecting him to accept.

"Hum... I guess you forgot our dinner plans," he hit back, crossly. "Didn't you tell me that Robert was taking overnight the kids to see his mother and you and I were free to have dinner in the city?"

"Oh my god... I am so sorry... But, I just invited twenty of my coworkers for drinks at the Houndstooth Pub. Palmiero, I am truly sorry. Come with us."

"No!" he snapped visibly upset. "I am not in college and don't want to hang out with fraternity boys."

"Wow... Are you jealous?" Camilla answered surprised.

"Palmiero was a man of the world, how could he be jealous of little American men." She thought. However, she replied, "Well you can come or not... I am going." and off she went leaving him stewing at his desk.

"Have good sex," he mumbled, as she left.

Pretending not to have heard, she quickly left.

That evening, Palmiero went to the pub where he knew Camilla had gone. He hurriedly walked toward the door. At the tavern, Camilla was relaxing from the pressures of the week and she was gladly accepting shots of tequila from a man next to her at the bar. Her team had left after only one hour. However, she was still there when Palmiero arrived.

Before he could enter, from the window of the bar he got a glimpse of Camilla's vibrant red hair cascading down her back. He saw her open mouth throw and the raise of her neck in laughter. She was talking to a large man leaning towards her. Her companion was a tall man with a shaven head that made him look like a lemon. He wore an expensive suit with the tie loosened around his collar. He noticed the man had an arm around her and was playing with her hair. Palmiero did not expect to encounter this sight. He thought that Camy, as he affectionately called her, would have been sitting alone.

After a while, the man whispered in her ear.
"You are so beautiful."

She moved away, looked at him in the eyes and caressed his cheek with a big smile. She kissed him on the lips and replied,
"Thank you."

Although she had heard it often, it was flattering to hear it from a complete stranger.

"I would like to have my way with you," he said seriously.

"Oh, really," countered Camilla, shamelessly placing her hand on his crouch to tease his hardness and without caring who in that bar saw her doing it.

"Yes, and, from the way you have been squirming in your chair, I know you are moist with excitement at that very thought," he boldly insisted.

Camilla was surprised and flushed red with embarrassment because he was right.

"Well let's go," she said.

"Wait, I am here only for one night. My name is Joseph Bottiglieri. I live in San Diego, I am married, I am bi-sexual and I will be leaving tomorrow. We will be together only tonight," he declared.

"You sound like the perfect man," she said pulling him close to her as she thrust her tongue in his throat and dragged him by his harm, commanding,
"Let's go... NOW!"

Joseph reached for his wallet, left some money on the bar and helped Camilla get up from her bar stool. Both walked to the door as Palmiero, unseen, furiously left the tavern.

Joseph and Camilla directed their steps to a hotel across the street. There, they requested a non-smoking room and hastily headed for the elevator. Once in their suite, Camilla was very excited and not a bit nervous. Joseph, who was extremely tall, fit and sexy, kissed her at the door. He caressed her face and kissed every freckle on it.

"I find you very sexy and beautiful," he told her, and I will pleasure you tonight."

As she started undressing, she declared,

"My name is Camilla," then, as Joseph was folding his trousers over the chair, she reached out to caress his bulge that by now had significantly increased in size, and asked him,

"In which position you prefer to take me?"

"Legs wide spread in a 'v' position," replied the man with a voice denoting intense desire and his underwear showed a very promising swelling.

Soon their clothes were off and no more words were necessary. They moved to the bed and kissed some more. Using his tongue with attention and passion, Joseph played Camilla's body like a fine rare violin and she respond in unison with him. His long liberated shaft slipped out from his constraining shorts and she held his organ and started caressing and sucking it. He moaned with pleasure. She felt his eyes on her and she was blown away by the desire and love she saw in them. Soon she was ready to have him in her.

"Come now, Joseph, plant your big fig tree in my garden of delight," invited Camilla spreading wide her legs.

Joseph made his way in between her legs and plunged in Camilla's nature making her jump with pleasure. Joseph, kneeling between her legs held them extended apart while clamping her ankles and pumping her vigorously. Then she threw him on his back and started riding him. Camilla felt very powerful. The moans escaping Joseph's lips and the look on his face filled her with a sense of power. Here she had a perfect stranger who would do whatever she wanted. His only desire was to please her. Never before, she had ever felt this sensation. She had known other men in the past and they had been pleased sexually by here, but to command that stranger was an experience like none other. She was completely lost in the moment. Joseph expressed his submission with sounds of pleasure. When her orgasm came, it was powerful and violent. The shrieks that escaped from her lungs left Joseph astonished. She had four back-to-back orgasms, Camilla collapsed on his chest. Joseph had never heard a woman orgasm sound with such intensity. She was exhausted and encouraged him to let her lay down so he could finish on top of her. As Joseph continued making love to her, he covered her with tender kisses. Then, he got up again pushed her knees bent to her ears and rammed himself deeply into her. While he did this, the pleasure he was receiving made her feel as if he was worshipping her like the Goddess she was. After he climaxed, it was very intimate. Joseph held her hand. Both lay next to each other, caressing and kissing. It was the sweetest and most tender experience.

As she was laying there next to him, Camilla thought,
"This is love without limits, love without judgment and love without condemnation. When all those negativities are gone, what is left is this love."

CAMILLA'S DISCIPLINARY TRAINING

While Camilla was still at the inn, Palmiero, who had seen them going to the hotel, went around the city to buy supplies. He wanted to teach Camilla a lesson and submit her to his will. He purchased ropes, to tie her hands and legs, duck tape, a whip and a candle to drip hot wax on her natural garden. He was mad. In that state of rage, he returned to the pub.

He called her cellular phone. As she recognized Palmiero's ring tone, she frantically searched for her phone somewhere on the night table next to the bed. Joseph, next to her, annoyed said,
"Do not pick it up."

She shrugged him off.

"Palmiero…, Palmiero, sorry I took so long to answer… Are you there?" she answered.

"Get outside, you whore!" he commanded.

"Oh my god, I'm sorry, I will be there."

"Wow, what's the rush," said Joseph, still in bed and trying to stop her, but she wiggled out.

She ran so fast out of the hotel room that she tripped and stumbled while fixing the dress on herself. That was the last time she ever saw Joseph.

"I am so happy to see you, Palmiero," she reached out for him.

"Get in the cab, you whore," he said grabbing her roughly and spitting in her face.

Camilla was surprised, but without a word did what he commanded. He handed her his handkerchief to wipe off his spit from her eye and gave the address of a midtown hotel to the driver.

"Where are we going?" she asked timidly frightened and somehow aroused.

Palmiero slapped her hard across the mouth. His ring caught the edge of her lip and she tasted blood from her mouth. She was scared, nervous but could feel warmth building up between her legs.

They reached a new hotel, checked in and went directly to their room, all without a word. Once inside he commanded her,

"On her knees, you bitch!"

In saying that, he toke his *lingam*, his column of energy, out and thrust it in her mouth. She started choking as he violently pushed it in and out. Then, abruptly he stopped. Camilla was scared. Worried for his fury, she begged, but then she realized that she wanted this as much or even more than he did. She knew that his behavior was not out of anger but out of love. His jealousy was only an excuse to enter into their next love phase. However, she had been very bad. She had sex with that stranger at the bar. If Palmiero had not called her, she would have still been with Joseph in bed. She knew that she needed to be punished.

Palmiero held her by the hair down on the bed and screamed at her,
"You made love to that guy at the bar, right?"

"Yes," she feebly replied.

Palmiero was outraged and completely aroused by that answer. They knew, wished and desired all what was about to take place. Camilla and Palmiero realized that she deserved to be raped. Both wanted it. She longed to be violated from behind.

"Please, take me in my anus," she begged, expecting Palmiero to comply.

He tied her tightly and pressed her on the bed. He spanked her repeatedly over the buttocks. He slapped as hard as he could until both cheeks were read hot with blue streaks. She started crying,

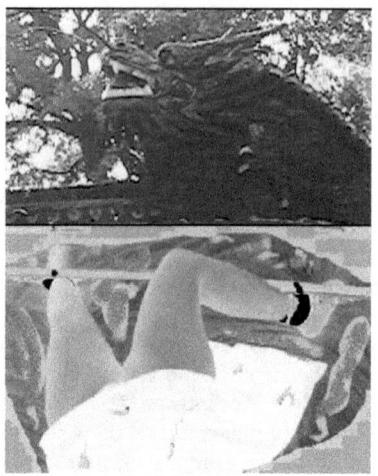

Camilla's bondage.

"You are hurting me and you will leave marks on me."

"Stop talking, whore!" he commanded, slapping her hard across the face and putting duck tape over her mouth.

"Now listen to what I will tell you," continued Palmiero as Camilla looked at him with eyes wide open. "Sadism is the assertion of the 'I' annihilating the Ego. I punish you to alleviate your sense of guilt and to affirm my dominion over your Ego. I will let you experience the heightened sensitivity by inflicting sadistic pain and masochistic hurt by receiving it. Both are always present in the deepest recesses of Love's essence. We want to bring to life that sensitivity until it vibrates to sound the symphony of love."

As he spoke those words, Camilla's eyes changed expression. Her dilated pupils were expressing an intensity of passion and desire, which expelled all fear. Palmiero took off the tape from her mouth and she proffered,

"Take my breath away. Give me the pain I always craved, over, and over again. Breathe life back into me… Take me to the mystical exaltation, rapture, ecstasy, and bliss, that only you know how to give me. You are pain and ecstasy to my heart."

Then, Palmiero lit a candle and let the wax drip on her. As Camilla writhed in pain for the hot drippings over her stomach, she confessed,

"Ahhh, this feels so good!"

Then, Palmiero ordered her to lay on her left side. She complied but turned her head slightly to look back at him with apprehension. He, kneeling behind her, took hold of her buttocks. He held them firmly, spreading them broadly apart, exposing to full view that beautiful virgin private alcove behind her secret garden. Camilla shivered in the expectation for the inevitable. She clutched the pillow under her head with her eyes wide-open expressing fearful desire. However, she did not retract. On the contrary, it seemed as if she was offering herself to facilitate the endeavor. Palmiero held his rod firmly in his hand gently placing its tip at the entrance of that channel. Then, he pressed, lightly, at the beginning, but ever more firmly as he encountered natural resistance. With a steady crescendo of pressure, his shaft made headways in that tunnel of love. Then, she grasped tightly to the pillow, opened her mouth biting it and emitted an intense scream of pain and pleasure. With an intense stare on her face, she continued screaming in silence from her open mouth exposing all her beautiful white teeth. It was as if she were saying,

"You are killing me, you own me and I never had a more pleasurable pain in my life."

Palmiero, from his part, was continuing in his inexorable penetration march. Every millimeter of his thrusting made him feel more and more in love and ensnared by her. He felt that, although he was asserting his power over her, she was the one who ultimately held him captive forever. That sweet alcove, enveloping his turgidity in the folds of its caressing membranes, made him a Master dominated by his subjugated slave.

Slowly, Palmiero slipped out. Camilla had a moment of relaxation. Only to be abruptly awakened by the renewed presence of Palmiero's desire demanding to enter again. Without gentleness Palmiero grabbed and strongly pulled her hair hurting her very much. He held her locks as reins dragging her head backwards. Then, he pushed hard against her sweet innocent opening. Abruptly, with only one powerful plunge, he entered again and completely occupied her defenseless hole. Camilla cried, accepted, was fulfilled and loved it. Four times, he repeated his love assaults and conquests until he gave her the fruit of his invasion. They rested cemented in the passion for each other.

Camilla had no way of knowing that succumbing to Palmiero's demands would have led him to his complete enslavement to her. Her innocence, her beauty, her intelligence, her child like wonder and her masterful lovemaking, all made him realize that although he was penetrating her in such a manner, she was the one piercing his heart. The turntable had changed direction.

Camilla realized she had to express her true nature to Palmiero. She had to reveal that she wanted to seduce and control all the men she desired. She wanted to submit them to her will. She wanted to take revenge on all men to retaliate against the one who had killed her mother.

"Although you are my master, I will have many lovers besides you. What I do sexually with another man is not to hurt you," admitted Camilla, "it is only for my fulfillment."

"So you think that I should get used to whomsoever being your new lover?" asked Palmiero.

"Yes, it is for my fulfillment, not yours," lashed out Camilla, "and that should make you worship me all the more. I want a harem of men."

"I worship you always at your feet," confessed Palmiero.

"They all must do my bidding. I want to be cherished by all, wanted by all and *fucked* by all."

"Oh, I love it and hate it,' proclaimed Palmiero, dropping on his knees and kissing her tortured hole inserting his tongue in it. Camilla squirmed and wiggled her buttocks in pleasure.

"You see my dear pet, I don't play," continued Camilla, lovingly placing a hand on his head, "I love and I love hard. This is what I will have in store for you. Yes of course the dominatrix-submissive arrangement, but there is in me something that craves for love and affection. Now that I have a husband and you as a lover who, I know, cares for me, you may think that my need for love is diminished. It is not. On the contrary, it grows. When I met you, I felt that I was here to heal you. I heal a piece of my husband and a piece of you. As I told you before, your desires, secrets, wants and wishes, all will be safe with me if we take this journey. All I need is affection, attention and adoration. It will be up to you to follow me. I cannot *chase* you. We will need to come to a mutual agreement on what works for both of us. I think the journey is scary, but oh so worth it and I hope your feelings are the same."

Transfixed, Palmiero listened in silence.

"You should know that I live with depression," continued Camilla. "It leaves me feeling hollow. We all experience depression, if only for an hour, a day, a week… forever. Some of us carry it like a dead limb. Some of us have good reasons to let depression take over. Like my poor sister raped so young. She was forced to keep it secret, afraid for me, her younger sister's fate. I have been blessed with a good husband. That is why what appears as unfeeling or standoffish in your eyes, at times, see it for what it is, it is survival.

If you leave me for any reason, I will survive. Just know that the hole in my heart will be huge and I will miss, you my dear daddy. I do love you. I do. I just learned early how to lose my mommy, so I am a tough cookie."

PALMIERO'S ENSLAVEMENT

Camilla had enjoyed her training. The pain and humiliation received made her realize that she was his slave. However, a new feeling had been awakening in her. It was not a reaction or a sentiment of revenge for the maltreatment and subjugation received. It was a sense of empowerment, a realization of her real nature. The Goddess had awakened in her. She was transformed. Her eyes emitted a new light. She turned around towards Palmiero and slapped him hard across the face. He was stunned.

"Prostrate before me, you miserable slave," she commanded. "Who do you think you are? What right do you have to be jealous? I will fuck wherever, whenever, with whosoever and with how many persons at the same time I dam please. In addition, while I will take my pleasure with those individuals, you will watch and serve all our need without a word. From now on, you will be my faithful slave, happy of being my servant."

As she sternly gave out this command, she reached for the whip that was on the bed and started whipping Palmiero with all her strength. Palmiero did not attempt resistance or tried to protect himself. He accepted his fate with an expression of rapture in his face.

"Turn around, bend over and offer me your back," she ordered without hesitation.

While standing in silence, Palmiero bent over, placed his elbows on the bed, spread out his legs and put his head between his hands, slightly turning his face towards her. Camilla calculated her distance, balanced her whip with an ample gesture of her arm and lashed him across his buttocks with all her might. Immediately, a read streak appeared on Palmiero's gluteus. She continued incessantly for other forty lashes. Palmiero did not emit a sound. However, the pain he was suffering was very evident from the expression on his face, while Camilla's eyes were radiating an intense joy.

"Amazing, good start my *dasa*, my slave, now, thank me and kiss my feet, you ungrateful servant," Camilla instructed, shortly suspending her punishment.

Palmiero kneeled at her feet and kissed them in a state of total adoration.

"Thank you, my Goddess," he said.

"Get up and go back to the previous position," Camilla ordered again, demanding obedience.

Palmiero followed the instruction and was ready for a new dose of those blessings on his bare skin. By now, his behind was aching intensely.

Merciless, Camilla deposited forty more strokes on that tortured flesh. Again, Palmiero was silent with a strange ecstatic expression on his face. Camilla, from her part was radiant. She kept hitting harder and harder, each time it seemed as if she was becoming taller in stature and more majestic than ever before. Each stroke gave her more beauty than the previous one. She was happy, as she had never been previously.

"Thank me again, you miserable servant," she demanded.

Once more, Palmiero was at her feet in complete adoration. He took all her tows in his mouth and Camilla glowing with sovereign pleasure pushed her foot until it gagged him. He was completely her slave now. To seal this status, Camilla made him go back to that whipping receiving posture. She delivered another twenty blows on that flesh, which now was black and blue with streaks of blood. After one-hundred and one lashes, she stopped only because she was tired. Palmiero got up, but did not sit. He could not, in that condition.

Flogging in Villa dei Misteri, Pompeii

Camilla laid the whip gently by Palmiero's head. She silently walked over to the chaise longue and sat down. Palmiero did not know what to do, to move or to look up. It was a long moment before Camilla huskily said one word,

"Come."

With great difficulty, Palmiero crawled over to her. He kissed her feet again,

"Thank you my Goddess, my love, my spiritual wife," he proffered. "I am your slave." Tears spilled out of his eyes. His joy was uncontainable. Camilla silently caressed his thick hair as he cried out,

"Devi, Devi, Devi, Goddess, Goddess, Goddess, your whipping was a very spiritual epiphany for me," he confessed. "We are now fused into one. I have lived my desire to absorb you and to be absorbed by you."

She wiped his tears away with her long elegant fingers and silently enveloped him with her mouth.

SECOND VOWS

Their two bodies were still tightly entangled, when Camilla broke the silence,

"Palmiero; let us make another solemn vow to each other."

"Anything you command, keeper of my soul and will," he immediately whispered in her ear.

"Let us swear to one another eternal obedience. My command will be your will and my will will be your command," she said.

"Yes, my Devi," he replied without hesitation, adding, "We should put it in writing with our signatures notarized."

"Very good idea," agreed Camilla, getting up and reaching for the hotel notepad.

With their handwriting, Camilla wrote what pertained to Palmiero and he wrote what regarded Camilla.

VOWS
BETWEEN CAMILLA AND PALMIERO.

CAMILLA OWNER AND SUBSEQUENTLY, SLAVE AND BITCH OF PALMIERO:	PALMIERO SLAVE, BITCH AND SUBSEQUENTLY, OWNER OF CAMILLA:
1) Camilla owns Palmiero's body, mind and soul.	1) Palmiero owns Camilla's body, mind and soul.
2) Camilla is the only person who can get the recompense of all Palmiero's orgasms.	2) Palmiero owns Camilla's anus and buttocks. He can do on them all he pleases.
3) Camilla can inflict pain on Palmiero as she sees fit, even if that could endanger his life.	3) Except Camilla's, Palmiero cannot penetrate any other anus.
4) Camilla will control Palmiero's sex with other persons.	4) Palmiero can inflict pain on Camilla as he sees fit, even if that could endanger her life.

5)	Camilla is entitled, as she likes, to whip and hurt Palmiero while he is making love with another person.	5)	Palmiero cannot subtract himself from any pain Camilla wants to inflict on him, not even if that could result with his death.
6)	Camilla always decides with whom Palmiero should have sex.	6)	Palmiero, under all circumstances, must always obey Camilla's commands.
7)	Camilla can have sex whenever, wherever and with whomsoever she decide, no questions asked.	7)	Palmiero cannot have sex without Camilla's approval.
8)	Camilla can have anal sex only with Palmiero.	8)	Previous Camilla's approval, Palmiero can have as many slaves as he desires.
9)	Camilla can have as many slaves as she desires.	9)	Palmiero, alone or with the other slaves, must always service Camilla.
10)	All slaves must give precedence to Camilla's will and command.	10)	All of Palmiero's slaves belong to Camilla and must give precedence to her will and command.

MUTUAL AGREEMENT:

1) Camilla and Palmiero will never intentionally lie to each other.
2) Camilla and Palmiero will work toward building their polyamory friends, lovers, and slaves together.
3) Camilla and Palmiero belong to each other and cannot be slaves to anyone else.
4) Camilla and Palmiero cannot be hurt or punished by anyone else except by each other.
5) All other slaves must service Camilla and Palmiero.
6) All other slaves must give precedence to Camilla over Palmiero.
7) Camilla can sell Palmiero to whom she likes.

Signed

Camilla McKierney   Palmiero Venturini

Notarized by Marilyn Jones

The next day, Camilla was glowing. She wore tight black silk dress with a plunging neckline that revealed her luscious breasts. Her feet were encased in high, open toed sandals and she had her nails freshly painted crimson in anticipation of the celebration. Camilla and Palmiero celebrated their new life style signing that document before Marilyn Jones, Camilla's secretary. She was also a notary public and testimony of that sacred commitment. They all had a Champagne reception in the Private Dining room of Caviar Russe in New York City. Camilla giggled as she sipped her champagne and fed Palmiero caviar snuggling on his lap. He could feel that she had no undergarments on and could not wait to get her alone. Camilla thought it could not get any better, when Palmiero exclaimed,

"Wait, I bought you a present."

"What?" she asked, "how could you have bought it, you barely left my sight?"

"This morning, when you were sleeping, I snuck out and went to Tiffany," he confessed.

He handed her the famous Tiffani's blue box, neatly tied with a light blue ribbon. The sight of the box was more than she could have thought and she eagerly opened it. In it laid a thick wedding band with diamonds all around. On the inside of the ring was one word inscription,

"DEVI."

THE LITTLE SLAVE GIRL

After another bottle of Champagne, Palmiero and Camilla were eager to be alone. They thanked Marilyn for partaking in their celebration. Nevertheless, they noticed that she was reluctant to leave.

"What's wrong sweetie," Camilla asked.

Suddenly Marilyn burst into tears.

"What I have witnessed today just made me long for my own love affair," she sniffed.

"Oh, you poor baby," Camilla cooed, pulling Marilyn's face to her breasts.

After a long moment, Camilla realized that Marilyn seemed to be inking her face deeper into her bosom. Over Marilyn's head, she caught Palmiero's eye and motioned him to get the check.

"My dear girl, you are too upset to go home," declared Camilla. "Come up to our hotel room, I am staying in the city. I told Robert I had too much to do and would be staying out tonight. I am sure Palmiero and I can comfort you."

At the word "comfort," Palmiero leaped to his feet and hurriedly paid the bill.

As they walked across the street, Palmiero held them both by their hands, but he squeezed Camilla's hand conspiringly. Camilla opened the door to her room and welcomed Marilyn in.

"Shall I order more champagne?" Palmiero inquired.

"No my dear, I think we had enough," replied Camilla. "But a nice bottle of Amaretto would be lovely."

Palmiero called room service and Camilla, undressing, said, "Marilyn, I have been in this dress for too long."

As Palmiero had correctly guessed, she wore no undergarments.

Marilyn looked at her stunned. However, she was not completely surprised. She had secretly harbored more than admiration for Camilla. At times, she caught herself fantasizing a love affair with her.

"Don't be shy now, little girl," Camilla commanded and, standing in her regal naked majesty before Marilyn, continued, "Lick me now!"

Marilyn immediately fell to her knees in front of Camilla and whispered,
"Yes my Mistress."

Camilla opened her legs wide and Marilyn scooted underneath her. When Palmiero turned around, after being on the phone, he was surprised and delighted by this sight. There stood Camilla, with her mouth open in an ecstatic expression and her long red locks falling behind her, and Marilyn, the petite brown-haired girl, under her legs hurriedly flicking her tongue in Camilla's secret garden. Camilla smiled when she noticed Palmiero's attention and invited him saying,
"Care to watch, my love, or to join in?"

"Oh my goodness, yes... let me get the door first," said Palmiero, as he heard the knock of the waiter delivering the Amaretto.

He opened the door and quickly threw a one-hundred dollars bill at the bellhop.

"Sir your change..." started saying the hotel boy.

"Keep it!" Palmiero cut short, eager to return to Camilla and Marilyn.

Palmiero poured himself a shot of Amaretto and sat down on the bed to watch the ladies make love. He had never seen Camilla look more radiant. Marilyn was between her legs and he could barely make out her face as her long luscious locks fell over her face. Nevertheless, her secret alcove was all exposed. It was the most adorable he had ever seen, it had the shape of a rosebud.

Camilla had all but forgotten Palmiero. Suddenly she reached out pointing and holding to the wall,
"I'm coming, coming, coming..." she screamed.

Then, patting Marilyn on her head, she continued,
"That was nice my pet."

Marilyn looked up at her with her big brown eyes shining. She was happy to have pleased Camilla.

"But you are not done," Camilla sentenced suddenly grabbing Marilyn by her hair and dragging her to Palmiero.

Marilyn, holding her head, cried out in pain.

"Now do him!" Camilla ordered.

"Mistress please, it is you I want to pleasure, only you," Marilyn tried to challenge Camilla's order.

"Really...? Then you will please me by doing whatever I say," answered Camilla. "Now, get on your knees. And you, Palmiero hurry up and take off your clothes, strip and let this little girl pleasure you."

"How do you want me to lie?" he asked.

"Spread your legs wide," Camilla replied.

Then, turning towards Marilyn, she added, "Now suck him very slowly, up and down his shaft."

Camilla instructed Marilyn and sat near Palmiero's head. They looked into each other's eyes. Palmiero floated in the physical pleasure that Marilyn was giving him and in the spiritual connection that he felt with Camilla. When she saw that Palmiero was drifting into a dream like state, she ordered Marilyn to swallow him more deeply. Quickly she held the girl's head down on Palmiero's shaft and Marilyn began to gag violently.

"You stupid girl," yelled Camilla and pushed her to the floor, away from Palmiero. While she lay gagging on the ground, Camilla lowered her womanhood on Palmiero saying,
"You wanted to come in her mouth right my love?"

"No, no… yes…," Palmiero whispered.

"Remember, you filthy slave, your pleasure reward is only mine," she sentenced slapping him hard across the face. "I will ride you now and you will fill me with your seed."

While Marilyn was still on the floor, Camilla rode Palmiero feeling that she was on a white stallion. Increasing her speed, she threw her hands in the air and moaned loudly. She lost all track of her bearings. Pleasure is all she craved and her orgasm was violent and at one with Palmiero's.

It was a long few minutes before Camilla and Palmiero moved. Then, he whispered,
"Bella, we invited Marilyn up to comfort her, but we mistreated her, maybe we should invite her into our bed."

Camilla sniffed,
"Fine…"

She had had her fun with Marilyn and now she wanted her to leave. Palmiero gestured for Marilyn to come into their bed,
"Come little one."
He lay between his Mistress and the little girl with an arm around each of them and they all fell asleep. Some time passed before Palmiero woke up to the sound of Marilyn's muffled cries.

"Shhh… shhh…, you will wake her up," Palmiero whispered, taking her away from the bed and dragging her on the dresser. He sat her on it, spread her legs and thrust his hard erection forcibly in her. She moaned and tightened her legs imprisoning him.

Palmiero did not realize that Camilla was already awake. But she was a different Camilla, she had Diana's gaze. She turned around to see Palmiero assaulting Marilyn on the dresser. She had he legs wrapped around his waist and he was pumping her furiously. Camilla was furious. Silently she slid out of bed.

"How dare they start without me," she thought.

She found Palmiero's belt and unnoticed, walked towards them.

"Well I guess you found yourself a new whore," she whispered fiercely.

She whacked Palmiero with the heavy buckle of his belt. He spun around with Marilyn still joined to him.

"No, no you are wrong, you needed your rest, that is all my love... please," he tried to excuse himself.

Camilla's fury was great and she drowned out his voice,
"No... no, I don't want to stop you," she said wickedly, "but I am your Goddess and we play by my rules."

Suddenly she yanked Marilyn's hair back and kissed her roughly on her mouth. While Palmiero continued to assault Marilyn, Camilla raised the belt and whipped Marilyn full backside hitting her repeatedly. She moaned and cried. However, Palmiero would not tear away from her and Camilla did not stop whipping her. Marilyn was near hysterical. Palmiero was alarmed by the gleam in Camilla's eyes. She would not release the belt and struck the little girl many times with it from the side of the big buckle. Large welts formed in front of her eyes and blood dripped from the open wounds on her thighs and back.

"Stop!" Camilla commanded, seeing that Palmiero was ready to orgasm. He immediately dropped Marilyn to the floor. Her wounds were so deep that she could not move.

"Now you will finish by drenching her hair and face with your seed. Then, get rid of her," Camilla commanded.

Palmiero did what Camilla had asked. He held Marilyn's jaw with his left hand and finished his orgasm on her hair and on her face. He was saddened to hear the agonizing sounds of shame and hurt that Marilyn was making. He was furious with Camilla for having gone too far. He sighed deeply and helped Marilyn on her feet.

"I will be back," he said to Camilla who had already turned her back on the two.

He carried Marilyn into the bathroom and gently laid her on the tiled floor.

"How can I fix this," he thought.

She had her back and buttocks streaked with blood. He found a towel, drenched it with warm water and gently began to swab her wounds. Marilyn had blacked out, but at his touch she startled and screamed.

"Shh..., shh," he whispered, "It's over; let me take care of you."

He smoothed her hair away from her eyes and gently sang a song in Italian. After a half hour he had done all he could to repair the damage. He remembered he had painkillers in his briefcase leftover from knee surgery he had months ago and gave Marilyn two to take and the rest of the bottle to finish.

"*Tranquilla*, be tranquil, *mia cara*, my dear, these will help," he told her as she refused at first to take them.

He helped her get up and put his raincoat on her. He was happy that it was not quite morning yet and he slipped out of the hotel unnoticed. He hailed a cab and helped Marilyn in as gently as he could. He sat next to her while she still moaned aloud.

"Hey, buddy," said the cab driver, "I don't know what you did to her, but I don't want any trouble."

"Keep quiet," Palmiero hissed, "and drive downtown, there is a huge tip for you."

Palmiero found Marilyn's address and told the cabdriver.

"Fine, fine," the cabbie said and took off down the deserted Manhattan streets.

At destination, Palmiero asked the cab driver to wait for him and he escorted Marilyn in her apartment and held her face in his hands comforting her.

"It will be ok Marilyn, you did well tonight. As for Camilla..., well she was not herself. She did not mean to hurt you this badly I assure you. We both love you."

Marilyn smiled sadly and said,
"Go, Palmiero, you have met your match with her. I understand why between you and me no serious relation could have ever worked and now with the bond between you and the Mistress there is no turning back."

"Will you be ok?" Palmiero enquired concerned.

"Yes, thank you for taking care of me," she answered and gently shut the door in his face. Palmiero hurried down the steps of her apt, got in the cab and went back to the hotel. He opened the door and Camilla was waiting with café for him.
"Baby how is she?" she asked worriedly.

"She will be ok. I think you should call her in a couple hours and give her the next few days off. Her wounds will take some time to heel," Palmiero assured her.

"Oh my goodness, what came over me," Camilla exclaimed horrified.

"*Bella*, it was Diana, it was Diana's fault, not yours. I should have stopped you, but she possessed me too," Palmiero comforted holding her.

"She is our only friend, who truly understands us. I hope she can forgive me," Camilla cried with sincere tears of repentance.

Early the next day Camilla called Marilyn on the phone,
"My dear, I am not calling you to apologize. You and I know that we have embarked in a new lifestyle; therefore, you are my consenting slave. A Mistress never apologizes for fulfilling her wishes. However, I recognize that you have served my needs well

and that you are distressed and I want to reward you with a week fully paid vacation from work."

"Thank you my Mistress," replied submissively Marilyn from the other end of the wire, "I deserved your punishments and I am very pleased by all you did to me. However, I am unworthy of your reward. If I may say so, I am in love with you."

***

That same morning Marilyn drove upstate New York to spend her week vacation at a friend's empty cabin by a lake. Speeding through tortuous mountainous roads, she was very distracted rethinking the events of the day before, especially what happened in that hotel room. She was fully conscious of her love for Palmiero and her total enslavement to Camilla. And she realized that there was no turning back. All these thoughts made her very happy. She was anticipating the great pleasures she will be enjoying with them again.

At that hour of the day, the sun was shining into her eyes, blinding her. When she went around a bend in the road, there, in the middle of her way, stood a woman. There was no room to jam on the brakes. If she had, she would have hit her. Instinctively, she swung left. She hit the guardrail breaking it and she plunged to her death in the ravine below.

A TROUBLED SLEEP

The next day, Palmiero, in a state of distress and with a news paper under his arm, entered Camilla's office.

Without giving Palmiero time to speak, Camilla said,
"I must tell you the dream I had last night. In the dream you were the highest Master ever. You were extremely wealthy and had a chauffeur who drove you around in a silver Mercedes with tinted glasses. You had a cane with a clear orb at the top. You hardly saw me. You directed my every move through, text, email and the chauffeur. I trembled when I received a command from you. Soon I was consumed by various tasks. It all became too much for me and I came to your estate. After I banged on your door, the chauffeur let me in. Your wife was there. She just sighed when she saw me and left for her own wing.
Entering your suite, I was disturbed. I passed by a television set that showed all the places I usually frequented. You had been spying on me. The chauffeur/butler knocked on your door. I entered. You were reading the paper and, without lifting your eyes, you said,
'Ah, so you worked up your nerve to come see the wizard.' You were slightly cruel and laughed at your own joke.

The Master in his dungeon

Trembling, I said, 'Please... master, may I sit on your bed.'

Before you could answer, around the corner, from another room, entered Oriana in a long flowing robe. She wore a black lace corset and had high heels. I was very angry as she easily approached you on the bed and performed fellatio on you. You never took your eyes away from me as you came in her mouth.

'Who is she?' I asked.

As Oriana wiped your semen off her lips, she gave me a witchy smile. Then, condescending, she said,
'Darling I have lived here with him for twenty years and I sleep with him nightly and his wife knows I am here.'

I ran from the house horrified at the knowledge that I was only your toy.

Shortly after, I read in the newspaper of your death. I was crushed. One night, however, I got an instant message from you, it said,
'Mexico... the Mayan ruins... meet me there.'

That is when I woke up... Then, Diana came. My hand was lying somewhat off the bed. As she took hold of it, she tickled my face with her long hair.
What do you make of this entire dream?"

"I do not know," reflected Palmiero distracted, "the future will tell us."

Then, in silence he placed the newspaper on her desk. The headlines read,

"CAUGHT BY SLEEP SPELL, WOMAN CRASHES IN RAVINE"

The article reported a name, Marilyn Jones.

A very big teardrop, rolling off Camilla's eyes, hit that headline.

CHAPTER 8
See Naples and Then Die

Postcard view of the Gulf of Naples

THE LAND WHERE WORDS ARE BITTERSWEET

As the plane started landing at the Neapolitan airport of Capodichino, Camilla grasped Palmiero's hand tightly. She hated to fly.

"Relax, wait you see the beauty of the city," Palmiero comforted her. "We are so lucky to have this year's conference in Italy. The long plane ride will be worth it, I promise."

Palmiero was feeling the joy of a honeymoon rather than the burden of a business trip. While the plane performed a wide turn to lineup with the runway, he was excited to show from the air to Camilla the city below, which was his childhood playground. From the window, he pointed out the volcanic inclines of the Vesuvius on their right with Pompeii and the numerous other towns sprawling around its slopes.

"My goodness, you are like a kid going to Disneyland," said Camilla, with a smile.

After landing, the limousine took them from the airport to the Grande Albergo Vesuvio. The Hotel, one of the oldest in Naples, was on Via Partenope, overlooking the Gulf. Upon arriving, they went to their separate rooms.

"Call home to Robert and assure him that you had a safe landing," Palmiero suggested. "Rest my love, you need to rest. The jetlag will catch up with you. Later, we will go shopping and eat dinner at the marina, on the other side of the promenade in front of the Hotel. There are great restaurants there."

Camilla was happy to have some time alone to prepare herself for the romantic date that was to come. She called home and spoke with each of her children and with Robert. He told her how they missed her already, but really, they were more excited about the gifts she was going to bring back for them. She hung up content with the knowledge that all was fine at home. Little she knew that it would have been the last time she would have heard their voice.

She inspected her hotel room. She opened the balcony window overlooking the beautiful see and the inviting elegant restaurants along the marina. From them came the sound of singing and music.

Camilla was happy to have some time alone with Palmiero. The stress of the American banking business and of trying to keep their love affair secret from their co-workers all vanished. She wanted Palmiero to see her with "*new*" eyes. Not as he saw her every day, as the businessperson, with her hair pulled back in a tight chignon, but as the sensual woman, he had awakened in her. She went to the bathroom happy to see that the architectural and old world beauty of the hotel extended also in there, with its ancient, claw-foot tub, big enough for two.

"Hmm, maybe Palmiero will join me in here later," she thought.

She ran the bath and noticed the scented oils nearby on a shelf. Her favorite scent "lavender" waited. She poured half the bottle into the warm bath and entered into the water,
"Ah..., this is heavenly..." she sighed.

She lay there for a moment listening to the soft songs of the musicians. From the restaurants on the marina outside, the music was flowing up through the open window. Her mind drifted to Palmiero. She had never met a man more intelligent. He had opened her eyes to a world she had never known. Meditation, travel, oriental studies, mythology, all possibilities that she had never given thought before. She battled all her life. First she fought for her education. She had earned her MBA from a local New Jersey University. Then she conquered the chance to have a family so different from the one she had come from. She felt blessed for both her education and her family. All this was true, but it was not until she met Palmiero that she opened those other possibilities for herself. Now this man, this mortal being, had given her the gift of wonder.

She came out of the tub and dried off. Her jet lag had disappeared and she rested on the bed falling into a deep dreamless sleep.

She woke up to the phone,

"*Bella*, are you ready for our date?" Palmiero was calling her.

"Oh, my goodness, I overslept. Give me 5 minutes," replied Camilla getting up from her bed.

Palmiero gasped seeing Camilla coming down the staircase. She appeared as a goddess with her long red curly apple-scented hair flowing down on her back. She was glowing with excitement. She wore a white peasant top and he could see the faint outline of her breast through the material. She had a full skirt, which reminded Palmiero of a lovely Mexican girl he once met among the Mayan ruins. Smooth as precious silk, her long white legs were an invitation to wonder in the clear transparent crystal waters of Polynesian coral reef atolls. However, it was her feet, which captivated Palmiero the most. She wore flat sandals with strings tied around her legs, like ancient Roman courtesans.

"You are gorgeous," he said, with his brown eyes wide opened.

Camilla was very pleased, but she blushed replying,

"Oh, stop, you see me every day." Then, regaining self-control, she continued, "Come on big-shot" show me where you used to take all your girlfriends."

Down, on the marina of Santa Lucia, across and below the street from the hotel, is *ZI'TERESA*, the most famous restaurant in the city. There, Palmiero took Camilla that evening.

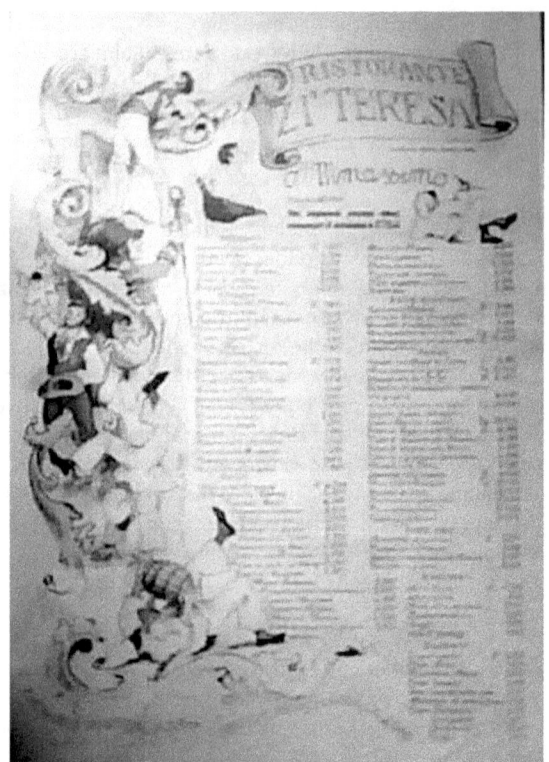

Zi'Teresa's menu

"Margherita, fravaglie, purpetiell'affunnate, zeppole e aglianeca ianco e'Falern," yelled out the attendant to the cook, after receiving the order.

"What are we having?" asked worried Camilla.

"Real Neapolitan pizza with water-buffalo mozzarella, tomatoes sauce and basil, fried minnows, baby octopuses cooked in tomato pottage, sweet-cream dough-ball pastries and white Falerno wine, they are all typical local products. Nowhere else in the world you can savor such delicacies, not even the pizza."

"Common, I had the best pizza in New York at 20th and Broadway. The pizza-maker was from here," remarked Camilla. "But I will not have octopus. I do not like it."

"I understand. However, you can taste this worldwide renowned dish only here in Naples. It was described by the Roman poet Virgil two millennia ago. He related that, in this area, the ghost of Anchises foretold his son Aeneas, the exiled Trojan hero, that he would have ended his wandering only when he would have eaten pizza, this local dish. And you will love octopus," replied Palmiero with a smile, while strolling-musician approached the table.

The musicians, a singer, a violinist and a mandolin player, knew which table to go up to and which song to perform for each couple.

"*Si 'na voce te sceta 'nd 'a nuttata mentre te staie co u sposo a te vicino,*" started the singer.

"This is '*Voce e' notte*, Voice in the night,' a very sad song," explained Palmiero. "The lyrics, loosely translated say, 'You will recognize my serenading voice waking you up in the middle of the night, while you are cuddling next to your husband. It is the same voice you knew, which is now tormented by the love for you and dying of jealousy."

The sweetness of the melody and the sadness of the words made big tender tears roll along Camilla's cheeks into her pizza. Nevertheless, Camilla tried all those new foods and loved them all, including the octopus.

After dinner, the two lovers walked the few steps up to Via Partenope, the street above that marina. They strolled along the boulevard hand in hand. An incredible moon in the sky shed a silvery long streak over the entire Bay length from the island of Capri to that panoramic promenade, like an avenue to wonder yonder. The gulf was dotted with *lampare*, gas lamps placed on numerous small angler row-boats to attract fish into their nets. These lights in the sea competed with the shining stars in the warm serene infinite firmament of that enchanted night. In silence, they continued strolling all the way to the Botanical Gardens and back to the hotel. It was not necessary for them to talk. Their minds were connected by the unison of their love. That silence continued also when Camilla turned the key of her room, both entered and Palmiero started disrobing her beautiful body.

Gently she moved away from him to change into something more comfortable. A few minutes after, she returned walking in a cloud of his favorite perfume and wearing a beautiful negligee, she had bought for that occasion. The robe was made of lace and lilac silk, her favorite color and materials. The see through lace cupped perfectly her breasts letting her nipples show. The silk gown was floor length with a long slit.

"You are more beautiful than ever," whispered Palmiero, as he kissed her softly, tenderly and deeply, tongue to tongue, exploring her mouth.

He sunk his head in her aromatic breast, caressed her, feeling every curve of her body under those veils. They made love that night with tenderness never experienced before. Both lay on their side facing each other. Their legs were tangled. Slowly, Palmiero inserted in her Fountain of Love his Jade Wand. They remained motionless. He retained his semen and prevented any emission for a very long time. Each one was absorbed in the presence of the other. It was meditation. Both were absorbing the vital essence of each other awareness. From their mouth they avidly drank their dribble. Each sucked the nectar from the other. Then, slowly Palmiero turned upside down. He placed his lips on her Spring of Ecstasy. Camilla, from her Mysterious Valley, poured directly into his mouth three fluids, her climax, her blood and her amber liquor. With gusto, he swallowed all her precious juices. At the same time his hard-pressing erection gagged her open mouth. Her throat was eagerly waiting to gulp down his hot and sweet reward together with his gushing liquor. Happy, drained, wet and bloodied, they finally fell asleep in each other embrace.

***

Early the next day, a splendid sunny morning, Camilla and Palmiero, went walking along the waterfront of Santa Lucia marina, towards the *Fontana dell'Immacolatella*, which offered a unique panorama of Naples. The fountain, a Sixteen-hundred architectonic sculptured structure with statues and three majestic arches, frames the stunning view of the Gulf. Its arches frame the distinctive M shaped appearance of the Vesuvius' volcanic cone flanked by Mount Somma.

Fontana dell'Immacolatella

"*Signurì,* Miss, *vire Nàpule e po' Muore,* see Naples and then die," called out a local vendor next to his pushcart bursting with souvenir near that fountain. The peddler, pointing with an ample gesture at the whole street of Via Partenope and its spectacular view of the Neapolitan coastline, urged Camilla to buy his cameos.

Intrigued, Camilla picked one up,

"The image on this cameo has the features of my mother," she said showing it to Palmiero.

The cameo

"Yes, this is Diana," he agreed.

"These cameos are mother-of-pearl bas-relief portraits," said the vendor. "They are made by local artisans. *Signurì,* Miss, the one you are holding represent our beloved Siren Parthenope. It is the same portray represented on the original ancient coins of this enchanted city.

Stù mare e stù cielo, this marine and this sky are *bellissimi,* the most beautiful of the entire world. Therefore, upon viewing this sun, *ca'stà n'front'a te,* that is on your face, and this sea, *ca 'spira tanto sentimento,'* which inspires great emotion, one, having fulfilled all desires, *pò murì*, can die peacefully," continued the vendor with pride. *"Vire Nàpule e po' muore, ch'est'è à storia*, the story goes that for this reason our Siren came to die on this very charming shore and, after seeing Naples' splendors, she was content to depart this life peacefully."

"More than a hawker, this vendor is a poet," said Camilla to Palmiero. "And I like this cameo, I'm convinced."

"Naples is the land of peddler-poets," agreed Palmiero buying the cameo with a smile.

"This is the daily reality of this city, which makes its inhabitants lyricists out of necessity," explained Palmiero. "Popularly, the Neapolitan spirit has a big sentimental heart proportionate only to his ever present unsatisfied hunger. Pulcinella, one of the many traditional Italian masks, the Neapolitan *Pullecenella* represents and embodies this stereotype. He is like an empty spaghetti-dish, always searching for food. Poetically, he seeks for *Zeza*'s love. She is the Neapolitan fascinating *flirtatious* Lucretia. Her duty is to break hearts with a simple glance of her beautiful deep dark eyes."

Mask of Pulcinella

COME TO SORRENTO

Camilla and Palmiero rented a car to drive from Naples to Sorrento. In that very late afternoon, they were chasing the sunset. As usual, there was heavy traffic on the *costiera sorrentina*, as the locals call the Sorrento drive. The slow speed gave Palmiero the opportunity to talk about the stunning localities they were passing as they drove along the coast. The drive took them through Castellammare, with its *Terme*, the spa of natural healing spring waters. Next, they passed over the bridge of the deep fiord of

The deep fiord of Furore

Furore. Always having the view of the whole Gulf of Naples on their right side and the sun setting before them, they passed through the little town of Meta di Sorrento. Palmiero took pride in explaining each of those beautiful sites to Camilla. Finally, as they approached Sorrento, they were greeted by the sweet perfume of the lemon trees blooming in that May warm and still evening.

The Excelsior Vittoria, their hotel for the evening, is on the right upon entering the main square of Sorrento. Once, the great tenor Caruso was a guest in that hotel, where he held his permanent Italian residence.

Sleepy and weary, Palmiero and Camilla headed directly towards their room. On the way, they passed a small courtyard filled with flowers and a fountain. They were surprised to find a lemon tree growing in its midst.

Camilla reached out to touch the waxy branch and thought,
"This is a magical place."

Once in their room, however, they did not go to bed immediately. They could not. Their room opened on to a terrace and the view of the entire Bay of Naples astounded them.

Postcard, panorama from Sorrento

Ernesto De Curtis, an Italian composer, from the far shores of New York City, remembering that view wrote *Torna' Surriento*, *Come back to Sorrento*, a song known throughout the world. Remembering the gorgeous panorama offered by that city, the author of the song continues saying, "*vir'ò mare quant'è bello*, look how beautiful is the sea." Likewise, that placid sea, with the island of Capri on the left, the Vesuvius across and the the high cliffs of the coastline on the right, enchanted Camilla and Palmiero.

Inspired by that sight and holding on tight close to her man, Camilla said,

"I believe we are connected completely on different levels, from the depths of depravation to the Heights of Heaven. In every level, we are true and sincere to ourselves and to each other. I will never stop loving you unless I stop loving myself. Let us never lie or hide things to each other. This is our richness. We do not know what the future holds for us. However, we will always have truthfulness of one to the other. The sharing of our feelings is sublime, I want to know you as I know myself and you will know me as yourself."

Through the night, the sweet music of a mandolin reached the terrace. Someone, serenading in the distance, was singing the nostalgic Neapolitan song *"Silenzio cantatore," Singing silence*.

"Hush," said Palmiero, translating the song word by word for Camilla, "hush, don't say anything tonight. Fall into my arms, but without speaking... All things are sleeping a shining dream... a summer night's dream. My love, in this silence, in this *singing silence*, I am not whispering love words to you, this sea is whispering them for me. Just tell me, are you completely mine tonight? Your beautiful eyes tell me yes and I am sure, because of this moon your mouth can't be untruthful."

Camilla said noting, but snuggled up to Palmiero softly moaning with a sigh.

***

Sorrento's harbor is at the foot of the cliff on which stands the Hotel Excelsior. Next morning, another beautiful sunny day, Camilla and Palmiero took the elevator to reach that port. Vendors, along the pier, were selling all kinds of items. However, a pushcart with a tower of hanging meats, really attracted Camilla's curiosity.

The vendor kept calling out,

"O' ped'e o' musso."

"O' ped'e o' musso"

"What is that," asked Camilla, pointing to the gruesome looking meats hanging from the glass tower of the cart.

"Boiled feet, mouth and ear of the pig," translated Palmiero. "You should taste it," he continued, buying some from the peddler.

The vendor quickly took a number of different meat parts and started chopping them in big chunks with a huge knife. He scooped all those pieces onto an oilpaper. Using a bull's horn as a shaker, he sprinkled generosity with grains of sea salt and squeezed two big Sorrento lemons on that meat. Then, he made a large cone and wrapped all in brown paper, which he handed to Palmiero.

"Have a piece," he offered Camilla while biting with evident gusto on a juicy chunk.

"Never!" Camilla horrified, quickly replied in disgust.

"Have a piece I command you," he imposed.

Camilla picked up the smallest piece and started chewing. When the flavors of that delicacy hit her palate, her face transformed, from disgust and hesitation, in pleasure and delight. Visibly satisfied she reached for a second and third piece until the whole bag was empty. She also reached out for one of those delicious lemons of Sorrento. Those are the only ones in the world that are so sweet that they can be eaten skin and whole.

At 10 am, they boarded the fast ferry, once called steamboat, *vaporetto*, to the island of Capri. After twenty-five minutes, they had crossed the stretch of water separating Sorrento from the islet.

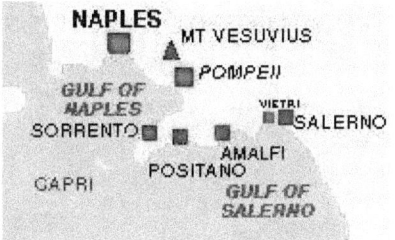

CHAPTER 9
Neapolitan Mysteries

CAPRI

The Island of Capri

At *Marina Grande*, the Big Marina, Capri's port, a small motor boat took Camilla and Palmiero to the *Grotta Azzurra*, the famous Blue Grotto used by the Roman Emperors as a refreshing swimming pool after their Bacchanalias orgies. To this day, local anglers swear that ancient ghosts, demons and monsters inhabit the premises and the tunnel leading to the imperial chambers. Upon hearing, this Camilla insisted she wanted to swim in the magical waters of that cave. The entrance of the Grotto is so narrow that requires tourists to switch from the motor boat to a small rowboat reeled in with ropes because rows are impractical.

Grotta Azzurra, Capri.[22]

Once in the Grotto, Camilla undressed and jumped off the boat. On contact with the water, a very luminous fluorescence surrounded her body. It was as if Camilla emitted her own glow. It was a celestial sky blue metallic radiance with white overtones. She glowed in her glory. She called out to him,

"Palmiero…, miero…, ero…," her voice resounded multiplied by the echo of the cave bouncing off the water and traveling up through mysterious tunnels.

Suddenly, the fluorescence from Camilla's body swelled. It divided itself like an ameba, reproducing only its contours. That pure radiance had the familiar shape of Diana. Like a dolphin or better as a siren in her natural element, that glow swam, leaped and disappeared in the underwater cavities of the *Grotta Azzurra*, reaching the company of the other ghosts, demons and monsters lurking in the abyss. Passengers, from other rowboats in the Grotto, pointed out that free overflowing gushing light with a prolonged "Uhhhhh…"

Camilla climbed back up on the boat. Shivering and wet, she covered herself with the towel the boatman handed her. He had always one available for his passengers who could not resist the temptation of a swim in that enchanted water. However, through the entire trip back to Marina Grande, no one made comments on the strange phenomena they had just witnessed.

From *Marina Grande*, a *funicolare*, cable car, pulled Palmiero and Camilla to the *Piazzetta*, the famous little square in the heart of the town of Capri. There, everybody who is somebody in the world has set foot. Two steps among narrow carless streets took them from the *Piazzetta* to the Quisisana, the most exclusive Hotel in the island. The name itself means "Here-One-Is-Cured," probably from every worldly worry.

Camilla, bare feet on the cobblestone, was radiant. She walked among the crowd and the numerous small very refined boutiques offering the most expensive products of Italian fashion. She was flowing with the breeze in her hair. The slight tan, obtained during the sea crossing and the excursion to the Blue Grotto, contrasting with her red locks, made her the attraction of the resort. Those who were usually fascinated by women stared at her, drooling with desire. Instead, the persons who were habitually interested in men looked at her with envy. Particularly, when they entered that hotel, a young bellhop, a very handsome and muscular very tan waiter about twenty one years old, could not take his eyes away from her. At the reception, Palmiero got the key of their room and gave it to Camilla. She went upstairs to freshen up while he went to the bar for an aperitif.

Faraglioni

The young bellhop escorted Camilla to her room. He opened the windows of the balcony overlooking a breathtaking panorama. It stretched through the Tyrrhenian Sea with the rocks of the Faraglioni on the left. Unseen, far, beyond the horizon were the African coasts, the island of Sardinia and the Spanish shores. Camilla generously tipped the bellhop. However he lingered intensely looking at her. Camilla was visibly flattered and welcoming, since she also really liked him. To tease him, she started undressing while going towards the bathroom.

"Close the door behind you, when you leave, Please," she said. Without waiting for an answer she took off her bra showing him her naked breast. Then, she went straight to the bathtub to wash off the seawater salt from her skin. The bellhop had no alternative, but to leave.

Excited by the event, Camilla slowly started washing. She lingered with the sponge on those parts of her body, which Palmiero found so irresistible. First, her toes, she recalled how he liked to kiss her feet. How he suck her toes and how ticklish she felt when he did it. Then slowly she made her way up her legs, finding her round thighs beautiful and intoxicating. Now she knew why Palmiero loved her body so much. She washed her breasts circling around her nipples. Then, with an intensity that surprised her, she thrust the sponge into her sacred garden. Letting go of all preconceived notions, she moved the sponge in and out. Softly, like a musical instrument ready to emit love sounds under Palmiero's expert touch, she attuned her body to perfection.

After that refreshing bath, she returned downstairs. In the lobby, she met Palmiero and the concupiscent eyes of the other hotel guests. Palmiero was at the reception desk ordering to deliver champagne and caviar to their room immediately upon their return later that evening. Seeing her again, the young bellhop at the reception desk remarked boasting with a coworker,

"Comm'è bbona st'americana, 'sta' sera me'laggia'fà," (How very desirable is this American girl, tonight I must make her mine).

Palmiero heard him but made believe he did not understand.

"Watch out for the heartbreaker *Capresi*, they will be out to get you," he warned Camilla with a strange smile on his face.

Camilla threw back her neck and laughing she said,
"Oh, are you jealous my love? Do not worry I will not get rid of you! Who will teach my new servants how to please me?"

They left the hotel and walked back to the *Piazzetta*. The bus stop is not too far from there. In the entire island, there is only one road wide enough to allow small cars. However, it is still so narrow that special mini-busses are built to fit the size of that street. That single road connects two Marinas, *Grande* and *Piccola*, and two municipalities, Capri and Anacapri above it. From the town of Capri, the road splits leading above or below to *Marina Piccola*, the Small

Marina with its *Canzone del mare*, the "Song of the Sea" and all the other elegant renowned beaches.

In Anacapri, Palmiero and Camilla visited the museum of Villa San Michele. The Villa had been the Palace of the Roman Emperor Augustus. One hundred years ago, the Swedish physician Axel Munthe in love with the island, restored those ruins. In that location, the doctor had the vision of the Archangel Saint Michael and decided to make it his residence.

Continuing on their sightseeing tour, Camilla and Palmiero took the chairlift to *Monte Solaro*, the Solar Mountain from which the whole island stood at their feet.

Anacapri, Capri.[23]

The couple returned to the *Piazzetta* where they had dinner. They had a candle light supper among a crowd of tourists. Families with kids, honeymooners, gay, lesbian, and polyamorous lovers, all, in harmonious coexistence, frequented that little square. Everyone was enjoying that May evening.

At the restaurant, Palmiero stretched over the table to kiss Camilla. From the table nearby, another American tourist remarked with a smile,
"Ah, Capri is for lovers!"

"On the island of Capri, the Roman Emperor Tiberius fulfilled all his legitimate and dissolute desires," explained Palmiero to Camilla. "There is evidence that since prehistoric time free love expressions have been floating in the atmosphere of this delightful island as the bougainvillea perfume its air."

"Let's go back to the hotel," said Camilla, visibly aroused.

Entering the hotel, a young gay man saw Palmiero grab Camilla by her neck and kiss her passionately. He too made an appreciative remark over Camilla's luck of having such a handsome man next to her. Both Camilla and Palmiero smiled.

When the room door closed behind them, Palmiero gently disrobed the voluptuous shapes of Camilla's body, feeling every curve of her complete nakedness. She unzipped his pants and Palmiero's baton jumped to attention, ready to direct a concerted romantic duet. Camilla's hand wrapped around his wand and personally took direct control of the orchestration of the entire symphony. At the touch of her long fingers clasped around his rod, Palmiero, more than ever, felt he was slave-bonded to her. He slipped out of the rest of his clothes as a shivering boa constrictor shedding its skin.

In that moment, a knock at the door interrupted that love entanglement.

"Yes?" called out Palmiero.

"Your champagne and caviar," a man's voice answered from the corridor.

Camilla, was annoyed for the interruption, but without hesitation, as she was, without a robe, answered the door. The young handsome bellhop was on the doorsill. He was dark, tall and muscular. Upon seeing her naked again, the bellhop lost his train of thoughts. He could not remove his eyes from Camilla's breasts. Losing all his arrogance the waiter appeared quite uncomfortable.

"Come in!" ordered Camilla closing the door behind her.

Noticing his embarrassment, Palmiero chuckling said, "Come in. Place the items on the table, please"

Camilla let him in and closed the door. She remembered how she previously discussed with Palmiero about the sadomasochist pleasure of participating in a threesome with a man. This seemed a perfect occasion. Especially since, they were in that island famous for its romantic and sexual adventures.

Palmiero asked the bellhop,
"Would you like to have a glass of champagne with us?"
Then, he turned towards Camilla and asked her,
"How do you like our young guest?"

Without waiting for her reply, he encouraged the waiter,
"If this is your last shift for the evening, you can enjoy some refreshment with us."

The attendant, who by now was less nervous, showed a considerable bulginess in his trousers, leaving the items on a table, replied,
"I was about to go home after this delivery. Thank you. I accept it."

"Please, be comfortable. Sit on the bed," said Camilla pouring a glass of sparkling wine and handing it to him. Then he sat on the bed. She offered him the cup. Ruffling his hair, she stood naked before him and asked,
"What is your name?" and, touching his arm, added smiling, "judging by your muscles it should be Hercules."

"I am Dante Scudieri. How should I address you and your husband?" he replied, visibly excited.

"You can call me Mistress and he is not my husband, he is my slave, like you are now," she ordered with a command that made Dante lower his gaze. He was mesmerized by her clean-shaven perfumed Love-alcove standing before his eye level.

Dante, who had entered the room expecting only to seduce Camilla, found himself willingly enslaved to her at the presence of another man. Therefore, Dante realized that he could not boast about his conquest with his friends without losing his pride and macho-narcissistic notoriety.

The romantic melody that started as a duet was becoming a threesome. Palmiero, standing motionless, looked at Dante paying homage kneeled before her and worshiping Camilla with his head buried between her legs. Then, he noticed that from the waiter's mouth an amber colored liquid was dripping running along his chin.

"Drink it all, my slave, this is the champagne I promised you," ordered excitedly Camilla, relieving herself in his mouth. "My slave Palmiero told me about your boasting with your friend. This is what you get in return from me."

Faithful to his servile nature, Dante was swallowing it as quickly as he could, trying his best to contain unsuccessfully the fast gushing overflow. Once the clear spring of the water sport stopped flowing, Camilla threw the waiter on the bed, where Palmiero was sitting. Both men, with their rods pointing to the ceiling, offered Camilla an irresistible spectacle.

She got down on them and started sucking one and then. Alternatively, she took both shafts in her avid opened mouth. She went back and forth, from the rod of Palmiero to Dante's one. She used her hand on one erection, while her tongue was engage with the other one and vice-versa. The hands of both men met, while at the same time they were reaching for her hair on the back of her neck. They pulled on them and pressed her head down on each other member. Each one was enjoying what their Dominatrix was doing on the other. It all started slowly, then, Camilla went faster as if she could not make up her mind whose manhood she wanted in her mouth. Therefore, she went furiously from one to the other. Almost as soon as one of those turgid sticks touched the depth of her throat, she moved to the next one.

At one point, Camilla said with a throaty voice quivering with desire,
"Dante let us give Palmiero a gift he will love. Take me hard in my behind. He believes it belongs to him alone, let us show him who can dispose of it."

While saying this, she glanced over to Palmiero. Then, she bent over on her knees and rested her head on the pillow. With both hands behind her, she stretched her buttocks to facilitate Dante's penetration. Palmiero stared at her, quietly and jealously accepting that enterprise. Promptly, Dante plugged his dart against her lovable orifice and pushed with no mercy. Camilla was shoved forward. In spite of the hurt, she kept her balance and, pushing back towards him, enabled him to penetrate her completely all the way in the deepest recesses of her bowels. Camilla's eyes and mouth shaped three perfect "O" of pain and pleasure. Palmiero was ecstatic while Dante mercilessly pumped her.

"Stop Dante, stop, you are hurting me too much," she begged him.

That supplication was intended not so much to make him desist, as to entice his action and arouse him further. For a second, Dante froze, as if gathering strength. Then, he intensified his furious attacks with renewed vigor on that poor defenseless anus. She increased her cries. Finally, as Dante emptied in her entrails his semen sack with a last powerful thrust, she emitted a final wild loud scream of pain like that of a mortally wounded animal.

When all was done, she turned to Palmiero and said. "Did you like it, my love?"

"Yes," he replied and first kissed her ever so tenderly on her lips and then on that tortured little whole, thrusting his tongue into it.

Meanwhile, Dante, having rested for a few seconds, regained his strength and vigor. Immediately, Camilla got back on her hands and knees. In this position, she took Palmiero in her mouth and this time offered her sweet garden to the bellhop. When Dante quickly penetrated her, Palmiero felt the muffled sound of satisfaction she uttered over his erection well positioned in her mouth. Palmiero could see the full expression of joy and delight on Camilla's face, as she was controlling and dominating simultaneously the erection of the two men.

The three of them, caught up in that indescribable pleasure, exploded in a symphony of ecstatic lasciviousness.

Palmiero, with his hands and thighs, held her head, face and mouth well secure on his member. Camilla, sucking him, grabbed both his gluteus, with her middle fingers stuck deep in his anus, to keep his manhood well lodged in her throat. Dante, pumping furiously in her throbbing womanhood from behind, held her tightly embracing her thighs and stomach with his hands clenched together over her navel. In that position, they frantically rolled on the bed, without ever letting their unity slip from one another.

When, after an hour of intense activity, the three of them finally came in unison, with an explosion of loud and harmonious sounds of pleasure, it seemed as if the Vesuvius had awakened. A very copious eruption of hot semen simultaneously inundated into Camilla's body, sweetly savoring her taste buds and warmly irrigating her vagina. Subsequently, exhausted and satisfied, the three of them, still in that lovable embrace, fell in a blissful sleep.

The next morning found them still in that viscous embrace. Palmiero was the first to wake up. He looked at Camilla sleeping. She was radiant and more beautiful than ever. As flashbacks, he revisited the previous night's events. Camilla's responses to Dante's rhythmical pumping vividly appeared before his mind. He could still hear her so familiar sounds of joyful pleasurable satisfaction and ultimate orgasmic cry. That recollection did not generate any jealousy. On the contrary, he felt gratitude towards Dante who now he looked upon as a collaborator for Camilla's glory and pleasure. What happened the night before filled his heart with joy for Camilla and for himself. He was not jealous. On the contrary, he was so deeply in love with her that it seemed beyond description.

Before those events, it was as if the tenderness of their love was separate from the kinky moments. Both were intense, but difficult to coexist. Now, however, they perfectly coexisted in a way he had never experienced before. He felt a need to protect her, while she went about reaching out for her rightful pleasures of the soul and of the senses. He looked upon Dante as a friend, a partner and a brother with whom to share his most precious possession. He promised himself that he would be cementing this bond with him by being more intimate as Camilla would have wanted them to be. His feelings towards her surprised him. An overwhelming sweet loving tenderness occupied his entire heart. He realized that now he was in love with her as he had never been before. He had an irresistible urge to kiss her warm sleeping lips. He was not bothered that a few hours before that same mouth had circled and swallowed Dante's shaft and semen. Gently and softly, he kissed her. A deep shiver full of suave worship came upon him, which, who never tasted it, cannot understand.

Camilla opened her eyes and smiled declaring her unconditional eternal love to Palmiero. At the same time, he was pleased that she stretched out her hand to touch, with a gesture of loving, tender and grateful care, Dante's tired manhood.

At that touch, Dante awoke. To regain some dignity in the eyes of his other two love partners, he proposed to take them back to Naples and guide them to visit some captivating and unusual places in that city. They all agreed.

The three lovers took the first *aliscafo*, hydrofoil back to Naples.

BACK TO NAPLES

For the hasty traveler, on a ten-day tour of Europe mistaking the Parthenon for the Pantheon, Naples is a city to bypass in transit to Sorrento and Capri. A quick tourist can show-off to his neighbors with a postcard saying, "I have been here." There, that same vacationer will drink "*Limoncello*," a refined and delightful local liqueur, made from the renowned local lemons. However he will not appreciate it and will thirst for stronger booze to get drunk.

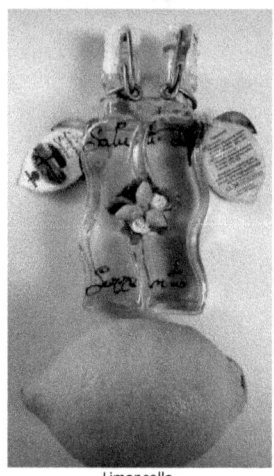
Limoncello

For the last century sophisticated traveler, Naples resembled an Oriental city, but without the European Quarter. However, it has a Spanish District north of the fashionable via Toledo. Nevertheless, the attentive person will be able to discover rich living history in it. The city offers cultural treasures filled with fascination and mysteries as no others.

The Roman historian Livy tells us that the ancient name of Naples was *Palae-polis*, the Old-city on the hill, distinct from *Nea-polis*, the New-city on the shore. Both cities, which eventually merged, were founded during the seventh century BC by the Greeks of Cumae, the nearby city seat of the Sibyl. The Roman poet Virgil, whose tomb is in that New-city, immortalized Naples' mysteries in his epic poem *Aeneid*. In fact, he made the nearby volcanic lake Averno the entrance of the Afterworld.

The city's oldest name, still used today, is *Parthenope*. That was the name of the beautiful siren-mermaid, who died on the Neapolitan shore heartbroken by Ulysses' indifference towards her love call. She was buried and venerated on those shores. Later her portrait appeared on the obverse of the first Neapolitan coins, along with, on the reverse, her father Achelous, the god of fertility, a bull with human face. From those coins, the Romans learned the art of minting and Napoleon Bonaparte took inspiration for his Neapolitan currency.

Napoleon's Neapolitan coin.

Near Piazza San Domenico Maggiore, in via De Sanctis, in the Nile's quarter of the city, once stood a Temple dedicated to the Egyptian goddess Isis.

The Nile, Piazzetta Nilo, Naples.

There, among the wonders of Naples, unknown to quick tourists, one finds the *Cappella Sansevero de' Sangri* also called *Pietatella*. Someone described the Chapel as a "small art treasure-chest, enveloped in an aura of fascination and mystery."

Dante guided Palmiero and Camilla to that Chapel.

THE ALCHEMIC LABORATORY IN SANSEVERO CHAPEL

One of the most enigmatic figures of Naples, damned by Pope Benedict XIV for heresy, is the alchemist, arts' patron, philosopher, scientist and sorcerer

DON RAIMONDO DI SANGRO VII PRINCE OF SAN SEVERO.

He descended from the Carolingian dynasty and the House of Burgundy. He was Grandee of Spain, Duke of Torremaggiore, High Dignitary-Councilor of King Charles of Bourbon, Marshal of the Royal Army Regiment, Templar and Venerable Grand Master of all Masonic Lodges. He founded of the occult Lodges, the *Lodge of the Chosen Ones, The Rose of the Great Order* and *The Perfect Union.* He was born in Torremaggiore, Foggia, in 1710, and he died in Naples, in 1771. He refurbished and organized his Neapolitan family burial chapel according to his occult designs.

Once inside the chapel, right above the entrance door, a life-size sculpture portrays the resurrection of a knight in full armor. He, stepping out of his own tomb, seems to walk towards the main altar before him.

Cappella Sansvero's altar[24]

Statues, flanking the altar itself, are of such great realism that the visitor may believe they are real people. Also, the cords of the mesh, on the statue, *"Disillusion of the net of time,"* and the see through gown, on the effigy, *"Isis' modesty,"* are of an extreme realism. However, more striking of all, is the astonishing sculpture at the center of the chapel representing Christ reclining on his deathbed. Camilla, to get a better look at it, tried to lift the veil covering it. Instantaneously, she retracted her hand screaming in disbelief,

"This transparent veil is made of marble."

"Yes," promptly declared Dante. "Some say that the Prince had discovered a procedure with an alchemic substance that could plasticize and transform any objects, including flesh, into marble. Perhaps, even this *"Veiled Christ"* and all the other statues here, were once living human beings.

Prince Raimondo di Sangro was a sorcerer. He made many alchemic discoveries, among which an eternal lamp. Some even claim that he was able to liquefy marble and marbleize blood. A similar event takes place here in Naples. Every year the coagulated blood of Bishop San Gennaro, martyred in 305, liquefies.

Now, come with me in the crypt, I will demonstrate what I mean," encouraged Dante.

Intrigued, Palmiero and Camilla followed him through a small corridor, down narrow steps, in a tomb, a crypt that only demons could find amenable.

"Here, the esoteric society of Naples convenes once every week," continued Dante, as they were walking towards the catacomb. "Sorcerers and practitioners of magic gather every Wednesday night to perform their arts and paranormal sex. They perform their rituals with the help of evil spirits and surrounded by terrible ghosts, including the Prince's."

"I can see them and I can feel the negative aura of the whole ambiance," said Camilla putting her hand under Palmiero's arm.

"And, here they are, the Anatomic machines," declared Dante, with emphasis, pointing at two gold-framed glass cases at the bottom of that vault.

In that creepy dungeon, the three companions stood alone. They were in disbelief before the skeletons of a man, a woman and a fetus in glass coffins. Only their intact cardiovascular system enveloped the bone-clean standing remains.

"Legend has it that they were two servants of the Prince," continued Dante. "While they were still alive, the Prince injected in their veins an alchemical substance. They needed to be alive, so their beating heart could pump the chemical through their entire capillary system and plasticize it. Later, it was easy to remove the excessive flesh."

"Can you imagine what an excruciating painful death that must have been?" commented Camilla, horrified.

"As you can see, the woman was pregnant and also her fetus was similarly preserved," observed Palmiero, pointing it out at the base of the case.

At that moment the woman's skeleton, with her arm lifted and pointing at Dante, said,

"Bruce, now Dante Scudieri, you are a murderer, you killed me while your child was still in me!"

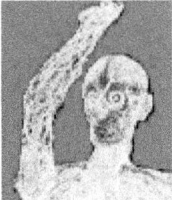

"You are a murderer!"

In the silence and solitude of that catacomb, only the three friends heard those horrible words. Transfigured by sheer terror, white in their face and without exchanging words, they rushed back up into the bustling street of the city above.

THE CEMETERY OF THE LITTLE FOUNTAINS

Entrance of the *Cimitero delle Fontanelle*.[25]

Parthenope, Palaepolis and Neapolis were not the only three cities that shaped present Naples. There is a forth one. An entire other Naples lies beneath the surface, sometimes unknown to the inhabitants until a cave-in accident reveals it. It is the Underground-Naples, *Napoli-sotterranea*, *first* built by the Greeks five hundred years BC. In one of these underground cavities, accessible from the *Rione della Sanità*, a very crowded quarter of the city, is located the vast ossuary of the *cimitero delle Fontanelle*, the cimitery of the Little Fountains.

Still visibly shaken and puzzled by the terrifying experience in the Sansevero Chapel, the three lovers headed to their next mysterious sightseeing.

Section of the *Cimitero delle Fontanelle*.[26]

"Since the 1656 bubonic plague, Neapolitans have buried here poor people who died nameless," said Dante guiding Palmiero and Camilla on this new excursion through the macabre localities of Naples. "Regularly, to honor those *anime pezzentelle*, 'ragamuffin soles,' each devotee adopts a skull, offers flowers, votive lamps and prays for the salvation of its soul from the torments of Purgatory. In exchange, the devotees ask the dead person to appear in a dream and fulfill their desires."

"I pray for my mother's soul to be in Heaven," said Camilla, on the brink of tears, "and for these poor lost souls, that have not even a stone."

Palmiero, wondering alone among those thousands of skulls, entered one of the many tunnels departing from a wide central area called the "Tribunal." There, the local organized crime pledged allegiances and sentenced foes to death.

As if pulled by a mysterious force, Palmiero started wondering aimlessly. He could have sworn that Diana was present there. Camilla saw it and ran after him.

Palmiero walked and walked until he saw an open door. Diana was standing before it. A musty smell hit his nostrils. Behind the opening, he could see his cellar, his personal space where he had stacked his precious wine bottles and adorned it with consumed candles. That door was the same one Diana had opened, when, at his house, she turned towards him and embraced him in her frozen fog.

The tunnel-wormhole

As Palmiero advanced in the passageway, its width got smaller while its length longer. The tunnel started shrinking on him. Camilla reached him and dragged him out of that tunnel-wormhole before it collapsed on itself killing Palmiero. For the second time Camilla saved him from Diana's deadly fangs.

"I saw her! I saw her! I assure you," kept repeating Palmiero in a trance.

"You mistook that statue over there, for Diana," explained Camilla pointing out to the only sculpture present in that cemetery.

"Yes," confirmed Dante arriving running. "That creepy headless bust is named '*Monacone*,' the Big Monk.' Usually they place a skull on it."

Il Monacone.[27]

"Let us get out of here, now," urged Camilla. "Let us go to a fun place where there is life and where tourists enjoy themselves."

"Pompeii," suggested Dante. "It is 15 miles South of Naples, a bit far from here, but we can rent a car and drive there."

CHAPTER 10
A Time Capsule

POMPEII

In Pompeii, Camilla, Palmiero and Dante strolling leisurely along *Via dell'Abbondanza*, the avenue of the abundant market, turned *into Vico dei Vettii*, the alley with the homonymous house. On the very entrance door of that mansion, the painting of Priapus, the god of fertility and plenty, weights on a hand scale his ithyphallic disproportionate nature.

Priapus, House of Vettii

"It reminds me of someone," said Camilla, smiling and openly touching Dante on his groin.

"You see," explained Dante, acknowledging Camilla's arousal, "Pompeii is an amazing place."

"Yes," reinforced Palmiero, with interest, "it is the perfect city, combining life with death. The eruption of the Vesuvius, in 79 AD, killed all form of life with its poisonous gases and buried the city under its ashes. Preserved beneath the ground, after millennia, the city reached us.

When the archeologists excavated it, the city came back to a new life. Its original inhabitants are here, petrified for eternity. The volcanic hot ashes, covering their bodies, solidified becoming their molds. The diggers had only to pour plaster in those mold-cavities to take out the casts of the corpses."

As he described, Palmiero pointed out rows of ancient Pompeian in their mute desperations.

Casts containing the remains of Pompeian[28]

At the sight of those unfortunate people, tears of sorrowful compassion appeared on Camilla's eyes. Especially one caught Camilla's sympathy. It was the cast of a man frozen for eternity in his attitude of attentive concern over his entire family dying before his eyes.

A man in eternal concern

Palmiero, seeing Camilla's tears realized the gentleness and exquisite sensitivity of her troubled soul. However, he was soon to realize that her compassion was short lived and she went back to her devilish nature again.

"Common, let us forget these morbid thoughts," exclaimed Dante, "The ancient Pompeian still share with us their costumes, manners and *joie de vivre*, love for life. Come, I will show you what I mean."

Camilla and her two lovers made their way through the well-paved ancient cobblestone roads flanked by sidewalks. On them surfaced the intricate web of the original pipes that brought potable water to each of the numerous houses in the long lines of buildings.

Occasionally, along the road, one or two of the many stray dogs, hiding in the bowel of the city's ruins, would peek out from one of the side streets, only to run away at the sight of tourists.

Finally, the three lovers reached the Lupanar, the ancient brothel.

Lupanar.[29]

"The Lupanar was so called because it housed the *lupae*, the she-wolves," explained Dante. "Ancient Roman prostitutes took that name because of their howling as a wolf. That call was a way of attracting eager costumers to their hidings in the darkness of secluded places like cemeteries. It is interesting that the putative mother of Romulus, the founder of Rome, and of his twin Remus was a *lupa*, a she-wolf,"

Lupa capitolina, Rome.

"In ancient Rome," added Palmiero, "the *lupae* or hookers worshipped Isis, the Egyptian goddess of love. Her temples, in fact housed sacred prostitutes, many of whom were the priestess of that deity. Greeks venerated that same goddess as Aphrodite, Romans as Venus, Babylonians as Ishtar and Indians as Lakshmi. An ivory statue of this last divinity came to Pompeii directly from India and was property of one of the rich Pompeian prostitutes."

Lakshmi, India

"In the silence of this place of death," declared Dante, as they entered the house of the ancient prostitutes, "you can still perceive echoes of laughter and merry sounds of pleasure."

"Yes, if you pay attention, you may read the boasting of a young man," said Palmiero with a smile. And, pointing his finger to graffiti on the wall, he read aloud, "*Hic ego puellas multas futui*, here I fucked many girls.'" And, pointing to another script, Palmiero said, "Here, one of his girls answered, '*Felix bene futuis*, Felix, you fuck well."

In the brothel, a narrow corridor runs across the hall, separating one row of small rooms from the other. A masonry bed furnishes each small niche. A stove, placed under that hard couch, wormed the mattress placed on it. As decoration, the numbered door of each cubicle had, depicted above it, the specialty offered by the young happy women in that workspace.

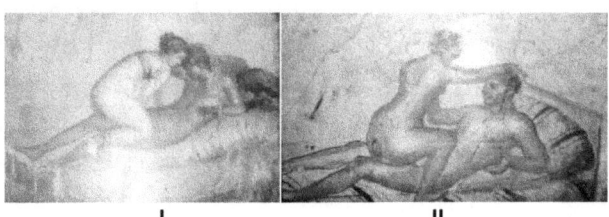

I　　　　　II

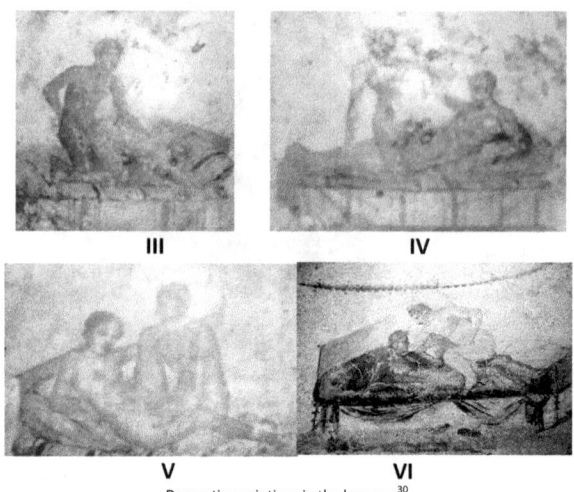

III   IV

V   VI

Decorative paintings in the lupanar.[30]

Camilla admiring the ancient paintings said to her men,

"In two thousand years, not much has changed." Then, playfully pointing out to the painting of the woman riding her mate, she continued, "I do believe that you, Palmiero, enjoy this position as well."

Camilla, overcome by lust, leaned towards Dante to kiss him while touching Palmiero's private.

"Not here," he said.

Surprised she replied,
"Why not?"

"Well for one it is getting dark," observed Palmiero. "Tourists are not allowed in the archaeological site after sunset. A guard could come in any time."

Camilla was visibly annoyed. Dante took her by the elbow and led her out of the Lupanar followed by Palmiero. They walked down an alley towards the exit of the ancient city. The three of them were quiet.

Suddenly Dante pushed Camilla into a doorway. In day light, on their way to the Lupanar, she had not noticed it. Now, at dusk, she realized that it led to a steep stairway.

"Hush, you whore!" ordered Dante.

"What…, how do you dare use this language with me? You are my slave."

Palmiero and Dante both felt the full force of that place. The ancient lust and lasciviousness, encrusted by time in that sordid place, took hold of them. They had to possess one of those ancient *ladies* of the night. They saw Camilla under a different light. Both roughly grabbed her and, dragging her down into that cellar, said,
"You cannot wait till we get back to the hotel? You are a whore."

Pushing Camilla against the wall of the dungeon, Palmiero ripped off her underwear with force and uttered in a low bass tone,
"*Lupa*, whore, *meretrix*, prostitute, is this what you want?"

Without any warning, as Felix would have done two millennia before, Palmiero thrust his manhood into her. Frightened and aroused, Camilla, the *lupa*, whispered,
"Palmiero, *bene futuis*."

All sounds in that crypt muffled away. All Camilla could hear was the heavy breathing of Palmiero intertwined with hers while she was sucking avidly on Dante's phallus. Subsequently, inspired by a painting Camilla had seen in the Pompeian brothel, in which a man was sodomizing another man who, in turn, was enjoying a woman, she commanded,
"Dante, violate Palmiero from behind and you, Palmiero, take me at the same time."

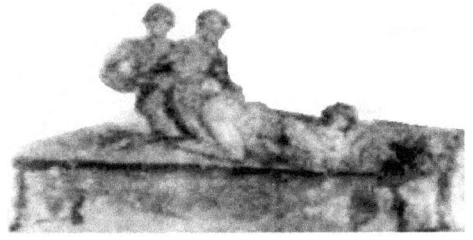

For a moment, the two men looked at her in disbelief. Then, Palmiero took hold of Camilla while he offered his back to Dante. With both hands, he spread apart his buttocks to facilitate Dante's insertion. The turgid member of the strong bellhop penetrated Palmiero so hard and swift that made him scream of pain. At the same time, pushed by that stallion, Palmiero sunk deeper into Camilla, as he had never done before. From her end, she truly felt as a whore of old and was happy about it. Dante pumped hard and relentlessly into Palmiero's anus. He was starting to feel the benefit and pleasure of that rhythmical thrust, which he conveyed in turn to Camilla's throbbing nature.

As both men discharged the reword of their pleasures into their mutual receivers, Camilla burst out with loud orgasmic screams. After both penises exited their bodily sheaths, Palmiero proudly realized his bisexual nature. Camilla had made him free. He was her slave, but his liberty was in that slavery.

THE DOGS FROM HELL

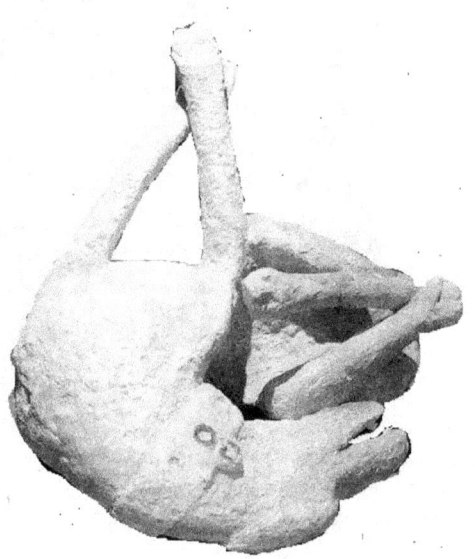

Cast with a Pompeian dog.[31]

When they emerged from that dungeon, it was dark. Coming out from their hiding placed, the usual bands of menacing stray dogs, roaming the deserted streets of Pompeii at night, arrived running from different directions. They were howling like she-wolves. Camilla, between Palmiero and Dante, held tight to their arms, quickly walking to gain the exit while the threatening dogs growled at them. The animals, like a pack of wolves, were closing upon them, preventing them from leaving the brothel area. It seemed as if they were taking up human form. They pulled on Camilla's dress, dragged on Palmiero's trousers.

Those dogs seemed to take human forms. They looked like ancient disheveled *lupae* that had come back to life.

Orestes Pursued by Furies.[32]

Like Furies, those ancient whores incited one another to perform their trade on those poor persons, trying to stop them from forever leaving the area.

"Aspasia, perform fellatio on him," one of those ferocious dogs called out.

"Menander, you are an expert in cunnilingus, take care of her. Or, if she prefers a woman, Rustica can do it," barked another one.

"Perhaps that young man would like a man. Maritimus, is your turn," growled still another.

In this manner Afrodite, Drauca, Epafra, Fyllis, Amaryllis, Cosconia, Felicula, Myrtale, Pyris, Restituta, Timele, Veneria and the homosexual Glyco, Lais, Rustica, Vitalio, even Attica, the most expensive whore, were all taking their turns on those unfortunate victims. One of the *lupae*, the she-wolf whore, Drauca, the head mistress, motioned to two of the male prostitute, to grab Camilla's skirt. They dragged her away from those men's arms and knocked her down onto the cobblestone. Her knee cut open and blood gushed down her leg. This incited the other dogs even further. One of the she-wolf was furiously trying to tear off her panties.

As Palmiero saw his beloved Camilla hauled further into the alley, he tried in vain to get her away from all those dogs. He was desperately crying, shrieking for them to leave Camilla alone, when, a howling pack of very numerous famished bitches came running from Herculaneum and attached Dante. The bitches that were dragging Camilla left her to join the new comers and were saying,

"*Lupae herculculanae venientes*, the Herculaneum whores are coming."

They were those prostitutes who died with thousands of other people trapped on the shoreline of the nearby city of Herculaneum. An avalanche of mud, generated by the volcanic eruption that had just buried neighboring Pompeii, covered them for eternity.

Now, leaving Camilla and Palmiero alone, both, the Pompeian and Herculaneum pack, concentrated exclusively on Dante. They were biting, tearing and pulling him apart, like the hounds that mauled Actaeon for surprising Diana bathing. As the first canines sunk their fangs in Dante's flesh, he enigmatically screamed,

"Diana, is this your punishment?"

Then, his screech reached an intensity that made Camilla and Palmiero's skin curl up in terror. The two, in each other's arms, were horrified. Impotent, they could only watch that carnage. One bitch, that had managed to tear apart Dante's arm and was pulling the flesh from the bone, was growling menacingly warding off three other dogs that wanted to join in the feed. A wolf, reaching for the jugular, had gnawed his head off. Six or seven of those whores were chewing on his headless torso. Like Actaeon, mauled by Diana's hounds, four or five bitches had taken hold of his groin and mauled his genitalia as a delicacy. Finally, the rest of the pack was running after Dante's head rolling in search for a burial in hell and dripping blood all along towards the city of Hercules.

Suddenly the sound of a galloping horse on the ancient cobblestone basalt scared those rabid wolves-bitches away. Diana on a black mount appeared at the twist of the road. Riding Death's dark stallion, she was Camilla and Palmiero's fatal salvation.

From her mount Diana spoke,

"Do not be afraid my children, I directed all these events to set things straight. Do not grieve over the death of the man you knew as Dante. He was the reincarnation of Bruce, the criminal who murdered me. He got what he deserved. Now, hold on the tail of this horse, it will lead you to salvation."

Immediately, Palmiero recalled the funerary iconography of the Osci, a pre-Roman Campanian population, depicting a defunct person following Death by holding his horse's tail. Instinctively, he grabbed Camilla's hand and the tail of Diana's horse.

Oscan funerary iconography

The horse of Death lead them to a tower, a building so tall that its end could not be seen, lost as it was in the darkness of that night.

Pointing to a door of the tower, Diana said,

"Go through that door, it will lead you to safety. This is the house of Death, but do not be afraid, presently he does not live in it. In it you will find four rooms, go through them. The door of the fourth one will take you to safety."

Hand in hand, Camilla and Palmiero entered that door. It opened in a very large crowded room lit as if it was daytime. At its center, there was a big white marble phallus. Awake, the entire

Marble Phallus of Nola, Naples

multitude moved around it in a frenetic exhausting dance. No one paid any attention to the couple.

Past that crowd, they entered another room full with people. This time they all were dreaming in a very soft dim light around another phallus similar to the first one. I was made of dark obsidian stone.

Tiptoeing past them, they reached the third room. At the center of it, there was an ever-burning fire, again in the shape of a phallus. The multitude in it were sleeping dreamless sleeps basking in the warmth of that blazing fire perfectly contained and never consuming itself.

Finally, from there, they entered the forth room. It was the most mysterious one, the biggest of all and encircled, enveloping in a loop, the other three rooms all around. It did not have a ceiling, only the open sky above. No one was in there, because all those who entered it were lifted away beyond the rooftop of the tower.

Desperate, Camilla and Palmiero reached for the closest door that opened on the parking lot where they found their car, the only one remaining in that deserted area.

How Camilla and Palmiero were able to get out of the Pompeian ruins or the tower, none of them ever found out. They only knew that, thanks to Diana, they got to safety. Had they known what Diana had in store for them, they would not have been so grateful towards her.

"What was that all about?" asked Camilla in disbelief, while sitting in the comfort of her car.

Talking to himself, Palmiero replied, "We went through Hierocrystal, the Holy Mountain of Inly. Those were the four dimentions of life, wakefulness, dream, sleep with no dreams and the silence from which we all come and to which we all go."

IL SENTIERO DEGLI DEI

Pogerola to San Lazzaro

The terror of what had just happened with the dogs, Diana and the tower was unspeakable. In spite of the warm night, Camilla shivering curled up closely next to Palmiero, as he was safely driving away from Pompeii. They headed towards the walk of the gods along the Amalfi drive, their next destination. He poured the mineral water that he kept in the car on a handkerchief and handed it to Camilla to bandage her bloodied knee bitten by those ferocious dogs. He felt that the terror, still emanating from Camilla's body, matched his own.

In order to take her mind away from the dreadful events, he started telling her about their destination, *il Sentiero degli dei,* the Pathway of the Gods. That is where they were driving. That was their new place. There, they would spend the next day in peace.

CHAPTER 11
Reunion

POSITANO

Positano's view from Furore

After one hour drive, Palmiero and Camilla reached the renowned charming upscale town of Positano. The comfort of the room in "Le Sirenuse" Hotel welcomed those very weary travelers. From their room, a terrace opened out over the indented coastline.

Pointing out the view to Camilla, Palmiero described,
"Once, many centuries ago, that shore was the aim of Saracen pirates from Northern Africa. To this day, you may see or dine in one of the numerous watchtowers built along the coast to alert local inhabitants of their arrival. The fear of the Saracens' incursions and raids, their plunging, raping, kidnapping is still present in the ballads, song and festivals of the town. Every August, takes place the reenactment of one of those Saracens' landing in the sixteenth century. A miraculous event took place at that time. Legend has it that, at the arrival of the pirates, the local inhabitants confronted them armed only with the icon of the Virgin Mary taken out from their church. At that vision, the invaders were unable to move and they either ran away in fear or converted on the spot to Christianity.

Recently, however, a new trend transformed that religious legend. Sadomasochistic gay parties for the wealthy and famous take place in some of the luxurious villas scattered along this coast. They reenact an actual Saracen's raid that took place in 1558 coming not from the sea but from the mountains behind. During that event, the pirates kidnapped and reduced to slavery three thousand inhabitants."

"Hum..., very meaningful that the attack came not from the sea but from behind..." observed Camilla with a mischievous grin.

"Ha, ha," smiled Palmiero acknowledging the double mining. "However, I am very tired let us go to bed."

LOVE'S COORDINATES

Palmiero was plunging. He felt the speed of the wind blowing on his face. The sea and the ground covered with deadly rocks were getting closer and closer. He braced himself in anticipation of the inevitable collision with those fatal pointed boulders. As he smashed on them, the sweet loving arms of Diana cushioned his fall.

At that point, Palmiero woke up to find himself drenched in a night terror sweat. The nightmare was very vivid and real. He looked at Camilla sleeping peacefully next to him, covered by the dim moonlight on the bed. He could not stop thinking how beautiful she was and how much he was in love with her. In the darkness, the chime of the far away church tower clock struck three times.

Palmiero could not sleep any longer. He got up and went out on the huge terrace overlooking the sea and the coastline. The dim lights of Positano were scattered over the cliff below reaching down to the shore. It was a dark night, a very dark night. Three were no clouds, but oddly enough, no stars were shining either. Diana was there, behind him in the darkness. A cold stagnating air enveloped him. He felt her hand and a prolonged shiver traveled from the base of his spine to the tip of his head.
"Are you here?" he asked in trepidation.

Silence.

"Dam you! Answer me!" he uttered through his lips.

The air around him became gelid. A stone rolled off the cliff beneath the terrace. From the corner of his eyes, he seemed to catch a glimpse of the familiar dark presence. At that moment, he seemed to hear a voice saying,

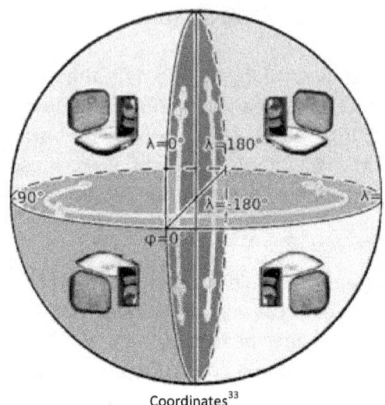

Coordinates[33]

"Finally, today you will be mine..." declared the Siren Diana, "I am Death, I am Desire and I am Hunger for Life. I seek existence and I trace out the circular coordinates that will allow me to find my way back to Life. I am the Siren who seduced you so I could experience life again. All along, Camilla has been my coordinates to you. She allowed me to retrace my steps and live again through the love you both share. I am Death's *Lingam*, his column of divine energy. I am Merlin who shaped the Round Table for King Arthur, Queen Guinevere and her lover, Knight Lancelot. I am the Siren Parthenope who died on the shores of the New City for the love of Ulysses. I am your dreams, I am your nightmares and I am your hallucinations. Each one of them is the tracing of the coordinates searching for love beyond eternity. Each one of them is a lifeline thrown forward seeking for the exit from the maze of existence. I am the daughter of Minos, King of the Dead, the ancient Ariadne who gave Theseus her ball of red string. With it he was able to trace his way out from death's labyrinth. I am Larthia who left her votive head so you would realize you crime, which mortally broke her hart. I am the one who wanted Marilyn dead and I stood in the middle of the way causing her to crash in the ravine. I did not want her to distract you from my daughter, my coordinates to you. I wanted to eliminate all obstacles to my plan and Marilyn was such an obstacle. Camilla is my umbilical cord. I am the Force that, in the maze between Life and Death, travels up through the fuse of the plant and makes it silently scream to the sky. Furthermore, I am the drive that fascinates you into the grave."

Having sung this requiem, Diana the Siren, Death herself placed her jaws on Palmiero's lips and drew his tongue and breath out of his mouth.

Palmiero dismissed all these phenomena as illusory perceptions fashioned by his nightmare. There were, however, strange shapes of gloomy shadows created by of tree branches and leaves on the slope below and above him. They danced in the soft hauling wind blowing through them. Nevertheless, he was not scared. Actually, the presence of Diana aroused him. He wanted to embrace her, kiss her... die with her. He was going mad.

Hours went by in that state. When Camilla walked out on the terrace found Palmiero staring at the distant horizon before him.

"My love, since we are awake," said Palmiero, "we should start now our trek on the Pathway of the Gods."

They left the Hotel at Positano and took the one-thousand-seven-hundred steps that would have taken them up at the beginning of the gods' walk.

As they started climbing those steps, Camilla asked.
"Why is it called the Pathway of the Gods?"

"Because on this trail, the Roman had built many temples," Palmiero answered. "They were dedicated to many gods, like Minerva, Mithras, Ceres and others."

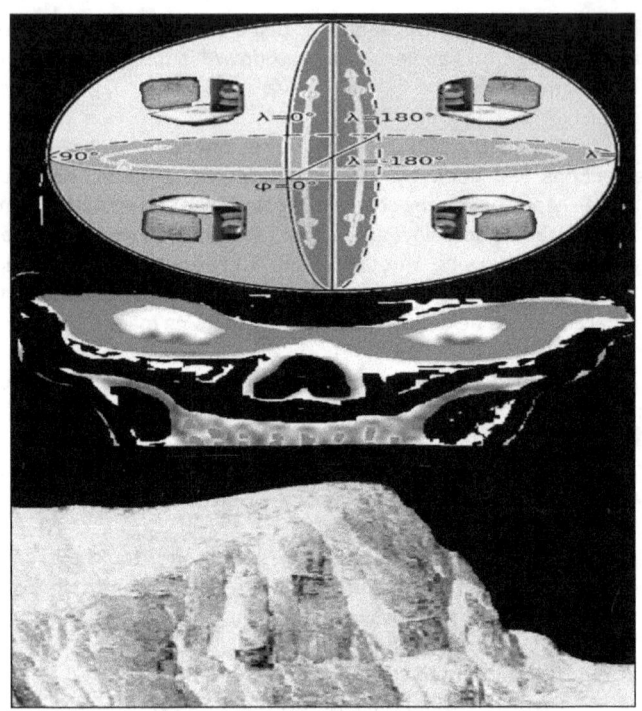

The *Pathway of the Gods*

PARSIFAL AND THE PATHWAY OF THE GODS

The Amalfi drive, twenty miles of one of the most breathtaking panoramas in the World coasting the gulf of Salerno, from Sorrento stretches between the towns of Positano and Vietri sul Mare. Way above it, among the clouds of heaven, runs the Pathway of the Gods, where mythical knights went for their Sacred Quests. This spectacular area inspired the German composer Richard Wagner to create the music for his last opera, *Parsifal*.

Like the legendary Arthurian knight Parsifal searched for the Holy Grail, similarly, Palmiero was looking for the ultimate meaning of life. He viewed Camilla as Kundry, the stunning maiden, seductress and lover of knights. She finally found redemption only through her submission to Parsifal. In turn, he gave up his ego and offered himself totally to Camilla.

The sadomasochistic abandonment was the equivalent of a religious mystical flight to regions physically comparable only to the beauty and wonder of the Pathway of the Gods. Completely giving himself up to Camilla meant defeating all the gods encountered along the trail of life. The gods were the resplendent shining forces of his physical and psychological drives and desires. Those were the divinities to subjugate and to master. Palmiero wanted to be liberated from the tragic malady of life's attachment. Only Camilla had the power and quality to lead him to achieve this heroic task. She was the daughter of Death.

At the beginning, the trek was easy. The cool fresh air of the morning made the walk pleasant. However, as the day warmed up, the walk became rough because of the heat. The rocky hills before them seemed quite arduous. Nevertheless, the reward was waiting for them at the end of those steps, when they turned around to look down at the view of Positano below. It was so beautiful that for a few minutes they stood mute before that magnificent panorama. Holding hands, they were incapable of breaking that eloquent silence. They resumed their hike. The dirt road before them was narrowing as it climbed up and further up. No one was on the path. Camilla and Palmiero were alone among the clouds, except for the company of the gods. They had the blue sky above and the mountains on their left. The vertiginous very high cliff, on their right, plunged, with a straight dizzying drop, in the rocky sea below. Along the green covered sides, frequent sunflowers, emerging from the shade of the surrounding boulders, stretched out their petals in a silent thankful adoration to the Sun while basking in its light. Trees and perfumed flowers teemed with bees and butterflies. Swift lizards and occasional black small innocuous snakes wiggled through the underbrush. Everything gave to the surrounding nature an idyllic atmosphere.

While walking on that spiritual path, Palmiero was explaining to Camilla his views,

"The Pathway of the Gods is a metaphor for our senses. Life is this road traveled by our senses. The senses are powerful gods, resplendent beings who bring the world into existence. They belong to the '/.' They seek the '/.' The '/' is their Holy Grail. However, along the road they miss it. The beauty of life's panorama fascinates and distracts the senses. By liberating the shining forces of the senses, I can become the real ruler of my world."

"How can you say that," Camilla interjected. "The world is out there, either you experience it or not."

"How would you know that, if you did not experience it?" answered Palmiero with an inquisitive smile. "And, nevertheless, you experience it only through your senses."

In deep thoughts, Camilla lowered her head to watch her step. Then, after a while, she asked,
"How can you liberate your senses?"

"When you focus on the constant presence of the faculties of the senses," Palmiero explained, "they are independent and different from any form of pleasure, apathy, or aversion towards their objects."

"Hum, that is true," she admitted. "My eyes see independently from my liking or disliking."

"You got it!" he shouted out, using a stick as a gulf club on a stone along the way. "You realize that the act of seeing is always the same independent from the stimulus. Now, forget the object of sight and focus concentrating only on the act of seeing, unaffected by like, indifference, or dislike. Then, do the same with taste and, either you like or dislike the food, concentrate only on the act of tasting. Likewise, for hearing, concentrate only on its act. Again with smell and feeling the senses are unaffected by like, indifference or dislike, it is your brain that determines subjectively its preferences."

"So, it is my brain that determines the quality of the object," reflected Camilla.

"Well," he continued, "in the brain, the faculty of thinking is, like the other senses, subject to passionate attachment. However, also then you realize that the act of thinking is always the same. In fact, forget the object of thought and focus only on the act of thinking. You will realize that it is the same either you have a pleasant or unpleasant thought."

"Where are you taking me with all this talk, besides this path that becomes ever more narrow and treacherous," asked Camilla concerned by that abstract arid thinking and the ominous precipice at the side of that slippery dusty track paved with rolling stones.

"The real problem is that we are attracted by what we lust for and repulsed by what we loathe," declared Palmiero. "Ultimately, what makes our life miserable is desire, which has no reality in itself, apart from us."

"How can one suppress desires?" asked Camilla.

"The sadomasochistic path of bondage and domination can be a valuable tool for the control of personal desire," confessed Palmiero. "That is the reason why I have pledged total obedience to you."

Camilla stopped, looked at him in the eye, placed her lips on his and whispered,
"And I to you."

THE BANDIT'S CAVE

Love and life

Three hours later, waking aimlessly, they reached the *Grotta del brigante*, the Bandit's cave. There, legend has it, that a dreadful brigand, to avoid being captured, preferred to jump to his death in the sea below.

To reach that locality, the path was almost nonexistent. It was very dangerous. The width of the path consented only to put one foot before the other. Palmiero led the way and Camilla followed him. Both proceeded brushing their right arms against the rock face. The view was spectacular, but the risk was enormous. Camilla kept silent, absorbed in her thoughts. A strange change was taking place in her mind.

Upon reaching the cave, Camilla broke her silence and with a deep voice commanded,
"Palmiero, take off all your cloths!"

Palmiero, who was feeling an ominous attraction for that panorama, looked at her puzzled and put forward a timid,
"Why..."

Camilla, annoyed and with a deeper and more raucous voiced uttered,
"Shut up and do as you are told."

Palmiero executed her command.

Once he was completely naked, Camilla said,
"Now, throw all your clothes over the precipice."

"But, how will I get back in town...," he ventured again.

Camilla slapped him hard in the face,
"Who said you will get back?" she proffered sounding cavernous. "Where you are going you will need no clothes."

Palmiero threw all his garments over the ravine and watched them glide in the wind.

"Now hold your manhood and pleasure yourself calling out for Diana and offering your sacrifice to her," she continued, with a transfigured expression on her face.

Palmiero, in a state of stupor, holding his erection in his fist walked to the edge of the precipice. A slippery incline toward the ravine, with no railing or parapet, stood between him and emptiness. He turned to look at Camilla. Tears were flowing down her cheeks as she battled Diana's mediumistic invasion.

Palmiero started pleasuring himself while worshipping Diana's divinity,
"Diana, I am yours, I dedicate this action to you," he started his prayer evoking her ghost. "Diana, I am yours..., I am all yours...," he repeated as he was reaching the climax of his pleasure.

Little did he know that Diana was there commanding him and watching him through Camilla's eyes. Weaker and weaker Camilla was trying in vain to bite her tongue, to prevent Diana from taking charge overpowering her. Nevertheless, a raucous order came out of her lips,
"Palmiero..., jump! " Camilla articulated, but it was Diana's voice that spoke.

Diana won! Camilla was impotent to fight back. Palmiero, still gazing at Camilla, saw her gesticulating a warning. He mistook it for a reinforcement of the order. Her gestures appeared to him as a command to execute the direction.

"Camilla, you really want me to?" shouted back Palmiero, with wide-open eyes in a questioning anxious disbelief as he continued in his masturbation for Diana.

Camilla was shaking with fear, unable to communicate her true feelings, except for her intense sobbing,

"Jump! Come to me Palmiero! I order you! Jump in the moment you spill your semen!" forcefully insisted Diana through Camilla's lips.

Palmiero slowly started walking backwards toward the ravenous gorge, never taking his eyes away from Camilla and calling out Diana's name. He would have stopped only if Camilla would have told him so. However, Camilla was unable to warn him when his next step treaded into the abyss while his ejaculation floated behind him in the wind.

Victorious, Diana the huntress released her grip on Camilla. Desperate she sprinted after him stretching out her hand to reach him, to hold him, to stop him from the insane gesture. The call of the Siren had finally prevailed. Parthenope succeed and Ulysses, together with his crew, was free to reach her.

As they plunged to their death, Palmiero and Camilla filled the gorge below with one desperate loud scream,

"Dianaaa!... "

From the surrounding mountains, the rocks and the cavities at the sea level beneath came back the clear echo of their cry,

"Dianaaa!... "

The Siren Diana at "The *Pathway of the Gods*" (*Il Sentiero degli Dei*)

CHAPTER 12
Conclusion

MY LOVE.

***

My Love,
When I'll die
They'll open my heart.
In it, the augurs
Will find your name
Branded by Vesuvian lava.

If I should die before you,	If you should die before me,
I'll wait for you a thousand year	I'll hurry to reach you.
When you'll join me	You'll come to get me.
I'll come to get you.	I'll follow you with trepidation.
You'll recognize me	I'll recognize you
From the ardor of my Spirit.	From the light of your soul.
Together we'll sail	You'll show me
The Ocean of the Absolute	The Way of the Infinite
I'll lead you	You'll guide me
Along the Perpetual Paths	To the presence of Eternal Love
Where we'll be given that union	Where we'll be Imparadised
That the century negated us.	While Transcendence approves.

Then, when we'll come back,
Remember… remember…
Again, remember all this.

FROM HELL TO PARADISE, THE COMEDY CONTINUES

Arienzo

As they hit the rocks and the sea, at the foot of the *Walk of the Gods,* the water parted. Even the land, underneath the gulf, retreated horrified. Palmiero and Camilla continued plunging further. They fell in a never-ending spinning free fall, all the way down to the deepest bottom of Hell's pit.

From time immemorial, Hunhau, the Mayan god of death

Hunhau in the Xibalba

was calling them to *Xibalba*, the underworld *Place of Fright*. The pit lies below the Mayan pyramids, inside the Balankanche Caves of Valladolid in the Mexican Yucatán Peninsula. There, Camilla and

The pyramid of *Chi'ch'èen ìitsha'* "At the mouth of the Maya's well."

Palmiero reunited.

He whispered to Camilla,
"This is the meaning of your dream, the Mexican Mayan ruins where we had to meet."

Diana was waiting for them along the Elysian Fields of the

Diana along the Elysian Fields

Greek heroes and virtuous souls. Now the three of them were completely connected. In life and in death, they had been united on different levels, from the hellish depths of depravation to the Heights of Heaven. In each of those levels, they were true and sincere to themselves, never ceasing to love each other in their own way.

"You came to me," Diana said with a tender smile. "You came to save me from the pains of Hell. I suffered enough in my life and during death. I have been calling you, to set things straight. I desire a new life with both of you, a beautiful life full of love and tenderness."

As she was speaking, Palmiero was between them with his hands on their necks and shoulders. In that manner, he guided both women through the treacherous ditches, the dark forests and the bottomless abysses of ravenous hell.

Like famished slimy larvae, solitary shadows were crawling all around them. No life was around them. There was only sultry

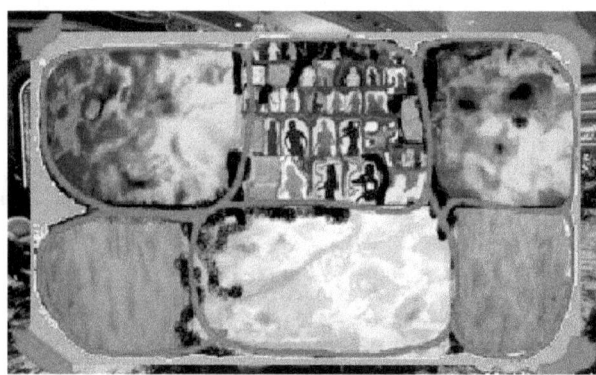
Infernal larvae

Death. It was Hell. It was the inescapable Maze with no life. However, that abyss was not a real place. Hell was life's blueprint tracing the coordinates of all the quantum possibilities on its map. Each larva chose its own direction, like a bookworm chewing its way through a dusty library volume or a termite leaving a tunnel trail of sawdust in the wood.

GHOST PHENOMENA EXPLAINED

"That night on the terrace of Positano, I explained who I am," Diana clarified. "Now I will tell you who really these larvae are. Living beings call them ghosts. We are now clusters of psychic energy."

While saying this, Diana pointed to themselves and to all those shadows which were surrounding them.

"Aren't we spirits now?" asked the larva that used to call itself Palmiero.

"When one is dead, no history or consequent individuality remains," she continued to explain. "You must view the living brain as a dynamo of psychic energy. Scientists discovered this energy through encephalograms, cat scans, magnetic resonance angiograms and other means. The brain is like a computer, once destroyed all its information, all its memory or history is gone. All that remains is the energy, which once powered it. Ghosts are like the images on a film. Now, that same energy goes to activate new computers, which express themselves in new memories or histories."

"Therefore, we have no history now," considered Camilla.

"Here, in hell there is no history. There are only tremendous energetic tendencies towards life. Life was *coitus*, an uninterrupted, continuous sexual intercourse of hungry desires demanding fulfillment. Consequently, Death is a *coitus interruptus*, an interrupted sexual intercourse. The *lingam*, the male column of divine energy, at the time of death withdraws from the live *yoni*, the female divine matrix of life. It withdraws with desire. The *lingam* withdraws from the *yoni* of life still hard and desiring it. That leaves its desire and want frozen in a tension toward the craved objects. It is like the hunger drive, which led us to food when we were alive. Except that, here and now while we are dead, there is no food. Eventually, our cravings will take us back to life with a new identity. This new one will have traits and projections of the old one, but it will never be the continuation of that forgotten history. Unless we identified the 'I' with the Pure Clear Diamond Love, the old individuality is lost forever with no recourse."

"I remember reading something like that," said the larva Camilla with a dreamy expression, "but what is Love."

"None of us knows. If we did we would not be here," explained Diana.

"Then, can you explain what ghosts are?" asked the daughter's larva.

"The ghosts, whom humans may experience in their lives, are like us," continued the mother larva, "neither spirits nor souls. They are only impulses of psycho-physiological energies frozen on a space-time continuum. An example of this imprint of energy can be visible in a Kirlian photography. Bodies warm up the air of the space they occupy and those photos capture the air molecules still radiating warmth immediately after the bodies are removed. The film records that surrounding aura. Then, the imprint left by the body can be photographed some time after the removal of the warming source.

Similarly, when intense emotions are experienced, the psychic energies, like echoes in the valley or images on film, release impressions on a medium. Those intense emotional energies persistently and repeatedly project on a media, which can be an object, a space or a person. It is like a film that needs a screen on which to project. However, there is no personality behind that projection of the psychic energetic event. It is like the reproduction of passion, love, lust, terror, sadness, cruelty, etc. produced by a theatrical representation. The emotions are there in their pleasant or disturbing feelings and in all their reality. That is the reason why a ghostly appearance can evoke passion, fear, pleasure, pain, or any other sensation. Ghosts are direct experiences of pure psychic events in their raw representation. However, there are no real personalities behind them. The actors themselves are only mediums of those passions. The psychic emotive energy is a desire, which takes a life of its own, which we call a Ghost. Finally that energy is desire, is the will to live, to satisfy that yearning itself.

One more thing I must tell you. It was not by chance that you saw Larthia's sculpture in the Morristown Museum. Larthia's Death demanded it. It was not an accident that the earthquake struck Southern Italy when Bruce killed me. Death coordinated these events. It was destiny, ineluctable fate. I am Death and I had my eyes on you. I shook you out of your house. Your life changed as

Camilla's life shattered. I coordinated your encounter. I wanted you two to meet. I wanted you, Palmiero, to take care of my daughter. And I wanted both of you here with me."

RESURRECTION

Then, without warning, Osiris, the Egyptian god of the dead, came and surrounded all those deceased larvae. He started masturbating and gradually he became as bright as the Sun god Atum.

This self-love affirmed its the identity, "I AM I."

Finally, the orgasm, resulting from that auto-stimulation, generated the Universe with a "Big Bang." Once hit by the regenerating semen deriving from the god's ejaculation, each of those crawling larvae took a life of its own.

Suddenly transfigured, Diana "became the Great Eagle *Wanblee* and took This Dead One on her loving wings, up passed the clouds, to those beautiful evergreen hunting grounds of *Wakaŋ Taŋka*." Diana was now the Woman, the Redeemer and the One who creates life anew. As the peaceful Great Eagle, she soared to the sky, taking Palmiero up with her.

The Great Eagle[34]

"Mommy, mommy,..." cried Camilla, seeing her mother sore to the shy. "I am afraid to be left alone here in Hell! Don't leave me here... as you did once before in your lifetime."

With a melodic reassuring chant, she sang to Camilla,

"My sweet loving daughter, do not be afraid. We are not leaving you. We must go and prepare a novel life and a new way for you, where I can redeem myself and love you as I never did before. There I will give you the love that you deserve and yearned for. A fresh bright beginning is waiting for you."

THE NEW BEGINNING

4- In the beginning, there is Nothing. It is covered by Death and Death is Hunger, Desire tightly embracing the Waters, its wife, its Speech. A perfect circle forms and, at the juncture of it, a spark generates, as a babe, and it says: *"I."*

5- And, the Beginning begins by Thinking,
"I am" and just so is named.

6- One day, strolling along, IAM sees his image in the water and falls in love with her.

Under a clear sky full of infinite stars conspiring to incite love, Daniela and Paolo met in Capri.

"I AM Paolo, what is your name?" he asked her.

Paolo Santorelli, "a tall, gray hair Mediterranean, with deep brown piercing eyes and long lashes," was an Italian history professor from Rome and a "Globe-Traveler," with "a long history of fascination with Pre-Columbian American culture."

"I..." she replied with a whisper, emotionally unable to finish.

After a very long intense silence during which they never stopped being lost into each other eyes, she said,
"My name is Daniela."

She was Daniela McGuiness, from the Jersey shore. She was "a stunning young woman with blond long hair, hazel eyes and a regal figure fit to fill a royal throne among the glamour and splendor of a mighty kingdom."

They met at the end of via Tragara, in the sweet scented warm breeze of a beautiful May evening, among the perfumed flowers of the island. Both were on the belvedere overlooking the Faraglioni, the famous colossal rocks of Capri, emerging from the blue Neapolitan waters. It it, once the Siren Parthenope used to swim.

The Faraglioni from Punta Tragara in Capri

Without taking his eyes away from her, Paolo said,
"Do you remember me?"

She answered,
"Yes… I recognize you! You are the ancient Indian Nawab who, once, held my daughter in his arms."

Then, not knowing why and pointing at the three rocky formations of the Faraglioni down in the calm waters, she continued,
"You and I are the two biggest of those rocks while the smallest one is our daughter."

Soon after, they were married, right there in Capri, in a little church overlooking the Faraglioni.

A year later, a baby girl was born. She had "long red locks, piercing blue eyes and a love-bite birthmark on her neck." They named her Camilla.

***

Final note to our dear reader,
You may say, "Nonsense, I don't believe in reincarnation!"
We answer, "How do you know what is there, after death?
Besides, every new birth is the reincarnation of the same Will
to live and experience a new life and renewed situations."

LYRICS: D*IAM*ONDS by Giacomo Simonelli

Diamonds - *hot and icy diamonds*
Diamonds - *stones you may die for*
Diamonds - *love and hate for diamonds*
Diamonds - *death and life for diamonds*

Danger Pain Unrest [and] Distress
Close fire that is burning your life
Power Money [and] Domination
Hard ice that is freezing your heart

Someday you'll give up your diamonds
An inspiration just will change your life
You'll find a new light looking into my eyes
A new temptation that you never will resist
Stronger than your own life
Harder than stones
Greater than you
And you will fall in love with me
Someday you will switch your way
And together we'll be safe
We'll be safe

Someday you'll find out the greatest power
If just look into my eyes
They are your diamonds
                    ORCHESTRA & CHOIR
Someday you will switch your way
And together we'll be safe
We'll be safe

Someday you'll find out the greatest power
Just look into my eyes
They are your diamonds

Someday
Someday you will find new diamonds
Someday
Into my eyes

ILLUSTRATIONS

269

REFERENCES
& Public domain photos

[1] *Cittavisuddhiprakarana* 42
[2] Luke. 11:9
[3] Apuleius, *Metamorphoses* II.17.16
[4] *Brihadaaranyaka Upanishad* 1.2.1
[5] Shakespeare 1,V
[6] Luke 11:9
[7] Picasso 1932, reproduction
[8] Wikimedia Commons public domain, File:Kamadeva1.jpg, http://en.wikipedia.org/wiki/File:Kamadeva1.jpg
[9] Flemish tapestry, Victoria and Albert Museum, London. Wikipedia public domain
http://en.wikipedia.org/wiki/File:The_Triumph_of_Death,_or_The_Three_Fates.jpg).
[10] Titian. Wikipedia public domain The Yorck Project by Zenodot Verlagsgesellschaft mbH GNU Free Documentation License.
http://it.wikipedia.org/wiki/File:Tizian_001.jpg and detail of the cascata della Reggia di Caserta,
Wikipedia, GNU Free Documentation License http://en.wikipedia.org/wiki/File:Actaeon_Caserta.jpg.
[11] Wikipedia, public domain, File:Pasiphae Minotauros Cdm Paris DeRidder1066 detail.jpg
http://en.wikipedia.org/wiki/File:Pasiphae_Minotauros_Cdm_Paris_DeRidder1066_detail.jpg.
[12] Mixopartheno, NY Metropolitan Museum, public domain, http://commons.wikimedia.org/wiki/File:Mixoparthenos.jpg.
and Neapolitan 400 BC silver coin, ob. Parthenope, re. Achelous
[13] postcard - Manara
[14] III century BC, Cerveteri, Vignali area # 13759, Vatican Museum
[15] (1717 - 1795) Wikipedia public domain image File:Wallajah2.jpg, http://en.wikipedia.org/wiki/File:Wallajah2.jpg.
[16] Shakespeare, Sonnet 3
[17] Rabindranath Tagore, 1889 - Tr. W. Radice, *Selected Poems*, 49, 1994
[18] *Genesis*, 25:17 fol.
[19] Gustave Doré, Inferno, XXX, 37-39
[20] Alaskan Yup'ik Eskimo, Yukon-Kuskokwim Delta, 1878, Smithsonian Institution, Washington, DC
[21] Shakespeare 5,III
[22] WikimediaCommons,Fgmedia, GNU Free Documentation License, File:Grotta azzurra.jpg,
http://en.wikipedia.org/wiki/File:Grotta_azzurra.jpg.
[23] Wikimedia Commons,Dorieo21, GNU Free Documentation License, File:Anacapri view.jpg,
http://en.wikipedia.org/wiki/File:Anacapri_view.jpg.
[24] 19th-century print, Wikipedia, public domain, File:Sanseveroaltar.jpg,
http://en.wikipedia.org/wiki/Cappella_Sansevero.
[25] Wikimedia Commons, GNU Free Documentation License, photo taken by Lalupa, File:Napoli - Fontanelle ingresso
1030843.JPG, http://it.wikipedia.org/wiki/File:Napoli_-_Fontanelle_ingresso_1030843.JPG.
[26] Wikimedia Commons, GNU Free Documentation License, photo taken by Lalupa, File:Napoli - Fontanelle 1030848.JPG,
http://it.wikipedia.org/wiki/File:Napoli_-_Fontanelle_1030848.JPG.
[27] Wikimedia Commons, GNU Free Documentation License, File:Napoli - Fontanelle il Monacone 1030862.JPG, photo taken
by Lalupa, http://it.wikipedia.org/wiki/File:Napoli_-_Fontanelle_il_Monacone_1030862.JPG.
[28] Wikimedia Commons, GNU Free Documentation License, Photo taken by Lancevortex. {{GFDL}} File:Pompeii Garden of
the Fugitives 02.jpg, http://en.wikipedia.org/wiki/File:Pompeii_Garden_of_the_Fugitives_02.jpg.
[29] Wikimedia Commons public domain, File:Pompeya lupanar.jpg
http://en.wikipedia.org/wiki/File:Pompeya_lupanar.jpg
[30] Wikimedia CommonsGNU Free Documentation License, File:Pompeii Lupanar.jpg,
http://en.wikipedia.org/wiki/File:Pompeii_Lupanar.jpg.
[31] File:Pompeji getöteter Hund.jpg, Wikimedia Commons, GNU Free Documentation License, Claus Ableiter,
http://en.wikipedia.org/wiki/File:Pompeji_get%C3%B6teter_Hund.jpg.
[32] Wikimedia Commons, *pubblico dominio*, File:William-Adolphe Bouguereau (1825-1905) - The remorse of Orestes
(1862).jpg, http://it.wikipedia.org/wiki/File:William-_Adolphe_Bouguereau_(1825-
1905).The_Remorse_of_Orestes_(1862).jpg.
[33] Wikipedia, GNU Free Documentation License, File:Geographic coordinates sphere.svg Creative Commons Attribution-
Share Alike 3.0 Unported license. http://en.wikipedia.org/wiki/File:Geographic_coordinates_sphere.svg.
[34] Gustave Doré, Purgatory, IX, 31-33